ESCAPE TO PERDITION

JAMES SILVESTER

URBANE
Publications

urbanepublications.com

First published in Great Britain in 2015
by Urbane Publications Ltd
Suite 3, Brown Europe House, 33/34 Gleamingwood Drive,
Chatham, Kent ME5 8RZ

A CIP catalogue record for this book is available
from the British Library.

ISBN 978-1-909273-79-5
EPUB 978-1-909273-80-1

Design and Typeset by Julie Martin

Cover by Julie Martin

Printed and bound by CPI Group (UK) Ltd, Croydon, CR0 4YY

urbanepublications.com

The publisher supports the Forest Stewardship Council® (FSC®), the leading international forest-certification organisation.
This book is made from acid-free paper from an FSC®-certified provider. FSC is the only forest-certification scheme
supported by the leading environmental organisations, including Greenpeace.

TO TIMOTHY AND GEORGIA,
with love bigger than the Universe and with apologies for the times I get things wrong. I can't apologise for the question mark tank top though; you are both just going to have to come to terms with seeing me wear that in public.
God bless xx

ACKNOWLEDGEMENTS

MY THANKS AND MY LOVE TO MIROSLAVA, for continuing to put up with me and for introducing me to so much of what would come to inspire this book. I really cannot thank her enough for her love, support and belief, though her choice of football team continues to disappoint me. My love and thanks as well to my parents and family for the encouragement and love you have and continue to show me and to my friends for keeping me sane over the years.

I also must express my thanks to Alan and Laura, without whom my life would be quite different and this book, if it existed at all, would be unrecognisable. Without their friendship I would not have got involved with Modradio, would not have made that first, fateful trip to Prague and would not have met the lady who would become my wife. Those two have had about as big an impact on my life as it is possible to have. Thanks guys.

Speaking of Prague, I must thank the erstwhile crowd of my favourite Blues Bar and Restaurant, some of whom I hope will enjoy reading this story with a touch or two of nostalgia. My thanks especially to Michael, Jamie and Phil for allowing me to reference them in this work, and, of course, to the genial Peter

Lowe, for letting me steal his name. I must also thank Rasti for his kindness in doing likewise.

Thanks to my colleagues at Modradiouk.net for putting up with the show over so many wonderful years and for all their help and support with publicising the book. Likewise, thanks to Bev and Etta of Whitefield library, in which I toiled on several occasions, trying to get the contents of my cluttered, disorganised mind down on paper.

Too many writers have influenced me to note here, but I would like to give a particular mention to the great Bernard Cornwell, who most kindly, responded to the email of a frustrated, wannabe writer several years ago with some simple but prudent advice. Thank you Bernard; this book is in part the result of you taking the time to reply.

Finally, my sincere thanks to my comrades at Urbane Publications, where I am proud to be part of a circle of mutually supportive and phenomenally talented writers. And, of course, to Matthew Smith. Without Matthew's unique approach to publishing and his willingness to engage with and take a chance on me, this book would still exist solely in my dreams.

Thanks one and all.

CHAPTER 1

APPLAUSE SHOT AROUND THE CONFERENCE CHAMBER like the cannonade of a victorious commander, reaching high into the rafters where cameras whirred and the cheers echoed. Down below, the man who had launched the barrage stood at the podium unmoved by the wave of devotion which threatened to engulf him. An ignorant observer might scratch their head and ponder how this man could inspire such praise; he was not after all what one would call a typical politician of the modern age. His suit, though tastefully elegant, hung crumpled over slightly stooped shoulders, and his large, once powerful hands gripped the lectern as much for balance as to add dramatic pose to his oratory. He was an old man, closer to his eighties than he had ever thought he would be, and did not belong to the photogenic, rent-a-smile band of pseudo-celebrities that comprised today's political elite. But this was Prague and this man was a hero.

More than a hero in fact; Herbert Biely was a legend. A legend of Prague's glorious Spring of 1968, that beautiful time when Alexander Dubček captured the hearts of the Czechoslovak people with his policies of liberal reform. Herbert had stood side-by-side with Dubček then as a youthful and impetuous high flier of the Czechoslovak Communist Party, proclaimed by all as a future First Secretary, tempered by the gentle wisdom of his older mentor. He had remained at Dubček's side as the tanks rolled through their streets and their Russian comrades sent soldiers to 'invite' them to Moscow to sign the Protocols. Upon their release he had remained with his mentor until the day they were parted by their Soviet overlords, ostensibly to serve as 'Ambassadors' but in reality to prevent them becoming focal points for rebellion and to offer them the temptation to flee. The Russians were fools to believe they could encourage either man to defect. They never would. They were proud men. They were Czechoslovaks.

The memories played flirtatiously through Herbert's mind as he raised his eyes from his notes and spoke in a rich, deep voice, unhindered by age, "I am a proud man, I am a Czechoslovak!"

The rows of supporters stood as one, adding cheers of passion to their stream of perpetual applause, while high in the gallery reporters pressed fingers to earpieces, the millisecond wait for translation a tortuous age.

Seated behind Herbert, the Party elite joined in the applause, some nodding sagely, their clapping slow and deliberate. Others jumped a little too eagerly to their feet, as much to be captured by the world's cameras as to show their support for the maverick before them.

Unfazed though he continued to be, Herbert had not lost his sense of theatre and he teased his entranced audience with silence, his sharp eyes flicking over the horde of faces gazing pleadingly back.

"Our divorce was not of our own volition; no multitudes marched through our streets demanding our separation.

Instead we were torn from each other's arms, from each other's hearts, by arrogant men who never asked nor cared that we, the Czechoslovak people, had no desire to be separated. Heroes of our one nation, Dubček, Havel, our own Karol Černý, argued against our partition, but the words of heroes counted for little in the minds of weak pretenders who chose wealth, power and influence over our bond as one people and future prosperity for our nation. In their quest for personal glories, they reduced one unified country into two asset-stripped playthings, ripe for the picking of the criminal and the corrupt, all the while rejoicing at the resentment which grew between us. And, my friends, we let them win, those arrogant, selfish men. Oh yes, we did. Like quarrelling lovers we have sulked and accused while ignoring the bond of family in our hearts. But we are ready now to acknowledge again that bond which they could weaken but never truly shatter. We are ready to share our destinies, to wipe our divorce from the slate and to marry our futures again."

He shouted the words above the pounding applause and with an old pro's eye he looked up to the gallery, a subconscious signal to the hacks to prepare for the money shot.

"We are ready to become one again!"

Herbert felt his resistance to the emotion in the room crumbling and, through a perfectly refined sense of occasion, he rolled back the years and lifted his arms from the lectern, holding them outstretched as though trying to embrace the hall. With a power in his voice he had first felt decades ago he reached his crescendo, "Naše rodina sešel , sdílení svých budoucích!"

The cannonade became an explosion as Herbert was engulfed in the feverous devotion of his followers and the flashing lights of the world's amused yet intrigued cameras. Above in the gallery his words were being spoken in a hundred languages and he allowed himself an inner smile as he thought what the world would make of his message. They were only a few short words, but ones which would provoke many more – 'Our Family Reunited, Sharing its Future'.

The handshakes came next of course. While the audience continued to erupt behind the bright white flashes that scorched his vision, Herbert was compelled to endure the indignities of modern day political posing. He left the lectern and stepped backwards towards his cabinet, his elite, all the time facing the throng of cheering people and waving dutifully as politicians should. He hated such posturing nonsense and loathed himself for succumbing to it. It was so much easier in the Sixties. There was little photogenic about Alexander Dubček, a balding, thin man with thick glasses and an ill-fitting suit. But he was a greater icon than a hundred of today's 'leaders' put together. Today the world's elite comprised of weak men and gutless women so concerned with saying the right thing that they invariably said nothing, masters of delicate thuggery who picked the pockets of the people while telling them they were giving more. To a person, thought Herbert, they were fakes, charlatans and worse, careerists; perhaps the most nauseating failing of all. Though he himself had been a 'young Turk' when he was the rising star of the Communist Party, he had toiled for his reputation and when the crunch came he had lived up to it. How many would do the same today? How many would stand by their people or their principles while staring down the barrel of a rifle or the muzzle of a tank's gun? They were pathetic, and worse, he knew many such people sat on his own party's rows behind him.

Herbert readied himself for the cold embrace of such

political friends, as they climbed from their seats and walked, arms outstretched toward him, each hoping to be the one to congratulate him first, showing the world the closeness of their bond. Well Herbert wasn't ready to be a careerist's stooge yet. With the natural skill of a gentleman, Herbert bypassed the proffered hands and reached out to the tall imposing figure at the back of the group, taking the man by surprise and pulling him to the front of the stage before wheeling round and scooping the woman at his left toward him, his arm paternally tight around her waist. These were the people he wanted with him at this moment; these were the two he could be sure of.

The man, similar in age but grander in appearance than Herbert, was Karol Černý, leader of the Party's Czech branch and another to come through the Prague Spring adorned with the earned label of hero. Černý had the look of nobility about him and carried that same air of aristocracy in his personal manner. A junior working under Herbert when the Russians came, he had impressed his superior with his fierce loyalty, just as Herbert had impressed Dubček with his own. Now he stood once more at his leader's right hand, his hair white, his physical strength sapped by age but his pride as fierce as ever.

Adorning Herbert's left arm was the stunning figure of Miroslava 'Mirushka' Svobodova; the woman who had helped Herbert build his business empire since the day he invested in the spa at Bojnice. A confident and capable Business Manager, she had stayed with him as his investment paid off and he had set about transforming Slovakia into the new hub of Central European tourism; an assortment of spa towns and ski resorts attracting the sort of wealthy clientele for whom global recessions were a minor inconvenience. And when Herbert made his decision to return to national politics she stayed, building the new Party together with him and Černý. She proved a key player behind its surge to resounding victory at the Slovak national elections, which elevated her to the position of Deputy Prime Minister of the Slovak Republic. From there the party, alongside their Czech comrades under Černý, had swept the board at the European Parliament Elections and were poised for victory at the Czech polls in just a couple of short months, Černý himself within touching distance of the Czech Premiership. The plan was simple: election in both countries would be a green light from the people to begin the process of reunification, and both Svobodova and Černý would be instrumental in the realisation of that plan.

These two, Herbert knew, had done more to bring about the prospect of a new Czechoslovakia than any of the hangers on and opportunists who now swarmed assiduously around them; and it was these two who deserved the limelight of this moment. Herbert sincerely hoped they would bask in it, not purely because it was deserved but because he himself was barely able to. The masterful oratory, which so encapsulated the still applauding delegates and which drew the careerists closer still around him, merely disguised the fact that he was tired; drained, weak and tired.

After Černý had delivered his own rousing speech to close events and urge the activists to ensure the Party's Czech elevation, the grand conference hall subsided into a low buzz with a few remaining delegates and the jabbering of journalists. The Slovak reporters were filled with questions and barely concealed awe for their Prime Minister and Herbert certainly owed the major Czech stations the courtesy of speaking with them, although he was careful not to steal Černý's prominence. Only diplomacy persuaded Herbert to speak with the flippant American girl in the power suit who congratulated him on raising his 'tiny little country' to international prominence in such a short space of time. Herbert, old and wise enough to swallow his offence, politely suggested that even small pebbles could cause ripples in the pond before bidding goodnight and excusing himself to find the Spanish news crew.

With the new British Foreign Secretary present, he knew he would be expected to speak to the British cameras and that he should take a precious few minutes rest, but he pushed himself on regardless. In truth, Herbert secretly enjoyed showing off his continuing fluency in several beautiful languages, but he inwardly conceded that he was perhaps giving one interview too many.

After the final 'gracias' Herbert sat down on the front row, feeling as hollow and empty as the auditorium was fast becoming. He prayed silently that the British journalist's questions would be brief and light. Pulling out the embroidered cotton handkerchief from his top pocket, an old gift from his late wife, he wiped his brow clear of the sweat which had started to form. Allowing himself a brief moment of self indulgence he ran the intricate delicacy of his wife's embroidery through his fingers and closed his eyes, wondering what she would have made of his performance. He chuckled gently, imagining her chastising him for everything from his choice of suit, to his speech, to his posture; never allowing her deep pride in him to go to his head and forever pushing him to do better. Though he told himself his return to politics was born from frustration at the then holders of power, in truth it had, in part, been to seek distraction from the solitude which stalked him as he approached his empty bed each night.

The moment finished, he pushed the handkerchief back into his pocket and sat up straight, adjusting his tie and brushing down his lapels in readiness for the next interview when he became aware of the person behind him.

"It'll be time for your injection soon." The newcomer spoke in a gruff Northern British accent.

Herbert swung his head round and smiled at the figure seated in the row behind him.

Peter Lowe, sometimes surly but most mostly affable, was the Englishman with whom Herbert had spent some considerable time over recent months. Herbert was fond of Peter, although his relationship with the Party was an unusual one. The whole inspiration behind the Party's conception was reunification, and with that goal came a raft of complications. Each country was a unique legal entity with treaties and obligations in place, each of which would require addressing in the event of reunification. While in many cases such considerations would be trivial and even mundane, others would be infinitely more complicated. Added to that, Herbert had gone from idealised hero of two nations, to Prime Minister of one seeking to influence the electoral outcome in the other; precarious ground even with the appointment of Černý as Czech Leader. For Herbert to be involved in the campaign at all necessitated careful negotiation of the political minefield, and the legal complications amounted to an international headache.

That was where Peter had come in. Shortly after the Party's overwhelming successes in the European Parliament elections, Herbert had received a phone call from Brussels offering congratulations on the Party's achievements and explaining the potential for unique problems that may arise from the results. As both Republics were, 'valued members of the Union', the EU wished to ensure that National elections in both countries were as smooth as possible and that neither nation would be subject to increased levels of tension or the possibility of de-stabilisation. To assist, they offered the services of a 'Relationship Manager', seconded from the Institute for European Harmony, an EU sponsored Think Tank, to serve in an advisory capacity until the elections were over. Peter Lowe was the chosen man, based chiefly on the fact that he worked at the Institute's Prague office and was acutely familiar with the Czech political scene.

Černý had angrily rejected the proposal, viewing it as nothing more than intrusive snooping, but Herbert was prepared to be more welcoming, recognising the need to keep the EU on board. Though Herbert suspected there was more than a little truth in the opinion that Peter was a 'snooper', he found himself liking the company of his new official liaison a great deal on a personal level. The two would often spend evenings working late in Herbert's office where the conversation would invariably turn to the Sixties and the days of free thinking and the best music; Peter extolling the virtues of the UK Mod scene while Herbert relived his love of the Czechoslovak 'Big Beat' sound. Herbert looked forward to those evenings and welcomed the chance to speak English and give his thoughts on the old Blues Masters over a glass or two of slivovice, or the rum that Peter so enjoyed. Against his better judgement, Herbert simply enjoyed being around Peter and he was pleased to see him here now.

"I know," Herbert nodded in response to Peter's statement, "but not here, later, away from the cameras." Abhorrent though the politics of image and style were to Herbert he had no desire to submit to the prejudices of the press by administering his insulin here.

Peter laughed and teased his friend. "Becoming image conscious are we?" he asked. Herbert laughed back and Peter stepped over the seats in front of him to sit next to Herbert on the front row. He looked fit for a man in his early fifties, and his slightly longer than average dark hair gave an impression of youth only countered by the hint of grey flecked through it and the lines beginning to pronounce on his face. Peter's suit too stood him slightly apart from others in the room. It was just as immaculate as theirs but was cut in a Sixties, double breasted style, accompanied by a thin tie, buttoned down collar and target symbol cuff links.

"You did well today," Peter said in an understated but sincere voice, "not that you need me to tell you."

Herbert smiled, "It is still always nice to receive compliments," he said. It was true, Herbert didn't need to be told how well he had done; one thing he had never lacked was the ability to hold an audience in his palm. Nonetheless he took his friend's compliment graciously.

Peter looked contemptuously round at the great and good of world journalism and with sudden aggression in his voice asked, "How many more of these jokers are you going to talk to?"

Herbert knew that had Peter been speaking with anyone else, 'jokers' would not have been his adjective of choice.

"You should be more tolerant of the press my friend," he said, the slightest twinge of sarcasm edging his words, "they are the bastions of freedom; the defenders of truth and champions of the oppressed."

Peter grinned widely, "Oh aye?" he said, "and I bet the sun stops shining every time they do up their pants."

The pair laughed and for a moment, and Herbert felt his tensions ease. Peter possessed an innate ability to bring calmness to a situation with a joke here and there or an arm around the shoulder when needed, and Herbert felt just the right level of relaxation ebb through his body.

"You are right of course to be cynical," the older man sighed, "in my day it was different, even under Communism." He gave a short half laugh, "You can say what you will about Soviet oppression – and believe me I have – but at least I didn't have to worry about what suit I wore, or whose hand to shake first or whether or not to bleach my teeth." Herbert's voice took on a whimsical tone, "When the tanks came for me, I could at least be sure it wasn't because of the colour of my tie."

"It was a different time," Peter said, joining his friend at the edge of his daydream, "a time for heroes and villains. Today's a time for photo shoots and bombing people because they wear a hijab and their father found oil in the back garden. There are plenty of villains knocking around these days Herb, but not too many heroes." The mood of relaxation was over as Peter's words brought the pair back to the reality of the moment.

"Bloody hell," Peter sighed, "We're sat here like Statler and bloody Waldorf and you've got bastions to talk to."

Herbert nodded and moved to stand before stopping and looking at Peter. "What are your plans for the evening?"

For a moment Peter looked uncertain before he answered, "Nothing much; a few glasses of the rough stuff, a bit of vinyl and asleep on the couch in front of a dubbed cop show I expect. Nothing beats Bodie and Doyle speaking Czech."

"Today is the anniversary of my wife's passing," he spoke with his usual quiet dignity, "I have arranged to visit the Church of Our Lady after finishing here, to pay my respects. I would be grateful for company if you feel you are able to come? Though I would hate to deprive Bodie and Doyle of your support."

For a moment Peter looked shocked and Herbert wondered if he had asked too much.

"Yes, of course, I'd be very pleased to." Peter's words stumbled hesitantly out and Herbert, wishing to save his friend further embarrassment put his hand up.

"Thank you, I am most grateful. Wait here and we can go on together."

Herbert took a deep lungful of breath and stood up. Gesturing over to where the British camera crews were waiting he thanked God that this was the last one for the day. "Why don't you come with me?" He asked Peter, "I'm sure the BBC would like to hear the EU's position on today."

Peter looked up with mischievous eyes, "The EU doesn't have a position on today Herbert," he smiled, "we wouldn't want to go interfering in the internal political arrangements of valued member states now would we?"

Herbert nodded his amused agreement, "Perhaps not."

"Anyway," Peter continued, "I've no wish to share a camera with him." Peter nodded over to where a tall, thin, not unattractive looking man with dark, swept back hair was offering charm and a politician's answers to the young reporter in front of him. "He's only here looking for his first big headline in the job."

"Really?" Herbert's eyebrows rose quizzically, "and what has Britain's dashing new Foreign Secretary done to provoke such disdain? As a patriotic Englishman are you not proud of his achievements?"

Peter grinned his wicked grin again, "Patriotic Englishman?" he said, "Not me Herb; I'm a good European." He winked and Herbert laughed once more before walking over to the waiting camera.

As he approached, Herbert could sense the discomfort of the young reporter and, he imagined, so too could Greyson, who was not so much answering questions as delivering a Party political broadcast. Herbert's first instinct was to let him. The press were, after all, only too keen to leap on the slip ups and mistakes of the political class, so they had little right to complain when the roles were reversed. However, he was not so keen for the day's events to be so blatantly hijacked by a politician from another country, even one as charming as Greyson, who owed no allegiance to the Czech or Slovak Republics and who's own Party's friendly overtures were politically motivated and far from cast iron. What was more, he could sense the chastisement of his late wife for not coming to the defence of an obviously bullied young woman, even though in life she would have insisted that no woman needed a man to stand up for her.

Struggling for a moment to supress the smile such memories provoked, Herbert steadied himself and stepped into the view of the camera, cutting the free flowing Greyson off in mid eulogy, grasping his hand, grinning broadly and looking him straight in the eye, knowing full well that the younger man would have no choice but to accept the politically warm embrace with equal fervour.

His senses still attuned to the reporter beside them, Herbert responded positively to her questions, praising the friendship of Britain's new Foreign Secretary and his Party and extolling the virtues of the new group formed through their joint efforts in the European Parliament. It was an immaculate performance from Herbert. He deftly deflected praise away from himself and towards Černý and the reunification movement as a whole, at once the statesman and the humble servant, utterly in control of the conversation. Greyson looked on with something approaching awe, or perhaps envy, in his eyes. And as quickly as he had arrived, he was gone, bidding goodnight to Greyson, the young reporter and the viewers at home, before turning and walking out of shot, leaving Greyson and his previously bullied reporter on an altogether more equal footing.

As the camera left him, Herbert's strong stride turned into a shuffle and he nodded to his driver and security detail, waiting patiently in the stands, his readiness to end the day's activities. He looked over to where Peter still sat, stoic, face uncharacteristically grim, eyes staring at nothing. It was now or never, Herbert thought, and he edged closer to his friend, placing his old hand on the younger man's shoulder. Peter's eyes shot up, his mind pulled from its introspection, and Herbert was glad to see a smile form on his friend's face.

"Are you ready?" he asked.

"When you are, Herb." Came the quiet reply.

Herbert held out his hand to Peter, helping him up from his seat, Peter returning the gesture with a protective arm cautiously hanging in the air by Herbert's waist. Herbert afforded himself the briefest of backwards glances at the auditorium, before turning back to his friend; the pair of them walking out, slowly and steadily together.

CHAPTER 2

HERBERT HAD NEVER EXPERIENCED SUCH A SILENCE between himself and Peter as they were driven away from the conference centre in the direction of Old Town. The atmosphere between them typically crackled with energy, the ease of their chemistry enough to break the ice in any room. Not this evening; Peter, reclined in the shadows, was deathly silent, lost, Herbert assumed, in his own thoughts. The only noise from the Englishman was his unusually deep breathing, as though he were trying to suppress a troublesome cough or else rein in an unwelcome emotion. Herbert himself was reluctant to break the silence, being likewise preoccupied with his own internal musings, much as the well-being of his friend was one of them.

The car journey proved mercifully swift, and as they stepped from the vehicle, Herbert could not help but notice Peter's grim countenance, his eyes resolutely avoiding both Herbert's own and the majesty of the Church. Walking slowly, as determined to take in the beauty of their surroundings as Peter seemed to ignore it, Herbert left his security by the entrance and selected a pew mid-way toward the altar, the great man struggling through a combination of age and confined space to drop a knee to the prayer mat. As he strained, he grew conscious of Peter's arm hovering impotently over his shoulders, and so with little more than stubborn determination, Herbert pushed himself down to save his friend from the nervous obligation of providing unsolicited aid, thus stripping Herbert of his dignity. The just audible sigh of Peter's relief as he did so brought a wry smile to the old man.

Retreating into his spiritual refuge, Herbert closed his eyes and his mind to all thoughts of interviews, egos and electoral politics. Whispered, prayerful words without a sound bite or slogan amongst them trickled from his lips before they too stopped and silence embraced him, punctuated only by the throb in his chest.

The tell tale sign of a creaking pew broke Herbert's serenity and alerted him to at least the physical discomfort of his friend alongside him; the old man's face stretching into an understanding smile as he opened his eyes and pushed himself painfully back to his seat, his stare still fixed ahead on the altar.

Beside him, Peter also sat staring forward, unblinking, his breath, it seemed to Herbert, short, as though he were exerting some great effort of strength to remain in his seat.

"You are not fond of churches?" Herbert's voice was gentle, paternal, tailored to put his friend at ease.

The younger man slowed his breathing, inhaling deeply into his lungs before quietly answering, "It's just been a long time."

Herbert's smile widened. He understood. "I have spent time away from the Church myself. There are few constants in life Peter; The Lord's joy at our return to the fold is one of them. I hope you may experience that yourself one day."

"I'm more inclined to think He's changed the locks in case I ever come back."

The small joke pleased Herbert, still conscious of the rhythmic thumping in his chest brought on by the day's events. He knew his words would not invoke a spiritual revival in Peter, but hoped they may at least serve to ease the tension that was palpably enveloping him.

"It must have been difficult under the Communists, being religious and all." The question was asked matter-of-factly and Hebert recognised his friend's attempt to steer conversation away from the state of his immortal soul.

"To be honest, I'm afraid to say I neglected to pay the proper attentions to The Lord in those days. I was young, eager to progress, passionate about my country. My heart at that time was so full of worldly concerns and the prospect of personal glories that I neglected to give glory where it was deserved. That is to my eternal shame."

"Don't be like that," Peter objected quietly, "The rest of the world seemed pretty pleased at what you and Dubček were doing in the Sixties; trying to make it a better place."

"For myself?" Herbert snapped his response and immediately regretted it, having no wish to add to his friend's discomfort. "No, I wanted to make Czechoslovakia a better place Peter, but I wanted also to take my place at its head." His voice was calmer, but the regret it framed could not be diluted. "I was loyal to Alexander of course, but I knew that one day I was destined to be his successor. I would have tolerated no other."

He felt his eyes dampening as he made his confession; the golden crucifix he stared at the only thing to retain it's clarity as the tears began to blur his vision.

"And where did my hubris carry me?" he continued. "Into exile, as my country fell to the Soviets and I spent decades in the wilderness, thankful for mere survival in the face of an empire I couldn't fight."

"That was always going to happen." It was Peter's voice which now snapped in irritation. "The Russians were never going to just stand by and let you and Dubček run around like the cats who got the cream, and saying a few prayers every Sunday wouldn't have changed that."

"Perhaps not," Herbert agreed, "But they might have changed me. I have been given a second chance my friend, the keys to the Promised Land. This time I have been sure to give glory where it is due and if people don't like it, well, that is their problem. Instead of lusting to be at my country's head, I am content to engage with its heart."

He drew himself up in his seat and dabbed at his eyes with his beloved wife's handkerchief, inhaling deeply as he did so. Beside him, Peter sat rigid, still staring ahead with a look of discomfort on his face, and Herbert gently placed a wrinkled hand on his knee.

"And what about you my friend?" Herbert's customary calm was now restored and he spoke to Peter softly, paternally.

"What about me?" Peter responded stiffly.

"Why did you come here tonight, to this place which causes you so much discomfort?"

"You asked me to come, remember?" Peter's responses were as curt and irritable as Herbert could remember him being and the old man could have sworn he heard the slightest of breaks in the broad, English voice.

"Yes, I know I asked you," he responded with still more calm and softness, countering the younger man's aggression with every word, "you could have refused, made any excuse. But you came."

"Does it matter why I came?" Peter spat, "Can't it just be because I was trying to be a friend?"

"If that was the reason of course," Herbert replied, "but there is something else. You have not been yourself now for several days; not the warm companion with whom I have spent so many hours, talking of music and movies and long dead heroes of days past. There is something troubling you. I thought if we could talk privately, away from the office I might be able to help."

"So you brought me to Church?" Peter almost sneered the words, his own eyes now filling swiftly.

"Church is a place for confession, of reconciliation. You have seemed on the verge of telling me something for some time now, but nothing has come; I will listen my friend, and will try and help if you will trust me with whatever is troubling you."

Peter's tears were falling freely now, though his head remained stiffly facing forward, unable, or unwilling to turn to look at the old man.

"You should have just quit." Peter sighed, drying his eyes. "Why didn't you just quit? You're an old man; you didn't need all this hassle."

"Why would I stop now?" Herbert responded gently, "This is the second chance I yearned for and I must see it through to the end. Whatever the campaign throws at me I can withstand, though I am grateful for your concern."

Herbert saw Peter close his damp eyes and bow his head as though compelled to offer prayer, but he knew there was a different reason for the younger man's posture and he waited for it to emerge.

"Herbert, I know how much this means to you but I'm your friend. There's so much riding on this, so much stress. It could kill you." Peter said. "Can't you understand that? A weak heart, advancing years and the weight of two countries' expectations on your back don't make for a good mix."

Herbert nodded. He understood only too well; indeed, the knowledge of his own mortality and the stresses he had placed upon himself were never far from his thoughts, but this... this was his mission, his purpose.

He smiled faintly, not attempting to counter Peter's warnings in any way. "I understand," he said, "and I thank you. But I cannot stop now."

"Your final word?" Peter's gaze remained firm, directly ahead of him.

"Yes. I let my country down, Peter. Had I been more active after the Revolution then maybe I could have spared Czechoslovakia from being torn apart at the seams. Instead I stood by, content to build my fortune and snipe from the side lines. No more."

Silence returned to settle between them, dampening the prospect of immediate resolution, until Peter finally tilted his head towards Herbert, his eyes still glistening but without the dampness of a few moments ago.

"I never told you this," Peter began, "but I wrote an essay about you at school. You were my hero."

The comment touched Herbert, though he stayed silent to aid his friend's flow.

"They told us you were a 'true man of principle'. How you'd

stood up alongside Dubček and the others, how you refused to sign the Moscow Protocols. They told us everything about the Spring, about Jan Palach and the protestors. We had black and white photographs of the Russian tanks rolling up Wenceslas Square lining the walls of the classroom. You were in a few of them, staring down the tanks, challenging the soldiers."

Herbert, always uncomfortable with flattery, shifted a little in his seat. "History often exaggerates," he said.

"I don't think so," countered Peter, "I've got to know you and I believe everything they said about you. If anything I think you undersell what you did."

Herbert was still determined to end any notions of hero worship. "I was a headstrong, arrogant fool," Herbert retorted, "And I'm a little surprised to find that disputes behind the Iron Curtain are grounds to become the hero of a British child. There were many people in many countries standing up to the Soviets, many for nobler reasons than my own. It did none of us any good."

Peter looked up briefly into Herbert's fatherly eyes then back to his feet. Herbert smiled in return as though he were a headmaster dealing with a nervous schoolboy.

Peter seemed distant, his voice taking on an almost whimsical quality as he continued with his memories.

"There was one picture of Louis Armstrong when he came over for the Jazz Festival, I think it was in '64? You were right next to him on the stage. I always liked to think that you'd been in the crowd, not as a politician or the face of the establishment, but just as a fan; just enjoying the performance. You were shaking his hand, thanking him for coming, for being there and playing for the people. That was why you were my hero."

The memory played in front of Herbert's eyes; such a beautiful time. Who would have thought it? The great Louis Armstrong, performing in Prague under the noses of the Soviets. Jazz was the voice of freedom, and there was Louis, sounding a blast of freedom in the heart of the Eastern Block; poking his trumpet under the curtain and blowing a reveille for the people. Herbert remembered it well. After the band had stopped playing and the people were cheering, Herbert had given in to his emotions and leapt onto the stage, grasping Louis warmly by the hand in unrestrained joy. Hardly the behaviour of a rising star of the Party, but Herbert hadn't cared.

He let his eyes close and began to realise that he was only half listening to the man next to him. The euphoria of the memories Peter was stirring complemented the familiar erratic thumping in his chest, accompanied by the light-headedness which told him he was overdue for his insulin. His sensations had begun to disconnect him from the reality of his surroundings, and Herbert found he was enjoying it.

He could hear silence once more and realised his friend had stopped talking. Herbert reached out and placed his strong, steadying hand on Peter's leg. Peter responded with a deep sigh.

"You're immovable aren't you?" the younger man asked.

Herbert nodded, reaching into his pocket for the thin metallic case that housed his insulin. He lifted a syringe and placed the needle discreetly onto the pale flesh, just visible below his cuff link.

"As immovable as the tanks proved in 1968," Herbert responded with a smile, pressing down on the syringe and releasing the fluid within.

At once, Herbert knew something was wrong. Where he had

expected nothing but the usual sting of the needle, he felt the smallest of tickles tracing his inner arm, as though someone had pushed a tiny marble into his vein. He clenched involuntarily as the marble reached his chest, bringing with it a discomfort Herbert had never experienced before, all consuming. Almost before Herbert had depressed the syringe, he had felt Peter's arm around his shoulder, saving him from the collapse that was overcoming him. He felt Peter's right arm wrap around his chest, holding him in a loving embrace as the discomfort in his chest bloomed into pain.

"I'm sorry Herb," Peter was whispering, "but you're not going to see the Promised Land after all." And Herbert understood that this was the reason for Peter's silence, for his tears. He could feel the weight of his body sinking downwards, still cradled in the arms of its murderer, who likewise sank to his knees with him, continuing his tearful apologies as they descended.

Herbert was gasping as his chest grew tighter, but that didn't matter. With enormous effort, he lifted his eyes to meet his killer's, and he heard the younger man spew forth a mix of apologetic explanation.

"I'm so sorry Herb, it was the kindest way I could think of; air embolism, it should be quick."

The flurry of words pausing, Herbert felt Peter embracing him tighter, pressing his lips close to the old man's ear.

"Shout for the guards, Herb. Shout them in."

Herbert understood what Peter was asking of him. If Herbert, with his last breath, were to shout for his personal bodyguard, waiting patiently outside the doors, if he were to scream the fact of his murder as his life left him, then Peter was doomed. He would be caught, red handed and inescapably. He might even find himself at the end of a retaliatory bullet from one of the more zealous members of the detachment. Without Herbert's condemnation, his death would be written off as the natural result of an old man with a weak heart heaping too many stresses upon himself. Peter was asking Herbert to kill him, to have his revenge even as he lay dying himself.

Peter was almost begging now, clutching his victim closer and closer, whispering his pleas, his apologies, his protestations that he had no choice, that if only Herbert had withdrawn from the election then it wouldn't have come to this. Herbert understood. Having lived under the KGB's constant gaze, he knew how such people operated and he understood that Peter probably really did have no other choice, or at least none that he would be allowed to live with. And Herbert knew that this man, his killer, was still his friend, and that his friend needed help, Herbert's help, not his aid in suicide.

Herbert could feel only pain now; his vision was blurring and he could not catch his breath, Peter's confessions fading in his ears. Somehow, he found the strength to lift his hand to Peter's mouth, silencing his words.

"John, thirteen, fifteen," Herbert wheezed, "John, thirteen, fifteen".

He saw Peter's face twist into confusion, then allowed himself a smile and closed his eyes, clamping his hand onto that of his friend for the final moments. The pain was gone and Herbert felt warm and relaxed, looking forward to the impending admonishing administered by his wife for his un-brushed hair and loosened collar, before taking his hand and leading him to the Almighty. The thought cheered him and he embraced the encroaching darkness with a smile. In the distance, he could hear Peter shouting for the guards, "He's down," he was saying, "he's down!"

Herbert could only hope, as the sound finally died, that Peter would one day understand that he had helped him in the best – and only – way he could.

CHAPTER 3

IT WAS LATE THE NEXT EVENING when a drunk and exhausted Peter finally boarded the tram to Žižkov, the ex-pat district where he resided and which teemed with Britons, Ukrainians and a hundred other nationalities gathering under Prague's graces. The stress of the last forty-eight hours pecked at his mind as he gripped the metal bar above his head for support, looking to the rest of the carriage like one of the typical drunk Brits come to celebrate a friend's impending wedding by vomiting over a foreign city. Despite the cold wind outside the tram, Peter was sticky and warm, his shirt glued to him by two day old sweat. When the young woman sat closest to him grimaced and moved to stand further down the carriage he became aware of his pungent odour. Well he couldn't help that, he thought, as he dropped into her vacated seat to the obvious displeasure of the tired commuters alongside him. The last day had been a nightmare.

The actor in him had come to the fore as Herbert's bodyguards had responded to Peter's urgent cries for help, his façade completely believed. Chaos had erupted around him. He had been swept along to the hospital in the ambulance where the great and the good of the Party waited in dramatic anxiousness for the object of their fakery to arrive. They rushed around Herbert's gurney as they had rushed to his lectern hours before, desperate to be the one with the sincerest tears and the most profound sorrow. The same cameras that had blinded him at his speech hours before glowed again, this time at his corpse. The only absentee had been one of the few whose grief was genuine; Karol Černý, who had given a brief statement to the press and retired to mourn in private.

Peter had allowed himself to drop back, having no wish to be part of this bogus outpouring. As Herbert's body was pushed through the hospital's inner doors and the plotters and schemers were stopped from going any further, Peter had found a battered chair and collapsed into it, sinking his head into his hands. Just as he had begun the surrender to the sound of his own weeping, he had heard someone next to him sniffing discreetly and turned to see the seated figure of Miroslava Svobodova quickly straighten herself and breathe deeply.

Unsure of what to do or say, he felt clumsily in his pocket for a tissue and handed it to her. She had accepted in an obviously forced show of politeness but made no effort to use it.

Peter had returned to looking at the floor, wishing to God that he wasn't there, and that she wasn't there, full of the resentment that he'd known would be pouring through her mind. A few times, Peter had thought she was about to ask a question but no words came. The anxiousness in Peter's chest had grown with the damning buzz of silence in his ears, to the point where he thought he would scream just to break the tension. In cold desperation to break the wall of ice between them, Peter had scrambled for something, anything to say.

"It was quick," he'd muttered, "he didn't suffer."

"You were with him?"

"Yes."

He'd made the mistake of glancing at her, only for his conscience to be pricked by the sadness in her eyes, her longing to know what had happened. He'd offered her a half smile.

"He asked me to go to the Church with him; he wanted to have a few minutes to remember his wife."

"With you?"

"I guess he thought you were busy, you and Černý, with election stuff and that."

"I'm sorry I didn't mean to snap, this is just... difficult."

"No worries."

She had spoken again, more quietly, without anger or resentment in her voice. "What happened?" was her simple question.

Peter had shifted uncomfortably, though the story was, by now, well-practised. He had been sitting with Herbert in the church, when the old man began to struggle for breath. He had clutched his chest and had passed away, despite Peter's best efforts and cries for help. It was a workable story, a believable one made all the more so thanks to Herbert's long standing gallows humour about his chest problems, and the very public knowledge of his heart attack a decade earlier. Party colleagues had since unwittingly played their part in embedding the lie by informing the press of how Herbert had privately confided in them of the worsening extent of his ailment. He hadn't, of course, but all good lies begat others, and Peter's was a good lie. But the thought of telling it again, to Miroslava Svobodova, had made him sick at heart. Nonetheless, repeat it he had, only to feel Svobodova's eyes on him as he stared at the floor; expectant, demanding of something more, some small detail or noble last words. Her dissatisfaction with his explanation had been obvious but he had had nothing else to give her and suspected she would be unlikely to take warmly to an admission of murder, or that his months of working alongside Herbert had been for less honourable motives than the Institute for European Harmony had implied when arranging his secondment.

Frustrated with her unwillingness to be fobbed off, Peter had opted for a new tactic of crass insensitivity, cutting off follow up questions before they could be asked.

"You'll be Prime Minister now, won't you?" he had asked. "Of Slovakia, I mean. It'll be a hell of a job for anyone to step into Herbert's shoes. I don't envy you, that's for sure."

The shock on her face had demonstrated a perhaps understandable ignorance of her impending elevation until his tasteless comment. Pleased at having prevented a further question, he had pressed on for the kill.

"And I suppose the polls will take a hit after this and it'll be up to you and Černý to drive the campaign now."

As his crowning move, Peter had exhaled an exaggerated breath, shaking his head to emphasise the enormity of the responsibilities which had suddenly become hers. He had felt the grip of the stare on him begin to loosen and within moments the sound of Svobodova's footsteps rather than her questions had filled his ears.

His thoughts back in the present, he wasn't exactly proud of how he had acted towards Svobodova, but the moments after a murder were not a good time to press Peter for subtle niceties. She was a strong woman, he mulled, and she would get over it.

He levered himself out of his seat and off the tram, staggering across the road to the graffiti covered door of his apartment building. Stopping halfway up the winding stone stairwell, the alcohol sapping his stamina, he sighed as he looked up at the rest of the steps requiring negotiation. With a huge effort, he heaved himself away from leaning on the cold, hard wall only to curse in alarm as something shot past his right leg, speeding in the opposite direction down the steps. He didn't have time to voice his surprise further before the object was followed by a tall, thin man in his early sixties, hurrying in pursuit, sweat beginning to break out on his bald head. Peter grinned.

"Evening John," he shouted after the man, "kids let the dog out again did they?"

"Little sods!" John shouted back up toward Peter. "It's the second time tonight!"

Peter's laughter lifted his spirits and gave him the energy to push on up the rest of the steps to his top floor home. It was always the same, he thought, when his Czech neighbour Andrea asked John, a fellow Englishman, to babysit the kids. John loved them dearly but they got up to some tricks and Peter chuckled at what other mischief would occur on John's watch.

Falling against his front door, he paused outside it long enough to make sure John was coming back up the steps muttering with the dog safely in his arms, then turned the key and stumbled through. Staggering a little, he shuffled into the cluttered living room and sat down, cross legged at the foot of the dusty bookcase, filled with an uncoordinated blend of vinyl and literature. His eyes struggling to focus on the titles his fingers were running over, he eventually stopped at a small, battered, leather bound book and pulled it from the shelf.

He muttered profanities to himself as he turned to the index and forced his eyes to concentrate on searching for the right page, his fingers irritably flicking at the stupidly thin paper, reminiscent of the only slightly thicker primary school grade toilet paper of years ago.

Eventually he found his place, his finger wrinkling the page as he dragged it across to better focus on the impossibly small lettering. As his blurring eyes struggled to take in the print, he swore he could hear Herbert's voice echoing his own. The words were simple, eating into Peter, "Greater love hath no man than this, that he lay down his life for his friend", John Chapter 13, Verse 15. Herbert's final words, a last message to his killer. The words sank into Peter, a final component to the emotional cocktail bubbling within him. Reaching up, he pulled a half empty bottle from the adjacent table, twisting the cap off with his teeth and spitting it against the pages of the book he still held in his other hand. He managed a brief swig before the tears began to leak and his throat clenched to prevent weeping, his body finally succumbing to the rigours of the past couple of days. The first night's sleep after a murder was a hellish experience which Peter had strained against submitting to, and as he felt his resistance waning he cursed in resentment and screwed at the page he had staggered home to read, tearing it from the book as he did so. And as the sleep he dreaded claimed him, his final lucid thought was the vain hope that this time, the faces of the dead would leave him in peace.

CHAPTER 4

PETER STUMBLED THROUGH THE NEXT FEW WEEKS as best he could. His cover necessitated his continued presence among the Party's hierarchy, although he was now very much, and very noticeably, pushed to the periphery. The intended rejection suited him fine. Had it been up to him, he would have retired to the sanctuary of his favourite blues bar the moment the job had been done and drunk until he'd vomited his conscience clean. As it was it was not his decision and he was left in the mind numbing limbo he now found himself in; unable to run, unable to confess, resented by all around him for the close bond he had enjoyed with the man they professed to adore and who had, unknown to them, died at his hand. And while he would rather have been someplace far away, Peter appreciated the distraction from introspection that his presence in this company afforded him. Since Herbert's death, Peter had not had a single night of peaceful sleep. He had expected the first night after the murder to be full of the usual nightmares, in truth he was as used to them as much as he feared their occurrence. But this time it wasn't just the first night; the next was no different, nor the following, and the effects were beginning to show. Every time he closed his eyes, he saw Herbert's face; eerily silent and deathly white, yet the stare oddly devoid of malice. Peter knew that such dreams were not good for his mental state, and he yearned, fruitlessly, for them to stop. He had begun to physically dread the onset of exhaustion and the irrational fear it would bring. In his waking moments meanwhile, a whirlwind had blown up around him, engulfing all others and leaving him the sole, curious observer. And there was much to observe.

As soon as the Party Executive had completed their night of professional mourning for the cameras, the already election frenzied offices had moved still further into overdrive. The funeral had to be arranged and the most opportunistic of the Party opportunists bid to turn the event into a meticulously stage-managed political event, featuring grief filled services at Prague Castle followed by live TV broadcasts of the hearse on its six hour drive via Bratislava to Herbert's home town of Bojnice, the roads lined with weeping mourners throughout. The thought made the bile rise in Peter's throat and he sighed a not entirely inaudible, 'Thank God', when the idea was vetoed by Herbert's children, a subdued Svobodova and an angry Karol Černý, the only absentee in those days. Eventually, the family acquiesced to a small, public memorial service in the Tyn Church where Herbert had died, followed by a private service and internment in Bojnice. No processions, no nonsense. Their one political concession being for the flag of the old Czechoslovakia to be draped over the coffin, in recognition of Herbert's stand for that country in the past, and his desire for its future restoration. The rumour in the office was that Herbert's family were refusing even to speak with Svobodova or Černý, for reasons that were unclear.

The funeral itself, which Peter did not attend, was the first occasion Karol Černý had appeared in public since Herbert's death. An understandable absence when mourning a friend, thought Peter, but dangerous behaviour for a Party Leader fighting an election. When Černý had arrived in the Party offices before going to speak at the memorial, Peter was shocked by how the events had noticeably aged him; his eyes still fierce but a little sadder, the stride still strong but weaker by just a degree. In the event, Černý said little in the office, not even bothering to throw his usual insult in Peter's direction, settling instead to fix him with a brief, but reassuringly contemptuous, stare.

The funeral over, the whirlwind continued with the still subdued Svobodova returning to Slovakia for formal elevation to the office of Prime Minister. Peter had no axe to grind with her and managed to offer a brief word of congratulation which had met a not too cold response considering his insensitivity of the night of Herbert's death. Then Peter once more found himself the resented outsider. Left largely to his own devices he suspected his role would end once the Party Executive had formalised the expected new power structure and elected Černý as Herbert's replacement as overall Party Leader. Černý had made not the slightest attempt to mask either his dislike for Peter personally, or his anger at the perceived intrusion into Party business by an outsider, and Peter was merely thankful that his posting would soon be over and he could begin the arduous process of washing Herbert's blood from his hands.

But then the unthinkable had happened. In a move which stunned Party Headquarters into silence, save for Černý's apoplectic rage, the news leaked through that the Party Executive had appointed Miroslava Svobodova the Senior

Partner in the hierarchy and overall Leader of the Party. The reasoning, ostensibly speaking, was sound; Svobodova was now Prime Minister of Slovakia in her own right while Černý, for all his greater experience, was merely a candidate in the middle of a campaign. Whatever he offered in gravitas, she countered in current status.

Peter guessed that the real reason was good, old fashioned misogyny. The executive members tolerated by Herbert as political necessities, no doubt saw in Svobodova someone they could control, an outsider easier to 'manage' than the old lion, Černý, who now prowled the offices with even greater predatory intent, willing someone, anyone, to challenge his authority. The misogynists were to be disappointed though as Svobodova made an immediate impact, pressing Černý on points of strategy and pushing him for joint exposure at key events, frustrating the old man still further.

To Peter, all this would have been amusing were he not so damn sick of it all. His detested superior had assured him that after decades of this work, Herbert was to be his final target. He hadn't said it in those words of course, he never did. Remy Deprez was not one to ever formally request a death; he relied on inference and hypothetical lectures to get the message across, and Peter had always intuitively understood what was required. There's been no contact from Deprez since Herbert's death, but that was not unusual and Peter expected he was merely being made to stew a little in the juice of his own guilt. That was one of the ways Deprez exercised control. Well Peter could live with that if it meant being finally free of the life he had endured this past quarter of a century, just as he could live with the disdain of his colleagues in the office. They spoke in Czech and Slovak about him when he was within earshot, not knowing, or not caring, that he had a fluent understanding of both. He had as much contempt for most of them as they for him, considering them wholly unworthy to bask in the reflected glory of the man he had murdered. Well screw them, thought Peter, pretty soon he would be sent on his way by that toffee-nosed bastard Černý and he could forget about the lot of them.

And that was precisely what he intended to do as he left the office that evening and walked through the rain across the cobbled streets of Old Town towards Jakubská; the street which was home to Peter's beloved bar. At least for the night Peter could forget each and every one of his problems, dead or alive, forget who he was and who he was compelled to be, and lose himself in his blues. And the blues that Peter needed to hear were on offer at only one venue in the city: The Smokin' Hot Blues Bar & Restaurant.

The venue was a blend of the best and worst Prague had to offer. Occupying the ground floor of a building tucked away in one of the many gothic streets leading off from the Old Town Square, the warm glow from its windows and the sound of blues flowing from the door offered a genuine sanctuary to weary souls. The small bar area, separated from the restaurant by a stone step and small archway, was populated by people who called this place home. The smell of Cajun cooking came drifting through, hoping to tempt the drinkers up the step. A couple of ex-pats sat on rickety wooden bar stools, their heads resting on their arms as they drifted in and out of intoxicated consciousness. Alone by the door, a student nursed a small coffee and flicked thoughtfully through the pages of a textbook, striving a little too hard to create the image of an intellectual.

On the next table sat a small cabal of American girls, thrilled at their first big adventure away from the States and keen to enjoy every second of their time in this country. In the corner, directly facing the archway through to the restaurant, Peter deposited himself at his usual table and quickly downed the beer that traditionally greeted his arrival. Sans tie and collar open, he sat hunched over his table, empty beer glass in hand, watching the big, shaven headed American singer wailing his blues to all. Peter turned his glance to the barman who returned his look and raised his eyebrows in query.

"Slivovice please Michael," Peter said, referring to the harsh plum spirit so loved in this part of the world. The first time Peter had drunk it still haunted his memories. It was foul, gut churning stuff and in truth Peter had never developed any affection for it. Only habit, formed through years of Czechoslovak hospitality when one never refuses the offer of a drink, compelled him to order it.

Michael nodded at the order and turned around to draw the drink. Peter allowed his eyes to drift onto the rear of one of the American girls who had come to the bar as he made his order. On most other occasions he would have indulged himself and woken up beside her the next day. This evening though, his libido was tempered with disgust, mostly with himself for spending his nights in the beds of girls less than half his age.

His daydreaming was broken as the figure moved to stand in front of him. The girl, having noted Peter's staring, had come to stand by his table, bringing with her the slivovice from the bar.

"Hi!" She said in an annoyingly chirpy voice, bleached teeth shining down at him. "My name's Faith."

Peter looked at her for the briefest of moments, quickly

47

suppressing any lingering desire to take advantage of her obvious naivety. He leaned towards her and took the proffered glass from her hand, a look of disinterest on his face.

"Mine isn't." He said this coldly, returning his stare to the bluesman, now accompanied by his fellow musicians.

When after a couple of seconds the girl hadn't moved he glanced up in irritation at her open mouthed expression and raised his eyebrow, silently daring her to say something. Hint taken, Faith returned unceremoniously and offended to her friends who looked hesitantly over at the surly Brit in the corner.

Peter leaned his head back against the yellowing wall and let the blues wash over him. The cold night air from the open door chilled his right side while his left basked in the warmth of the bar. Smiling to himself, he closed his eyes and drained the slivovice from his glass, curling his lip as the harsh spirit burned its way down. He idly pondered whether to chase it with another or move on to rum, but that decision could wait; the music had captured him. He could still remember when he first listened to a real blues record. Not the kind of over-played cover bastardised by bubble-gum pop stars, rapping over classics and calling it a 'tribute'. Peter winced. He had known bluesmen in Prague who had wept after hearing the wailings of legends tortured into what today's 'stars' insisted on calling R'n'B. Well it wasn't what Peter recognised as R'n'B. No, Peter remembered like it was yesterday. An old '78, loaned to him by his mate after that bitch had left him. He had always been a Mod, enjoying the energetic passion of all things soul and beat, but he'd never spent too much time on the blues that started it all until then. Peter remembered every crackle on the vinyl as he had huddled next to the speakers; strangely nervous, as if

Robert Johnson was pleading with Peter for sanctuary from the Hell Hound on his trail. The music had stayed with him ever since, becoming his refuge and his comfort, and while he would always be a Mod in his heart he was a bluesman.

His friend, Rasti, Smokin' Hot's owner, would often tell Peter he should say the odd prayer, but Peter did his praying through the music. That was what bluesmen did. And he knew the blues were played here every night and he could sit and listen and keep his conscience quiet for a few hours.

The dream burst as Peter heard a familiar cough coming from the door, ending his brief respite from purgatory. His eyes still closed, he sighed at the arrival of the man he knew was standing in the entrance. Opening his eyes, Peter ignored the doorway and looked over to Michael who raised his eyebrows in response. "Rum." Peter said.

Remy Deprez was a tall but not very well built man with a thin nose and impeccably cut black hair, his face and lips each as pale as the other and the eyes a sunken grey.

Peter took the offered glass from the barman and looked across at his superior standing in the cold doorway. He breathed a short laugh before turning back to watch the bluesmen play. The new arrival walked parallel to Peter's table and looked down through the restaurant to where the musicians were hitting their stride. "Perhaps we should go somewhere a little more discreet…" he began over the sound of hot piano and applauding diners.

"I'm watching the band," Peter immediately countered in a harsh voice before raising the glass to his lips and swallowing the rum. "Another one please Michael," he said to the barman as he slammed the glass down. Peter smiled to himself as he watched

Deprez's face twitch at the open insolence but the Frenchman offered no rebuke; his desire to challenge his subordinate apparently receding at the site of the empty glasses and Peter's clenched hand tapping erratically on the table. Instead, he took off his heavy overcoat and hung it on the hat stand next to the bar.

"Fernet." He directed the barman then seated himself at Peter's table, distaste growing in his face as the blues at the far end of the restaurant stepped up a gear.

Peter, eyes closed again, tried desperately to block the knowledge of Deprez's presence and concentrate on the music, but to no avail. His respite was over and though he ached for the freedom to listen to his blues, the suffocating shadow of the man sat uncomfortably alongside him choked the life from his desire. Opening his eyes he took his freshly replenished glass in his hand and downed its contents in one gulp. Slamming his hands on the table he stood up and marched to the door. "Come on then, let's go," he snapped impatiently, looking back at the ir-ritated Deprez who now moved to quickly finish his own drink. He tipped a wink at the barman. "I'll be back in a bit Michael," he said, "keep my tab open." Michael nodded in agreement. Deprez was suddenly at Peter's shoulder and the two were walking out of the door, the sound of the blues receding.

Peter stuffed his hands into his pockets and looked down the cobbles towards old town as he always did when leaving the bar. The illuminated spires of the Church of Our Lady before Tyn peeped over the row of buildings like a beacon in the black sky but the comfort Peter usually drew from the sight was absent tonight; they refused to soothe a man who had committed such evil within their walls. Deprez stood next to him, his amused smile still on his face, and the pair began stepping slowly along the stone walkway.

"Why did you have to pick now Deprez?" he asked irritably. "You've been happy to leave me dangling this long, why pick tonight to chew my ears off when I'm trying to relax? Herbert's dead, what more do you want?"

The smile disappeared from the Frenchman's face as his thoughts quickly turned to business. "The fall out hasn't gone exactly as predicted." Deprez's deathly pale face looked even whiter in the cold rain. "Reunification is still probable if one believes the opinion polls."

Peter's face contorted as the pair walked slowly down the deserted street. "And that's supposed to be my fault is it?"

"No," Deprez shook his head, "we just expected things to turn out differently that's all, particularly with Miroslava Svobodova in control."

"What does it matter who's in control as long as it's not Herbert?" Peter asked in irritation.

"Don't be naïve Peter," said the Frenchman, "if Karol Černý had been made senior Partner in the leadership one would have expected support for the Party to continue; he is almost as big a hero as Biely. But Svobodova should have been a different proposition. She's a woman; a young woman." Deprez paused as though her gender itself should have obvious cause enough to make his point.

"And?"

"And she is a nobody, she is no heroine of the Spring, she wasn't even in politics until Biely took a shine to her." Deprez sounded distant, as though voicing his internal ponderings aloud. Peter was in no mood to offer sympathy.

"So she's fooled you. You thought she was a nonentity and instead the people love her."

Deprez grimaced. "It's fair to say we expected her reception to be somewhat different than it has turned out to be. We thought without Biely to hold it together the Party would fracture and support would fall away. Then we could forget all this reunification nonsense once and for all."

"And instead she's proving herself a competent leader and Černý's kept his gob shut. I saw him on the news the other day, talking about his new leader bringing an age of prosperity to the Czechoslovak people. Looks like you misjudged that one Remy."

Deprez shot his mocking subordinate a look. "You seem remarkably comfortable with the prospect of a new Czechoslovak Republic for an employee of the Institute Peter."

Peter shrugged, enjoying his superior's moment of discomfort. "I'm not arsed either way Remy. You don't need my opinions; you just spin me three times and point me at whoever needs killing."

Deprez had not taken his eyes from Peter and narrowed them as they walked. "Well I'm sure you will have an opinion on this Peter; The Child believes that we can still turn this situation to our advantage after all."

Peter froze at the mention of The Child and the pair stood still in the middle of the street. "What makes him think that?"

"He feels we have an opportunity to ferment suspicion and distrust on a par with those back in…." he trailed off.

"1992?" Peter growled.

1992 was when Peter had started hating Remy Deprez. It was when Deprez had betrayed Peter, a betrayal he still feared retribution for. It was also the year Czechoslovak legend Alexander Dubček died. Although Dubček had been tacitly against the movement for Slovak independence in 1992, he nonetheless looked set to become Slovakia's first President; an International Statesman respected the world over with the potential to turn Slovakia into a beacon for the new Europe. It wasn't to be. Instead he ended up dying in a hospital bed ten weeks after a car crash from which his driver walked away unscathed. The Slovaks cried foul, but the investigation found no suspicious circumstances and his death was officially marked down as a 'tragic accident', while the Slovaks endured a succession of weaklings and pretenders in Dubček's place, looked on by the world as the poor relations of the more glamorous Czech Republic.

"You want it to be like 1992?"

Deprez nodded uncomfortably. "The Child thinks invoking such feelings will eradicate the unification movement and ensure Eastern Europe remains fractured and divided, dependant on the support of the established European hierarchy to survive in the face of any suspected Russian aggression."

Peter nodded his head in anger, listening to the same old stories re-played with new characters. "And just how does he plan on doing that?" Peter asked, already knowing the answer.

"The Child feels, hypothetically speaking of course, that a major event such as the death of another prominent pro-reunification politician, such as Miroslava Svobodova for example, would provide the appropriate response."

Peter stopped dead, his worst suspicions confirmed. He flung his clenched fist into the stone wall beside him and cursed as the pain penetrated his alcohol-numbed senses. "You promised me Herbert would be the last one!." Peter's eyes were those of a condemned man whose expected reprieve was withdrawn at the last moment. "I was supposed to just be a spy! He was a harmless old man; a bloody hero!"

Deprez glanced quickly down both directions of the street to be sure they were alone and stepped closer to Peter, his aggravation overcoming his fear.

"Harmless is hardly the word," he said quietly, "since he insisted on gracing the world with his return to politics he managed to effectively turn Slovakia into a one party state and was on the verge of re-uniting with the Czechs. We didn't go to all the trouble of breaking the country up after the Cold War just to let a relic from the Sixties put it back together again! Can you imagine the damage to the project if he'd succeeded?" Deprez's eyes flicked again from left to right then focussed on the fool in front of him. "All that was supposed to end with Dubček. If the Czechs and Slovaks unify then all at once they become the focal point for all the ascension states. Instead of towing the line we give them, they could very well form their own power block in the Union that could in time disrupt the Institute's control. And the more confident they grow the more divided the Union as a whole will be, conceding on more and more points out of fear the new bloc will encourage Russian interest if their demands are not met. We cannot let Europe's future be dictated by a loose collection of post-communist shitholes, when it is infinitely better that they remain internally divided but under our overall protection."

Deprez visibly relaxed, the frustration in his face giving way to the calm countenance of a teacher, patiently explaining a problem to a troublesome student. "The established hierarchy have to stay in control. The balance cannot be threatened, not by Greece or Ireland collapsing, not by Britain dissenting and not by grandiose Slavs and gypsies trying to do things their own way. It is we who maintain control Peter, for the good of the Union."

Peter grimaced through the barrage of logic without moving his eyes once from the cobbles at his feet. When he was sure it was over, he inclined his head, just slightly, upwards and focussed on this man that he despised.

"Fuck you Deprez." Peter spat out the bitter words, glaring fury at the Frenchman before him. "Fuck you!"

Deprez twitched a little, always wary when Peter's feral side reared its head, but reasonably sure its potency was diluted by the mixture of beer, rum and slivovice thumping through Peter's brain. Cautiously he stepped forward, trying to add a touch of steel to his voice.

"I'm only letting you know the situation Peter," he began, "I'm just voicing The Child's opinion that things would be much smoother if Svobodova wasn't around. They'd be smoothest of all if she were dead before the weekend. Probably best not to hope for another car crash though, not so soon after Haider. They'd be smooth for you Peter; I'd be off your back, for good this time. How you take that information is entirely your own affair."

"Bastard! You're ordering me to kill her, just bloody say it." Peter mumbled like a sulking child and pushed his hands into his pockets.

Deprez shook his head at the pathetic sight before him. "I don't need to Peter do I?" he said quietly, "I've never needed to. You are no spy; you're a murderer."

Peter broke off his eye contact and turned his head back up the street to where the blues came dancing through Smokin' Hot's doors.

"You know the situation Peter," Deprez straightened his tie and pushed the hair back from his face, "I'll wait to hear from you."

Peter watched him walk away towards the bright lights of the Old Town Square then turned back towards Smokin' Hot. "Bastard!" he said again, and set off back to his shot glass and his blues.

CHAPTER 5

SEVERAL HOURS LATER Peter staggered out of Smokin' Hot's doors and leaned against the wall in front of him hoping the cold air would dilute the dizziness brought on by his last shot. He knew Rasti would have let him sleep in the restaurant if he'd wanted to but he needed another drink and even in his intoxicated state he didn't want to impose upon his friend. Instead Peter set off to find one of the round-the-clock sports bars that lined the streets behind Old Town.

Peter found the entrance to the place he was looking for, inset into a graffiti-ridden stone wall and after pausing for a few more deep breaths he went down the stairs into the basement bar below. The fresh air that threatened to sober him a little was replaced in his lungs by the hot, thick atmosphere of his new surroundings. All around him lay the scattered remnants of the latest night in Prague. Mostly men, all sat hunched at small tables as far from each other as possible, hands cradling small beers or smaller shots that looked untouched to Peter's eye but were held possessively, like crucifixes against unseen vampires. They were the usual suspects; a couple of stragglers from stag groups, separated from their friends and unable to find their hotels, waiting nervously for morning in this suddenly intimidating city. Others were travellers presently arrived at Florenc on the night bus, seeking inexpensive shelter before continuing their journeys in the morning. The rest were comprised of refugees from domestic arguments who had fled to this sanctuary before rows with partners went too far, while a couple of aging prostitutes sat closest to the door, their pimps slightly further back eying Peter up. There were only two rules here – stay awake and keep yourself to yourself. Peter had lost count of the number of times he'd seen homeless people scurry into places like this having scrimped enough money together for one drink, trying to make it last all night, only for them to be violently ejected after falling asleep in the unfamiliar warmth. He wondered how many of tonight's guests would successfully hold out until morning.

Crossing to the bar he ordered a shot, drank it and asked for another and a coffee from the impassive Czech bartender who refused to open a tab. Peter slapped the money on the counter, and carried his drinks to a small table in a corner alcove from where he could keep his eye on all the occupants of the room. The smoky air was complimented by the dim noise from a small TV on the wall showing basketball highlights and from which, along with a couple of framed football shirts alongside it, the venue claimed its 'sports bar' status. In the corner opposite Peter, a battered slot machine was being cursed at by an unkempt drunk who complained to all who would listen that it was broken and unfair before depositing further coins inside it.

Peter downed his shot and was content to spend an hour or so sat in his not too uncomfortable chair before going home and facing the unpleasantness of sleep. The heat in the air though shook Peter's resolve and he felt his eyelids begin to droop, making his eyes sting from a combination of exhaustion and second hand smoke. Having no wish to be roughly escorted from the premises, he forced them open once more and focused on the bright television image glaring from its alcove, and slowed his breathing into deep, sickeningly warm gulps.

Peter noticed from the periphery of his vision, a dark figure rise from its table and move slowly in his direction. The movement distracting him, he turned away from the TV and towards the shuffling shape, straining vainly through the dim light to make it out, while shadow continued to hide its visage. As it continued to move towards him, an air of grim familiarity enveloped Peter. Its face was still hidden in the poor light, but its shape and its movement sparked instant recognition in Peter's mind. Impossible! Peter couldn't move, but continued to stare open mouthed, eyes streaming as the figure moved closer, now only feet away. Relentless, as if deliberately ignoring Peter's fears, the figure stepped forward, the light bleeding onto it as it moved into full view and Peter looked, pale and silent, into the face of Herbert Biely. The flesh grey, the mouth robbed in murder of the smile it had possessed in life, but the eyes still somehow sympathetic, with just the tiniest glimmer of the warmth Peter so well remembered. Peter could only continue stare in dread. He was immobile, paralysed, as Biely leant purposefully forward, arms outstretched towards him....

Lost in the disorientation of waking, it took a few seconds for Peter to place exactly where he was. The two strong hands jerking him up from his seat by the front of his jacket quickly brought him back to reality and he swore in Czech at his attacker, knocking the bigger man's hands from his chest and instinctively adopting a coiled, if unsteady, pose in readiness for a fight. Scanning the three men in front of him he recognised the surly barman, stood further back from the other two, a look of smug triumph on his face, while the others were the rougher looking men he'd mistaken, or not, for pimps when he'd first come in.

"Vypadni! Churak!" The bigger of the men snarled at him; the profane order to leave obvious to all, even those ignorant of the language.

Peter looked, in contempt more than appeal, at the other patrons in the bar, the smarter of whom were keeping their heads down and their eyes averted, casually flicking the pages of day old newspapers. One or two of the Brits risked the occasional wide-eyed glance over at Peter before hurriedly returning to nurturing their still untouched beers.

Peter inwardly shrugged and chastised himself for expecting help; he'd left plenty of people in similar binds to their own fate over the years. Instead he quickly assessed his chances of taking the three men on single handed and making it across the bar and up the concrete steps to the street in one piece. The barman would drop with one punch, Peter reckoned, and the bigger of the other two was probably beatable quickly – from the look of him he was more flab and weight then muscle and strength. But the other one, the slightly shorter guy, was a different prospect. He'd take some beating even if Peter wasn't still half asleep with a nightful of alcohol in his gut. And even if he did manage to floor him Peter had no way of knowing if anyone else in the bar was in on the deal; he could drop the three of them and make it to the door only for three more to block his path. Even if he made it out of the bar, it wouldn't take long for his attackers to recover and pursue him, probably phoning their bigger, harder friends up the road to join in the fun too. Swallowing his pride, Peter reluctantly unclenched his fists and moved away from his table. "Ok, ok," he said, "dobrou noc."

He backed away from the trio, keeping eye contact with them until he reached the steps where he turned and shot up them three at a time. Reaching the top, the freezing night air punched him in the face and Peter cursed as rain began to fall. Checking his watch he reckoned he could manage to squeeze in a few hours' sleep before he had to get ready for his meeting with Svobodova which had been arranged earlier that day. It was a meeting he was not looking forward to in the first place, but was now complicated further by the necessity of her death at his hands. He had no desire to murder Svobodova but neither did he have any choice, however unjust that may be. Better to just accept the fact that they were both victims of other people's power plays, get on with it quickly and quietly and let the Institute play puppet master once again. Afterwards if he still felt worthless he could come back here and let the three arseholes downstairs finish the job.

His introspection was curtailed by the freezing puddle that splashed over him courtesy of the speeding taxi hurtling on up the street. In sheer resignation, Peter, his vocabulary exhausted of expletives, began to trudge slowly back in the direction of Smokin' Hot. His limited desire to journey back to his apartment washed away in the puddle, he figured to throw himself after all on his old friend's mercy and ask to sleep in the restaurant for a few hours. He knew he still had a couple of suits and shirts there somewhere, kept in reserve for times such as this, and while Rasti might insult, chastise and threaten to kill him for leaving only to crawl back and wake him, as an ex man of the cloth Peter knew he would let him in eventually. And he hoped to God that Herbert would let him sleep.

CHAPTER 6

ALTHOUGH SLEEP PETER DID, it was as disturbingly unpleasant as it was deep, punctuated by images of a placid Herbert and a hundred vociferous others, whose screams morphed into a constant pounding in his head upon waking. Confused, he looked sharply around, gasping air into his lungs, trying to determine where he was, only for the movement to increase the pain in his head threefold. Clutching his face in his hands and forcing his breathing to slow down, he blinked the blurring out of his eyes and focussed, probing his mind to recall how the night had ended. He was back at Smokin' Hot, he knew that much.

Peter sat up. He had been lying half covered by a sleeping bag across two clumsily thrown together tables, his rolled up jacket shoved under his head as a damp pillow. To his left, on the floor, lay the remainder of last night's clothes, pulled inside out and carelessly strewn, while to his right stood a dirty metal bucket, presumably intended to capture any vomit he may have ejected. Peering into it, Peter found it mercifully empty. His vision regaining some clarity, he recognised one of his emergency suits, housed at the restaurant for just such an occasion, pressed and hanging above the archway in front of him. God bless Rasti, he thought.

Peeling himself out from the sweat drenched bag, Peter gently hauled himself from the table and stood, bare feet on the cold tiles, stretching the aches from his body brought on by his cramped night. The extended movement re-fuelled the thumping in his head and he froze still again, eyes clenched, willing the debilitating pain away and silently yearning for a few moments of complete stillness and quiet.

His solace was ruptured by the peel of mocking laughter that came from behind him, and Peter unclenched his eyes and cursed. Turning slowly around, he stood in the dubious glory of his nakedness, in front of the small, Romani cleaning lady, standing in the archway to the bar, pointing at him and screeching with laughter. Thinking it pointless even to cover himself, Peter sighed deeply and, his booming head unable to search for the necessary Czech translation to explain, confined himself to cursing again. He collected his suit and offering her an exaggerated bow, stepped through the bar and into the outer corridor where the toilets and a rickety shower were housed.

The majority of the cannon fire in his head washed away with the slow trickle of water and what remained was quietened by the steaming, black coffee waiting for him at the end of the bar as he stepped back in, somewhat cleaner and far more appropriately attired.

Rasti was nowhere to be seen, presumably out meeting his suppliers as usual, but the still chuckling old cleaner had mercifully remained to refill his cup with the rich Colombian blend provided courtesy of the small company run by a couple of Rasti's friends. After two or three cups Peter almost began to feel human again and stood up to leave, quickly feeling in his wallet for a spare note to supplement the wages of the cleaner who offered him a theatrical wink and wolf whistle in return.

The smile on Peter's face at his less than dignified start to the day soon disappeared in the cold, fresh air, bringing with it the realisation that he was on his way to meet the very woman who's newly proposed death at his hands had led him to wake up naked and hung-over in the first place. The grim irony almost drew a harsh laugh, but Peter stifled it, instead cursing the biting cold around his throat and the absence of his favourite silk, paisley scarf.

Getting away with murder wasn't easy, despite what Hollywood had to say, and it sometimes amazed Peter that he had done so successfully and repeatedly for quite so long; over a quarter of a century in fact. For much of that time, the apparatus of the Institute had been behind him, but even so it was achievement he had once felt a peculiar pride over, but no more. Herbert's death had been problematic enough, but the combination of his age and ill health had lent itself so beautifully to a cover of natural causes, that it was considerably easier than normal. Svobodova would be a different proposition. A young woman (politically speaking at least) in her forties, she was the very picture of good health with no complaints or conditions for Peter to take advantage of. No, with her, it would have to be an accident and organising something appropriate with such limited access to her was the puzzle occupying Peter's mind as he walked to Party Headquarters.

The puzzle had stayed with Peter as he'd stepped into the building and waited for the call to Svobodova's office, and it remained as the meeting was delayed hour by hour by hour.

When the call finally came darkness was falling and Peter was still fully in the throes of pre-occupation, but Svobodova's opening question wrenched him back to the present.

"So what did you do to him?"

Peter squirmed, she couldn't know could she? He looked straight into her eyes for any hint of accusation and relaxed a little as she broke into a smile.

"Sorry, what did you do *for* him? It's been a while since I spoke in English."

Peter marvelled at the effortlessly seductive way in which Miroslava Svobodova leaned forward at her desk, her hands clasped together on the oak surface, cleavage subtly but deliberately exposed above her tightly buttoned waistcoat. Catching himself, Peter quickly moved his eyes up to her commanding, if somewhat mischievous eyes, and noted her raised brow as she waited for an answer.

Svobodova was beautiful, unquestionably so, her features punctuated by faint, delicate lines which simultaneously betrayed her years and added a layer of experience to her attractiveness. That same experience haunted her eyes at least as much as they glinted with a peculiar coquettishness. To Peter, methodically absorbing and cataloguing each detail of her appearance and surroundings, these small imperfections only emphasised her magnetism; her maturity adding to her natural beauty more than lipstick and blush ever could. She was unique in Peter's mind, and for the first occasion in almost as long as he could recall, he felt the buzz of nervous anticipation teasing his senses; a sure fire indication that he was close to being intimidated by this woman, although not so much that he neglected to guard his answer.

"This and that," he said, "Just informal advice really."

"About?"

"Anything and everything – everything that would have a wider impact on the EU as a whole at any rate."

She smiled at his obfuscation. A nervous looking aide entered the room with a tray of coffee, placing it on a side desk and handing a small, white cup and saucer each to Svobodova and Peter before scurrying out once more. When the door closed, the politician stood up and moved to the cabinet behind her, pulling from it a glass bottle, half full of a transparent liquid all too familiar to Peter.

"I admire that you still keep his confidences," she said, "I hope I can rely on you to be similarly discreet about Party affairs in his absence." She poured two glasses of the spirit, handing one to Peter, who grimaced slightly at the imminent return of alcohol to his system. "Anyway," she sat back down across the desk from him, "It would appear his faith in you was justified; I understand now why he asked you to go with him the night he…." She tailed off and Peter's grimace deepened at the reminder.

"Listen," he began, "About that night, I'm sorry I was such an insensitive prick, I just needed to be alone and it was the quickest way I could think of getting rid of you."

She downed her shot slowly, not breaking eye contact with him.

"Honest as well as discreet," Svobodova remarked.

"When I need to be." A short silence descended and Peter thought, for a moment, that he was about to be ejected, which would make the successful execution of his assignment all the more complicated. The brief flutter of uncertainty faded though as a smile toyed with the edges of her mouth.

"No apology necessary, it was a strange night, particularly for those of us who he called friends."

Chasing the alcohol with her quickly drained espresso, Svobodova's mood seemed restored.

"My apologies," she began, "I'm afraid this meeting will have to be 'on the go', I have to be somewhere else."

"Oh, ok…" Peter began to respond as Svobodova stepped quickly up and walked to the door, gesturing to Peter to follow her. As they left the room, the cavalcade of security proceeded to walk them through the corridors to the basement at the rear of the building, whereupon they were ushered into the waiting black official limousine. Even as they were seated the politician was on the front foot again.

"You don't mind?" she asked, not waiting for an answer, "you'll be able to make your own way home I'm sure?"

"Sure," Peter responded, with the voice of a man whose consent was already assumed.

As the car set off, Svobodova leaned back, not quite relaxing but dropping down a gear, her eyes never leaving Peter's.

"So," she began, her tone conversational, "having spent all that time with Herbert in private, what did you think of him, of his vision?"

"The official answer?"

"Your answer."

"He was an absolute genius."

She laughed. "I know that," she said, "but why do you think so?"

Peter realised he was being tested, pressed on exactly how well he really knew the landscape and the background to the reunification movement. He didn't mind such quizzes, they were par for the course and, in truth Peter was a bona fide expert on the region's politics, a necessary side line of his true occupation. Pausing only to adopt a sage expression he mimicked his host and leant back in the comfortable leather seat, taking advantage of the poor lighting that masked him.

"Herb knew all those years ago when the country split into two that there was no real passion for independence. Ok, people were in favour of decentralisation from Prague, but not necessarily to the point of separation. Klaus and Mečiar never held a referendum to determine the public's will, they pretty much just divided the country up between themselves and made damn sure they came out on top. In reality the split was an arbitrary decision by men in smoky rooms, with the side effect that there was a sizeable chunk of the people who felt betrayed by their leaders. Whereas Havel and Dubček eventually reluctantly accepted the split and remained active, Herbert took a step away from it and flat out refused to run for Slovak office on the grounds that he would always consider himself a Czechoslovak. So he went away and amassed an enormous fortune in business and toured America and Europe on the lecture circuit. Eventually he started popping his head over the parapet again and when the new governments started selling off your national assets, like High Tatra, he started buying them back and investing in them. He turned a tidy profit too, with the help of people like you."

He paused to judge her reaction to his last few words; a smile and a theatrical bow of the head.

"In fact," he continued, "that was pretty much the only bit of criticism people could throw at Herb: a former socialist making money on the back of Slovak heritage. Whereas Dubček was always a reforming socialist at heart, Herbert had no problem with the finer trappings of capitalism, but he justified it over the years with the amount of jobs he created and the massive regeneration he sparked. Still, it was about the only stick that Čurda's lot could beat him with. But Herb never forgot that significant numbers were upset at the break up. He watched so many youngsters leave the country to make money elsewhere when you joined the EU and he realised that one day they'd want to come home and make some changes, so he positioned himself to take advantage of that. He invested his fortune in the spa towns and resorts, and used his global influence to attract the best clientele. Then he built his Party around the idea of tempered capitalism with a huge focus on community bonding and social responsibility that everyone remembered as the best parts of Communism. It was largely through his efforts that the Slovak GDP started to rise at a higher rate than the Czech's, so for once Slovakia wasn't being treated as the poor neighbour. The knowledge that you weren't going to be anyone's doormats anymore helped erode some of the natural resentment that had built up and more people were happy with the idea that reunification would mean a real partnership. And all the time he was bringing the Slovaks to his side he was mobilising his old Czech allies like Černý to work their PR magic in Prague and remind people that the new dawn promised during the Revolution had never really happened, fermenting the idea that the Czechoslovak family had been torn apart against its will."

"You make it all sound very simple," she said, "surely it can't have been as easy as that."

"No." conceded Peter. "I mean to be completely honest he

was helped by the lack of any real opponents in Slovakia. After some of the stuff that went on under Mečiar's watch a hero of Herb's stature could have swept the board at the elections without even having to open his mouth. But getting the Czechs on board was harder, particularly with Čurda as President; although personally I think Hedvikova is the real power in that Party."

Jaroslav Čurda was the Czech President and a vociferous opponent to Herbert and his dream of reunification. Technically only an interim President, following the surprise departure of Zeman several months earlier, he was nonetheless a cunning, if not particularly clever, politician and was enjoying the place atop Czech politics that his current position afforded him. Needless to say, he had responded less than favourably to the two pronged attack of Biely and Černý in advocating reunification, knowing full well it would likely signal the end of his own luxury and influence. Daleka Hedvikova meanwhile was the incumbent Czech Deputy Prime Minister and an altogether more formidable opponent; less experienced and somewhat colder than Svobodova, but dynamically energetic and possessing of a sharp political intelligence.

Peter continued, "Herb's masterstroke was his European Parliament campaign. Until then no-one had really thought reunification was a serious proposition but he and Černý managed to show both countries what a united approach could achieve, orchestrating the campaign around genuinely Czechoslovak issues, presenting you as one country and one people with favouritism for neither, and you totally swept the board. Čurda's lot don't have a single MEP left, which is probably why he hates you all so much."

Svobodova nodded at Peter's exposition, while the car sped through a deep puddle, splashing water against the tinted window.

"Yes, Čurda," she mused. "He's an odd one. We'd expected opposition from Zeman but… so strange, that business…"

"Yes, a lot of people thought so," coughed Peter, unwilling to encourage too great a degree of questioning down that route. "But at least the elections were brought forward as a result."

Svobodova's impish grin was back. "So what is next for us, Mr Lowe? How do you think Herbert's vision will progress under my stewardship?"

Peter opted for his usual tactic when asked to stroke a politician's ego: blunt honesty. Besides, he probably owed her that much given how it would all soon be immaterial. "Well you're not perfect by any means."

A raised eyebrow was her only response, so Peter continued.

"You don't have Herbert's gravitas and you don't have the status of Heroine of the Prague Spring to fall back on – but you make up for that in general competence. It doesn't hurt either that you're a beautiful woman."

"So I am a pin up?" She asked in a stern voice that implied she had long grown tired of such criticisms.

"Not at all. You know as well as I do that it isn't so much beauty that's important as image. Thatcher was hardly a pin up but her image kept her in power years longer than many expected. In your case you've managed to combine your natural beauty with a projection of strength and intelligence meaning men respect you and women see you as proof that they don't need to compromise their femininity to be successful. The feminists and students adore you; they see you as the face of the future – a kind of Slovak, female JFK. You're a winner all round on that score; the uncrowned Queen of Eastern Europe so the western press say, more popular than Merkel ever was, or Thatcher too for that matter. Demographically the only groups you don't carry are the ultra-nationalists and some of the more hard core older generation who have a problem with a woman in charge. But that's why you need to keep that old bugger Černý on side."

Peter thought he saw the first signs of a blush on Svobodova's face that was quickly suppressed.

"A Slovak JFK?" she quizzed. "That implies I have nothing to offer but a bright smile and vacuous promises of Camelot."

"I disagree," Peter's voice was un-fawning and clinically professional. "You certainly benefit from the Camelot factor, like Obama did, in that there are chunks of the electorate who'll follow you without even knowing your politics, just because you're a symbol of change. But you go deeper than that. Herbert wasn't exactly a politician for the digital age but he and Černý managed to build a strong Party in spite of that; using their reputations, but backing them up with facts and details. As the inheritor of that, you benefit from the fact that the public have already bought into your Party's ideals, and now have the Camelot/Obama factor to go with it. Politically, the cards really are stacked in your favour."

"What else?" she asked, her voice lighter again. "You said I was by no means perfect but then proceeded to flatter me."

"Well you get some stick for being a bit eccentric. The waistcoats don't really help deflect that." Peter's eyes dropped again to her torso to illustrate his point.

Svobodova grinned her impish grin again. "I'm surprised

to hear an aficionado of Sixties culture suggest I should dress more conservatively."

"Oh I don't," Peter countered, "I think a bit of eccentricity is absolutely fine, in fact I think you could stand to play up to it a bit more." Her mischievous grins were infectious and Peter found himself warming to her, actually enjoying the playful, flirtatious tone to their conversation. "In fact I reckon you could carry off a pocket watch pretty well if I'm honest," he said.

"A pocket watch?" She laughed out loud and Peter was pleased to see the crack in the veneer. Before he could answer though, a telephone in Svobodova's armrest began to ring and the young woman composed herself and pressed the speaker button.

Peter instantly recognised the severe, booming voice of Karol Černý bellowing to Svobodova in his native Czech tongue, which she responded to in kind, occasionally glancing her eyes up at Peter.

Words flowed quickly as the car sped along and Peter struggled to translate, picking out that Svobodova was 'on her way' before hearing his own name mentioned. As it was spoken, the line went momentarily quiet, before Černý spoke again, in English.

"Since you insist on keeping that panák in your employ," the booming voice began, "I suppose our conversations will be in English from now on."

The insult twisted Peter's gut and against his better judgement he heard himself responding. "I might be a stooge," he said, "but I'm not a bloody tourist, I live here. And I can speak Czech quite well thank you." Peter said the last words in

Černý's language to hammer home his point to the old man.

Another silence was followed by a curt ending to the call from Černý and a statement that he would contact Svobodova again, later.

Svobodova shrugged at Peter. "I would apologise for Karol, but you should know what to expect from him by now."

"You gave into him." Peter was matter of fact and said the words without judgement or condemnation.

"How so?"

"You spoke to him in Czech, not Slovak."

Svobodova laughed heartily. "Is that all?" she asked. "Mr Lowe, it's the same language."

"Not true," countered Peter recognising her bluff, "if I'd said that you'd slap my face. To an ignorant foreigner they might sound the same but the differences are pretty big really."

Svobodova sighed a little, her laughter receding. "No, you are right. The truth is, Mr Lowe, that when a Slovak speaks to a Czech the conversation will ninety-nine times out of a hundred be in Czech. It's like a sort of natural deference almost, certainly in Černý's case. I don't like it but it's pointless to argue about it."

"It'd piss me off." Peter said in blunt honesty.

Svobodova laughed again, her veneer once more splintered. "It pisses me off too," she said, "but such is the way of the world. If you think that's bad you should listen when we speak to the Polish, they will always expect us to defer to their language. But to be honest Mr Lowe there are more important things for me to worry about than regional dialects." Her voice became more serious as the briefly relaxed pressures returned to line her beautiful face. "We are at the pinnacle of a campaign to bring our countries back together, to do literally what your Benjamin Disraeli said metaphorically; create one nation where two now exist. I don't think picking fights about which dialect to use will be helpful in achieving that."

"You should be careful though," Peter's voiced displayed equal concern, "little things like that that will be gobbled up by the press. Fifty years ago regional dialect wouldn't have mattered to anyone but these days it's exactly the kind of thing the media will use to attack you, to make one side or the other look like the junior partner. The anti-reunification lobby will pick your every word apart and if they can highlight any split they'll have you."

The new Prime Minister simply smiled in response, as if, Peter thought, weighing up some great conundrum in her mind. And then just as suddenly, she snapped forward and peered through the window.

"We are nearly here and I've taken up too much of your time already, I'm sure you have things to attend to. Thank you Mr Lowe."

Her closure of the meeting was a little more abrupt than Peter had expected, and caught him a little off guard. Again, he thought, probably all part of her tactics to dominate and control her conversations.

"No problem," he replied, "anytime." He likewise sat upright, straightening his tie and readying himself for the walk home from wherever he was, but Svobodova spoke again, her customary smile back on her face.

"Anytime?" she questioned. "How about right now?"

"What?" Peter grunted, surprise overriding politeness.

The car drew to a halt and Svobodova waited for the driver

to open the door. Turning her head back to Peter, she grinned.

"Do you like football?"

"Yes," stuttered Peter, imagining a brief chat about favourite teams and intoxicated night time walks to stadia for vital fourth round cup matches, before the door swung open and he was blinded by flashbulbs and floodlights as Svobodova stepped out in front of Prague's Generali Arena.

Following behind her, Peter saw that they had been swept up in a veritable fleet of similar cars, each carrying the great and the good to the ground. The endless stream of dark suited men that poured from the vehicles dragged Peter's thoughts back behind the iron curtain, while the illuminated stadium and noisy crowd counterbalanced his perception. Security once more descended on them, carving a path through the thunderous noise to their seats in the Executive boxes, where Peter took the opportunity to look around at his company for the evening. The box was a who's who of Czech politics. Away to Svobodova's left sat Černý and his aides, engaged in hushed debate about a myriad of topics all un-connected with football, while on the front row, parallel to the half way line sat the Czech President, Jaroslav Čurda, alongside the formidable, Daleka Hedvikova, and the glove puppet currently occupying the Prime Minister's office, Vladimir Rukavice. They were all here to watch the Czech Republic and Slovakia play a friendly.

As the noise of the crowd increased, Peter struggled to feel comfortable in his surroundings. The anonymity of a football crowd usually afforded Peter the freedom to truly relax, and blend without ripple into the sea of the good, bad and worse of society that comprised it. He had spent many a day in such waters, where even the finest of people surrendered their composure to the rocky lurching of the foamy tribe, belching approval or roaring displeasure at the targets scurrying across the muddy green below. Never once had he been intimidated by bellows or sneers, and never had he felt the slightest bit out of place. Tonight though, he sat Neptune like above the waves, tucked into the Executive Box, the occupants of which, for the most part, stayed as quiet and sombre as the crowd below were loud and passionate. The exception to the unwritten rule of emotional sobriety was Miroslava Svobodova, whom Peter found himself sat beside, and who cheered each tackle and hollered for each shot; her face enveloped in unbowed enjoyment.

The ball skidded into touch and players briefly crowded around a stricken youngster on the ground. Only then did Svobodova turn to Peter. "My friends call me Mirushka," she said, "so please, no more 'Ms Svobodova' nonsense."

He grinned back at her, "You wouldn't want to know what my friends call me," he said, "but fair enough, Mirushka, whatever you say." They carried on with their mutual smile until a roar from the crowd dragged their attention back to the game playing out before them. The young Slovak Number 7 had smashed a shot against the underside of the bar, rattling both it and the predominantly Czech crowd, before the imperious Czech centre back calmly collected the ball and played it smoothly along the ground toward his midfield anchor man.

"I have some business to attend to in Bratislava tomorrow." Mirushka leaned her head towards Peter but kept her eyes rigidly on the game. "But when I return I'd like you to clear your desk from the main office."

Peter was unsure what surprised him the most; that she would bring him to the game only to fire him, or that he felt such acute disappointment by her request. Working for the Party had become a personal hell in the days since Herbert's death; his legs dragging him up the steps to the office each morning as though they led to the gallows. Freedom from his cover was what he had dreamed of, in those rare moments of sleep the nightmares afforded him, but now that she had actually said the words, he cursed how much more difficult his mission would now be, but more that he was being sent from her presence.

"Oh, sure," he responded, flustered. "I mean, I understand of course; I was Herbert's contact, you don't know me from Adam…"

She turned her head back to look at him, her smile returned to her face. "No, Mr Lowe, you don't understand; I'm not terminating your secondment, I want you to be part of my personal advisory team." She laughed at the confusion on his face.

"Oh, right," he said quietly.

"Herbert always spoke very highly of you," she said, "I could never understand why he would tolerate your presence, but now that I've met you, spoken to you, I think I do. So, are you interested?"

Peter was flustered again, but this time with a nervous pleasure. "Yes, yes of course I am!" he answered sincerely. "But there's one condition though."

"Name it," she said, her smile still bright.

"If I'm going to work for you then no more of this 'Mr Lowe' nonsense; call me Peter." He grinned a wide grin back at her and held out his palm. She took it and held it tightly.

"Welcome aboard. Peter."

Their hands stayed fused together, their eye contact unbroken, as the stormy sea below them erupted in exultation.

CHAPTER 7

MIRUSHKA AND HER ENTOURAGE had left for Bratislava immediately after the game, unhappily so after watching her National side losing 2-1 to the Czechs, which took the edge off her relaxed positivity. But at least it meant that Peter didn't need to see her today and that was how he liked it. After getting back to his apartment, he had cursed himself for having given in to more than a passing interest in her; there was no point further complicating what had to be done. He had made the mistake with Herbert of getting too close to his target and the result was sleepless nights and guilt drenched hangovers. His awe of Herbert and his friendship with him had allowed, as a clever man somewhere had once put it, a death watch beetle into his soul. He wasn't inclined to make such a mistake again. He liked Mirushka a lot more than he thought he would, so it was unquestionably better to avoid her until what had to happen, happened. With her, for the day at least, occupied in Bratislava with election strategies, photo-shoots and laborious telephone battles with Černý, Peter had the time to plan her death in detail.

The first sound he heard the following morning was a smash and his own voice swearing as the glass bottle, whose contents he'd used to push himself for barely a couple of hours into the clawing clutches of sleep, slipped from his fingers onto the hard, carpet-less floor below. He swore twice more before opening his eyes to the light streaming painfully through the thin, faded curtains, causing his brow to furrow and the thumping in his head to beat harder. His left arm swung to the cabinet beside him, his fingers fumbling for the pills. Stuffing four in his mouth, the arm returned for the bottle of days old water standing guard by the tablets. The warm, stale liquid was nectar to Peter, nudging the pills down his throat and bringing reluctant life to the parched desert of his mouth. His breakfast finished, he flung his legs out of the bed, bringing forth another expletive as his heel made contact with a shard of glass from the bottle he had already forgotten about breaking.

This would not be a good day, he thought, hissing as the remnants of rum on the glass flowed in with glee to attack his wound. Pulling the shard from his heel he hobbled to the bathroom to wash and find a plaster. How could he be so stupid? He could have made any excuse not to have accompanied Mirushka to the game, not to have sat next to her, not to have spent the evening pretentiously flirting with her. But he had gone, he had flirted and, once more he felt the doubts and hesitations gnawing at him just as they had with Herbert, only this time more so.

Shifting the weight in his left leg to the unscathed toes, he leant his arm against the wall behind the toilet and continued to berate himself as he went about his morning ablutions, damning his idiocy with each stroke of the toothbrush and scrape of the razor.

His apartment was a disaster zone, the freshly broken bottle and speckled red trail now running to the bathroom, only adding to the shambles in which Peter lived. Hobbling over to the dust coated unit that guarded his bed, Peter slid open the top one and lifted a pair of faded boxer shorts out, revealing the dull, black gun that lay beneath them. For an experienced murderer, Peter possessed an almost religious hatred of guns. That wasn't to say he was unaccustomed to using them; indeed, his aim was, in his mind, unparalleled, although these days the grip encouraged callouses on his palm and firing aggravated the arthritis he had begun to feel in his knuckles. Nevertheless, employing his talent with firearms had long since repulsed Peter; sniping from dark corners robbing him of the veneer of nobility that he, in his less lucid moments, liked to convince himself he possessed in his willingness to despatch his victims via more direct means, and while looking into their eyes.

He focussed on the gun, nestled in his underwear, as though it were an estranged lover, whose presence was as unwelcome as it was unavoidable.

The torn page, from the night he had returned from Herbert's murder, still lay where he had dropped it in the small living room opposite the bedroom door; a paper thin jewel in the flat's chaotic mess. It caught his eye as Peter, clean and presentable in a fresh black suit, blue shirt and paisley tie, headed for the door and he shuddered as he stared at it. The sound of aggressive car horns duelling down the busy street outside tore him from his thoughts and he move to the door with a slight limp, slamming it behind him as his annoyance returned along with the throbbing in his healing foot.

His mood did not improve on his journey to the Party Office, the only positive to come from the previous day being his move from the main office to Mirushka's private staff, giving him the access he needed to properly prepare and sketch an outline plan for her demise.

His planning was interrupted by the nervousness at the office that soon turned into blind panic as the latest polls came in throughout the day. Football, of all things, proved to be the cause of the biggest 'wobble' in public support for the Party since its conception, causing Černý to scowl, the electoral strategists to ponder and those that had thought to celebrate the Czech victory by donning replica strips to squirm. As the buzz of anxiety around him intensified at the reports of the Party lead being slashed to single digits, Peter allowed himself a moment of euphoria in the hope that Mirushka's death would not, after all, be necessary, before cursing his sentimental foolishness. The telephones in the Private Office never stopped ringing and Peter found himself fielding calls from the length and breadth of both Republics, testing his thin patience and stretching his interpretation skills to their limits.

The working day passed with the chaotic mood of the Party showing little sign of abating. Peter slunk silently away from the pack, heading back up to the comfortless tomb he called home; the focus brought by his assignment successfully binding the nervous exhaustion within him.

Once at the flat, he quickly changed into a simple black polo shirt with white trim, grey jeans and a black, high buttoned, knee length jacket fastened up to his chin. Grabbing and opening a bottle of Czech beer from the otherwise sparse fridge, he made for the door but stopped cold at the entrance to the living room. In truth, Peter had hardly been back to the flat in the weeks since Herbert's death, relying instead on Rasti's generosity, and when he had, he'd been functioning purely on autopilot – shit, shower, shave then back outside in a fresh suit. Virtually every corner of the flat remained as it had been on the morning he'd awoken there, head typically pounding, aching fingers clutching a torn tissue thin page. The book he had torn it from still lay discarded on the floor in front of him just as he had left it; motionlessly accusatory, the crumpled page that had distracted him that morning alongside it. Peter stared wide eyed and strangely nervous; his left hand unconsciously toying with the softly jingling keys in his pocket. He lifted the bottle to his lips and took a swig, unblinking and silent as the cold, carbonated ale washed over his tongue and down his throat. The chilled liquid's contact with the small cavity in one of his back teeth made him hiss and curse, breaking him free from the invisible grip.

Though Peter cursed his own illogicality and bid superstition be damned, he could almost feel the twisted, wrinkled page observing him, condemning him. Slowly, too slowly for his own liking, ashamed at lending credence to his foolishness, he crossed over to the room and on blind yet reluctant instinct he stepped quickly inside and picked up the source of his discomfort, stuffing it into his pocket before turning on his heel and slamming the door to his flat behind him.

Arriving at the stop just as a dirty red and white tram heaved itself into view, Peter fumbled in his pockets for a ticket and jumped on, sinking into a vacant seat. Wedging his beer between his thigh and the hard plastic chair he became conscious of the anchoring weight of his eyelids and he blinked hard, scanning for something, anything, on which to focus, to spare him further torture. Fixing his eyes on the back of a figure sat several seats ahead of him, Peter listed its features to keep his mind active; the black overcoat covering hunched shoulders, navy scarf wrapped tightly around the neck…The list continued until he ran out of features to comment on, but still Peter stared, willing away the exhaustion. But as the stare continued and as if feeling the tired eyes burrowing into it, the figure slowly turned and Peter stared once more into the eyes of Herbert Biely.

He woke with a jolt, jarring the bottle and spilling some of its contents on his leg and the floor before he composed himself and grabbed it. One or two passengers glanced disapprovingly at him, disturbed by his sudden exclamation upon waking, while others buried their heads into papers, turned up music or stared impassively through the windows, determined at all costs to avoid eye contact. Cursing quietly, Peter tried in vain to wipe the spilled ale from his leg before abandoning his futile efforts and sitting back again. A louder curse followed as he felt his eyelids continue to droop and he stood up in defiant resentment of his exhaustion.

The tram was pulling into a stop and Peter checked through the windows for his location: Pavlova. Partly through a desire to let the rain wash the beer from his jeans but mostly through fear of falling asleep again, Peter disembarked and proceeded to follow the main road down to Wenceslas Square, his emptier bottle grasped in his hand. About five minutes later, soaked and cold, Peter reached the square and stopped to rest by the imposing memorial to Saint Wenceslas. Leaning against the drenched monument and lifting his bottle to his lips to stop the biting rain diluting it further, his heart sank at the illuminated sight before him. His beloved Prague, a city of culture, of history and beauty dressed up like some cheap harlot and made to dance for the people that violated her. Like a vandalised portrait, all around the square, the black as pitch night was punctuated with neon lights, fast food outlets, clubs, strip joints and bars, while prostitutes, dealers and pick pockets hung around in dark alcoves waiting to take advantage of the drunkards inside. This was why Peter stayed away from Wenceslas Square. Seeing Prague like this was like watching an adored teenage daughter stagger home from a debauched night out, tights laddered, bra unhooked and virtue in question. Or akin to watching an ageing loved one deliriously reject sobriety and descend into alcoholic stupor.

Draining the last of the beer from his bottle Peter glanced up at the figure on the plinth above him who likewise gazed at the square that shared his name with a look of offended nobility.

"Sorry mate," Peter said aloud hurling the empty bottle into a nearby waste bin, "but at least I can't be blamed for this."

Stuffing his hands into his pockets he set off through the ocean of sin before him, the waves of thieves and hustlers that lined the square parting for him as he walked Moses-like through their midst. The look of grim disapproval on Peter's face told them to stay away clearer than any words could and he wore it for that reason. He didn't have time for crackheads and whores and if anyone was unwise enough to follow him down the square extolling the dubious virtues of the latest skin bar then they'd wake up in a hospital bed if they woke at all. He needed a drink and he'd be damned if he was going to have it here. What Peter wanted was the only sanctuary Prague still begrudgingly allowed him, the shelter of the Smokin' Hot Blues Bar with its uncomfortable chairs and cold draught blowing through its never fully closed doors. He wanted his usual table and his usual drink while the usual Thursday night duo wailed their usual blues. Anything else would be a deviation and a deviation would affect the concentration he needed in abundance, for there was murder to be planned tonight.

He could already hear the blues calling to him from Smokin' Hot as he rounded the corner onto Jakubská and headed inside, but before he could make it through the entrance he felt a buzz in his pocket. Thinking it a message from Mirushka, a giddiness embraced him and he pulled his phone excitedly from his jeans, only for the warmth to dissipate as the name 'Deprez' appeared on the display. Touching the message open, his pleasure at least partly restored at the unexpectedly positive words it contained.

'Poll data requires assessment, suspend project pending full analysis'

"Result!" Peter leapt up and punched the air, shouting out his words without concern. "I'll suspend the fucking project mate, no problem!" He'd done it! The slimy bastard had done it for once; he'd studied the polls, seen the lead slip and decided *Mirushka* didn't need killing after all, at least not right now. Well Peter wasn't going to let this opportunity pass by; tonight he was going to celebrate.

He swaggered into the bar with his widest smile in many a day affixed to his face, radiating cheerfulness to all patrons. Behind the bar, as usual, was Michael, who raised an eyebrow at his regular's demeanour.

"Bottle of champagne please, Michael." Peter stretched his grin wider still

Michael's raised eyebrow was joined by its associate.

"Champagne?" he asked, failing to disguise the surprise in his voice.

"The best you've got. Time for a little celebration, I reckon, I've been moping about for too long."

Michael turned to the fridge to pull one of the rarely ordered bottles from the back. "I couldn't swear this is any good," he said honestly to his customer.

"Then put it back." Michael and Peter both turned to see Rasti coming through the door. Dressed in his usual attire of cargo pants, faded t-shirt and battered leather jacket, somewhat damp, dirty blonde hair partially masking his round, cheery face, the big Czech gave Michael the usual arm around the shoulder in greeting as he walked around the bar, then turned to his friend.

"Why would you want champagne?" he demanded. "You wouldn't even know what to do with it. That's like ordering egg and chips every day for a lifetime from the same café only to waltz up one day demanding lobster thermidor."

Peter's laugh carried an air of indignation. "Piss off," he countered, "I'll have you know I used to drink plenty of champagne back in the day."

"Back in the day perhaps," Rasti said, "but that day was a long fucking time ago. No self respecting champagne wants to end up being pissed against the wall of a sports bar by a man who doesn't appreciate it."

Peter shook his head at the passion of his friend's disapproval, which, if nothing else, had helped maintain Peter's currently lighter mood.

"Look mate," he eventually said, "I just felt the need to relive the old days a bit. Call it nostalgia or whatever."

Rastislav was Peter's friend. Peter's good friend, the pair drawn to each other by their shared love of the food, the drink and the blues served up at Smokin' Hot. Rasti was the restaurant's head chef and owner and loved his venue so much he spent most of his free time there; so much in fact that Peter wondered exactly when he was supposed to be on duty. Rasti was a naturally big man, not fat, just big; but his voice carried an unexpectedly paternal calm. The frame gave the impression of a 'gentle giant' and Rasti's casual and laid back demeanour added to the perception. A small cross dangled from his neck, a reminder of his days in the Priesthood, and now the former man of the cloth stood in a half-full blues bar, leather coat flung onto the stand in the corner, talking champagne with a man he didn't know to be a murderer.

"Well, if I'm going to drink champagne with you," he said, "it isn't going to be the piss we stock here. Come on upstairs to the office with me."

Giving Michael a hearty slap on the back, he escorted his friend through the enclosed beer garden and up the narrow stone steps behind the wooden door. Above the restaurant were a collection of rooms that came with the lease but which were rarely, if ever, used. When Rasti could be bothered he rented a couple out to visiting business people but for the most part they remained empty, except when used to accommodate a drunken Peter, which had happened more often of late. One room though, which Peter had never been inside, housed Rasti's office and the Manchester man felt a childlike pang of curiosity as Rasti opened the door.

The room was surprisingly spacious, piled high with folders and poorly stacked papers. In the far corner stood two large chillers filled with row upon row of green bottles, resplendent with foil tops and each with its own label carefully facing up.

"Nice gaff." Peter was genuinely impressed.

"What's the occasion?" Rasti stood between the two chillers, awaiting Peter's answer, "good news or drowning sorrows?"

"If I was drowning my sorrows I'd have stayed downstairs with your usual piss," Peter grinned in response.

"Good fridge it is then." Rasti slid over to the fridge on his right, swinging it open and stooping to run his eye over the labels.

"You have a good fridge and a bad fridge?"

"One for good champagne and one for bad; I need something to toast bad news with."

"You toast bad news?" Peter grinned quizzically at his friend's revelation.

"I'm a good Catholic," came the response, "I rejoice in The Lord for everything, but I'm not going to celebrate a tax bill with the Dom Perignon '96. There's a particularly foul bottle around here somewhere in case they ever tell me I'm dying."

"How come we've never done this before?"

Rasti shrugged. "Because we're always downstairs with the bands."

The big Czech pulled two dark green bottles from the rack, letting the door swing shut and returning to sit opposite Peter at the large, paper strewn desk, clunking a bottle in front of each of them and pulling the foil from the top of his own.

Peter raised an appreciative eyebrow at the label and likewise began to peel his way to the wire cage housing the cork.

"Glasses?"

The chef puffed out his cheeks, the thought seemingly occurring to him for the first time. Looking around for whatever was within reach, he pulled two mugs down from the shelf adjacent to the desk. Quickly examining them he opted for the one with the naked lady handle and tossed the other to Peter.

"You'd better have that one."

"Oh cheers mate," Peter replied a little sarcastically, as he peered inside to find a small but determined ceramic phallus fixed to the inner base.

"I'm not sure Madame Bollinger would approve."

Rasti shrugged again. "If she shows up she can have my cup. She's probably too posh for this place anyway."

"And you carry off your commonness like a champion." Peter grinned, extending his now full vulgar cup towards his comrade.

"Second only to you my friend." Rasti returned the grin and clinked his own crude mug against Peter's in the most mildly offensive toast either man could remember.

"To..?" Rasti quizzed.

Peter pondered for a moment. "To the temporary and ideally permanent suspension of superfluous and wholly unnecessary caveats of already laborious big wig orchestrated bullshit projects."

Rasti blinked. "And all who sail in her." He said.

Draining and refilling the cups, Rasti held his aloft again. "And to the imminent birth of a new Czechoslovakia."

Peter drank to his friend's sentiment, suppressing the twinge of guilt it awoke in him.

"Bloody hell, not you too."

"Why not?"

"No reason, you've just never struck me as being particularly political, that's all."

Rasti shook his head. "I'm not, but this election isn't about politics, it's about choice, about the future of the country. Or countries…"

The topic sat uncomfortably with Peter and he reached into his pocket, nervously toying his keys.

"What does it matter, really? Czechoslovakia was always an artificial state, who cares where someone draws the boundaries this time?"

"Because this time it's us who decides where they are drawn!" Rasti looked as enthusiastic as Peter had ever seen him. "This is the first time someone hasn't just come along and told us what would happen. Nazis, Communists and even the men supposed to be our leaders, just so they could be kings of their own little castles. This time the people have a choice and that's really all I want."

He sat back and refilled his mug once more.

"Anyway," he said, "from now on, this is a politics free zone."

"You're right!" Beamed Peter, slapping the desk, happy that the conversation was over. "Time for some music!"

"You want to go back down?" Rasti asked.

"No way! I mean the guys are brilliant, but I need something different tonight, something to move to."

Peter was wired, rising from his chair and pacing the room and turning to his friend. "You've still got my tables haven't you?"

Rasti nodded. It had been some time ago that Rasti had borrowed Peter's turntables to host a DJ night at the restaurant and since then they had gathered dust up here, along with several boxes of records loaned from Peter's extensive collection.

Rasti gestured to the cupboard which housed the artefacts

and Peter grinned like a child at Christmas, quickly and expertly setting them up.

"You're in for a treat now mate!" he laughed. "And I want to see you dance!"

Rasti took in the peculiar sight with interest and shook his head. "Believe me Peter, no-one wants to see that."

"Course they do! Crack open another bottle and get up on the floor."

Whether due to Mirushka's unexpected reprieve or the offensive mugs of expensive champagne, or a combination of both, Peter felt as light headed and light hearted as he could remember and he was determined to enjoy it, cramming in as much fun as possible while he could.

He peeled a precious vinyl gem from its sleeve and ran his thumb over the circular edge like it was a blade waiting to cut through his misery. He placed it delicately on the turntable and lifted the needle.

A blast of hot electric organ exploded from the speakers, accompanied by a piercing horn section and a twang of understated guitar, delighting Peter and shocking Rasti upright. Peter stepped away from the tables into the middle of the room and span around, rocking his shoulders and twisting his legs into an echo of the dances he used to do, like a neglected engine, slowly creeping to life after the proper injection of oil.

"How can you sit still to this?!" he bellowed at his friend.

"Because I might look like you." Came the reply.

"Only if you're lucky."

Giving in, Rasti got up and pulled another two bottles from his 'good fridge', as Peter twisted and turned, and joined him in the middle on the floor.

"Well," the big Czech started, "you asked for it."

And they danced. Uninhibited, unashamed, heaving with laughter as champagne bubbles forced their lips apart. They Whoop-ee'd and Wang Dang Doodle'd, they Waded and Testified, they Begged and Hushed and Dusted Brooms, as though the salvation of their very souls depended on the shuffling of their feet and the strutting of their stuff, to the vinyl Peter masterfully spun.

He played until their dancing became a stagger and their shuffling became a hug, inspired as much by the need to stay upright as friendship, until the needle scratched on tunelessness, signalling the end of their interlude and pre-empting their collapse into their respective chairs.

The laughter continued, driven now by exhaustion rather than the hilarity of earlier, and Peter's mind began to wander once more, at least as far as his intoxication would allow.

"It's all about the choices." Peter muttered to himself, but loud enough to stir Rasti, who promptly staggered up and towards the door.

"It's too late for a deep and meaningful," he yawned, "I'm shagged and I need to make sure Michael's locked up properly. Are you staying here tonight?"

Peter nodded, "Room for a little 'un with you?" he teased.

"In your fucking dreams mate!" Came the response, punctuated by the slamming door.

Peter knew he should get up and go to one of the spare rooms, to crash in an actual bed, but he simply couldn't be bothered, preferring instead to stick his feet up on the desk and let his all too rare contentment keep him warm. Tapping his foot in time to the memory of the tunes he had played, Peter, for the first time in weeks, willingly closed his eyes to the oncoming rest, satisfied that it held no horrors for him tonight. And as he slipped drunkenly into sleep, his freshly unconscious mind neither cared about, nor even registered, the softly buzzing telephone in his jeans pocket.

CHAPTER 8

HE AWOKE WITH A GASP, jarring forward so hard he nearly fell from the chair, the sudden movement cricking his neck from its uncomfortable position and forcing his body from the twisted pose it had stiffened into overnight. Peter's sleep had not been the revitalising sanctuary his intoxication had led him to expect, and he sat still for a moment, shaking the nightmares from his delicate head. His mouth dry, he sat up looking for anything to dampen it, finding half an obscene cup of flat champagne which made him grimace as he drank it. The liquid disappeared like a thimble of water into cracked earth and his mouth felt none the better for it, only more sour and matching his mood.

The by now semi-regular routine of shower, fresh suit and fresher coffee followed, all courtesy of the absent and apparently unaffected Rasti, before he dashed out at a run to reach Party HQ and the returned Mirushka.

Peter's giddy anticipation of seeing her again was tempered by her granite expression as he walked into the room and the coolness in her voice as she instructed him to accompany her and the nervous young aide, Adrianna, down to the waiting car once again.

"Where are we off to?"

"High Tatra."

"Slovakia? You've just come from there! I thought you had engagements in Prague today?" Peter was still breathless from his run and struggled to keep pace with the two women.

"And I've had them," she shouted over her shoulder, "the Radio interview and Thought for the Day at 6:00am, the choreographed commute with the people at 7:00am and the joint appearance with Karol for Breakfast TV at 8:00am. Now I have to be in Tatra for the afternoon tea with Party donors; they won't accept being pushed back again."

"The schedule was agreed months back, but we didn't know you'd be Prime Minister then." The young aide sensed a rebuke from her boss, who smiled reassuringly back at her.

"It's no problem," Mirushka soothed. "What good is election season if it can't keep me busy?"

The three reached the car, the driver, Ivan, waiting patiently as ever by the open door. Once inside, Mirushka collapsed into her seat and let out an exaggerated sigh, before looking over to Peter and finally giving him the smile he had craved.

"I'm sorry to surprise you," she said softly, "but I have a feeling I will need you with me today."

"My pleasure," he grinned back. "Happy to help."

The car set off, picking up speed as two police motorbikes pulled out alongside it as escort and Mirushka's demeanour became once more rigidly professional, gesturing to her aide.

"Adrianna."

The young woman handed her a raft of day old newspapers.

"Just look at them!" She threw the folded sheets over to Peter who didn't need to look to know what she was referring to.

The same picture had adorned the front cover of every paper in the country the previous day: a grinning Karol Černý sat a few seats away from a grimacing Svobodova as the Czech Republic's winning goal thundered into the net. Each headline offering some pithy, witty joke about the 'end of harmony' or 'trouble in paradise'.

Peter was unmoved. "They're just having a laugh with you," He attempted, "Elections are open season on politicians, you know that, and you've never struck me as someone too concerned with what the papers had to say."

Mirushka was unconvinced. "It's not just the papers Peter, it's the polls."

"Well we're all worried about the Poles."

Peter's joke was met with a look of mild disappointment. He shrugged it off. "Look, the response is obvious isn't it? You just tell whoever asks that you look forward to the next round of internationals containing the new Czechoslovak Side; what a team that'll be."

Mirushka nodded sagely. "That's why your Institute speaks so highly of you Peter. Now, both of you, if you don't mind I'm going to grab a couple of hours sleep." She settled back and closed her eyes. "This car is about the only place I can call home these days," she yawned, "but at least I have somewhere away from the world to mull over strategies and policies and rogue polls…"

Mirushka fell silent while young Adrianna pressed herself into the other corner and busied herself with papers, files and reports.

Sat opposite the two of them, Peter said nothing, his smile having receded back into his lined face. 'Your Institute',

Mirushka had said, 'rogue polls'. Her words, and the realisation that he had not looked at his phone since the previous night, compelled him to draw it from his pocket, dread thumping through his chest with each beat of his heart, pounding louder as he stared at the message that lay in wait for him.

'Rogue polls,' it read, *'reunification still likely. Suggested you continue with project as planned and avoid unnecessary delay to ensure successful completion of overall strategy.'*

As the car sped on, rushing through the peppering of new rain, Peter sank deeper into his seat, the elation of the previous evening now ripped from his body. He was once more the ageing murderer, staring across the car at his victim. And he felt sick to his very soul.

CHAPTER 9

THE NAUSEA WAS A PERMANENT FEATURE of the journey, bringing with it a return of the granite expression Peter had worn for much of the past few weeks, the perfect accompaniment to his silence. Svobodova had remained sleeping for virtually the entire journey, a small mercy for which Peter was not ungrateful, and when she had awoken, he feigned sleep himself to avoid conversation. There was to be no more foolishness on his part, no more sentimentality. Svobodova must die.

When the car arrived at the Tatra mountains, Svobodova stepped from it, fresh and Prime Ministerial, having swapped her high heels for snow boots and her suit jacket for a long, winter coat. Peter travelled in her wake, a dark suited spectre of misfortune, a few short paces behind her as they travelled their choreographed path to the tourist centre. She caught his eye only once, as she stepped into the small cable car and gestured for Peter and Adrianna to take the one behind, an eyebrow furrowing for the briefest of seconds her only acknowledgement of Peter's dark expression. Peter continued to stare through the glass at his target, reluctant to lose sight of her even for a moment in case his clarity was disturbed and he fell back into introspection; a luxury he could not afford until the job was over.

Hanging back as he stepped from the carriage and the party moved into the luxurious dining area overlooking the mountainside, he observed her movements, her body language, recording each facet in his mind as she circulated the room before moving out onto the small private balcony for the obligatory 'top of the world' shots.

The balcony was narrow and was fast becoming cramped as photographers and well wishers spilled onto it, pushing Svobodova back against the rail and causing her for the first time to look flustered and irritated by the cameras surrounding her. Two of her security detachment, led by a young, well-built Slovak with a goatee, began to push the guests back, while some photographers ducked and slid and pushed themselves forward, eager for one more shot of Eastern Europe's Uncrowned Queen atop the snowy mountain with the sun setting majestically in the background. As they pressed forward, Svobodova stepped back, her boots betraying her as she slid backwards towards the gap in the rail and the perilous edge of the mountain. An arm shot through the crowded bodies, hooking her around the waist, halting her slide and pulling her up to her feet.

Ensuring she was steady, Peter released his grip and smiled sheepishly as Mirushka beamed once more for the cameras, gesturing to Peter, who felt in that moment like sliding off the mountain himself.

"My hero!" Mirushka joked to the laughter and applause of the relieved crowd.

"Bollocks," whispered Peter.

———

Hours later and leaning on an altogether different balcony rail, Peter looked up at the fairy tail castle dominating the view, framed by the densely forested hillside. Even with dark clouds hanging over it and the rumble of thunder in the distance it was beautiful. On the other side of the hill, beyond Peter's sight lay the resort that had been the catalyst of Herbert's Slovak regeneration; fine hotels and the best restaurants cradling the rejuvenated spa that Herbert had loved so much. The whole complex housing the great and the good blended seamlessly with the stretch of traditional taverns, pensions and eateries that lined the road leading up to the castle; an exemplary and natural mix of the old and the new. Closer to Peter were oblong apartment blocks that typified the communist era; grey and soulless to the outside world but inside bustling with the neighbourliness and community spirit so absent in the enlightened west. The balcony Peter stood on belonged to one such apartment; the Svobodova family home, empty these days but previously the hub of Mirushka's life. On the ground below stood a car full of security and Peter saw a black suited operative standing silently by the communal door. He knew that the young agent with the goatee, whose name, Peter had learned was Rado, would be standing outside the flat's front door and he guessed that he wasn't the only security presence inside the building. Peter took a deep lungful of the fresh, clean air and closed his eyes. Bojnice couldn't have been less like Prague but it had a magic all of its own. His chest felt lighter than it had done in years and he spent a few seconds just standing there filling and emptying his lungs. His relaxation was interrupted by Mirushka's voice coming from inside the flat calling him to the kitchen.

He walked through the lounge and into the small kitchen,

where a wooden table and two chairs had been set up; a faded tablecloth hastily thrown over it. Peter had cursed himself for the incident a few hours earlier which was now being displayed as the final item on news reports across both countries, leading him to turn his phone off to avoid the inevitable furious rebuke from Deprez. It had not been a big slip, and would probably not have resulted in any harm to Mirushka, but instead of taking the chance, Peter had opted to play the hero, with the consequence of having his face plastered across the media for the whole region to see. And when Mirushka had publically rewarded her 'hero' with an invitation to dinner, he had at least managed to whisper his insistence that it be in private. Though she had agreed, he was more than a little surprised to find himself swept up in the car on the two hour trip away from the snow to Bojnice, while the remainder of the entourage enjoyed the luxury of the Tatra resort.

Sitting down, Peter looked up at Mirushka who stood at the stove, her back to him, toiling over a big pan of what smelled like cabbage soup.

Hearing the scrape of his chair, Mirushka ladled big portions of the soup into bowls and placed them on the table. "It's all very well dining in luxury with corrupt politicians and perverted diplomats more interested in what's in my bra than the menu," Mirushka sat down opposite Peter at the small rickety table, "but sometimes a girl likes to cook in her own kitchen, away from prying eyes."

Peter felt a pang of admonishment having enjoyed her form while the soup was cooking but judged by the mischievous smile on Mirushka's face that she was teasing him. He grinned his own impish grin, thanked her for the soup and took a big spoonful.

Having lived in this part of the world for so long, Peter was an aficionado and huge fan of the region's cuisine and he smacked his lips as the hot, sour liquid went down.

He looked up at the tired beauty of the woman sharing her meal with him. The make up was gone, her hair dishevelled and her face tired. The bags under her eyes betrayed her exhaustion and seeing Peter's gaze she hung her head slightly, allowing her hair to mask her face. Peter still stared, admitting to himself that this was the most naturally beautiful woman he had ever known, and it struck him just how difficult political life must have been for her.

Men like Herbert and Karol Černý were gentlemen of the old school, far above the tactics of others who would regularly barter career advancement for a little 'close personal attention'. Peter finished chewing the chorizo in his mouth and swallowed. "It must have been difficult to get where you are now," Peter voiced his thoughts matter-of-factly, "I expect there were a number of men jealous of you."

Mirushka swallowed a spoonful of her own soup and shrugged slightly. "I am not an apologist for laziness Peter nor do I blame all the evils in the world on white, middle class males, but it is true that being a woman in politics is hard." She reached for the bottle of slivovice on the table and poured measures into the two glasses that had been waiting next to it; brushing her hair back from her face she offered one to Peter. "If you are plain and unattractive you are ignored, and if you are pretty people assume you are stupid and treat you like a model. They may just as well strip us naked and write 'Vote For Me' on our breasts." She downed her shot and took a quick swallow of water to chase it. "And then there is always someone who thinks you will take him to Heaven in exchange for the key to the executive bathroom; if you say no pretty soon the newspapers are saying that you are a lesbian."

"That shouldn't matter in this day and age."

"Unfortunately not everybody is so enlightened."

"Has that ever happened to you?"

"Of course, back in the early days. I was an easy target. I have never married so it is easy enough for a journalist to insinuate things and make their little comments. But so what? I would rather be screwed by the press than by those pathetic little men." Her last words were spoken in a quiet, bitter voice and Peter downed his own drink and picked up the bottle to refill their glasses. Mirushka took another spoonful of the soup and carried on, "But it was different with Herbert. Herbert was very, very kind."

"I'd never doubt that for a minute." Peter responded. Mirushka put down her spoon and elaborated needlessly on the late man's many qualities.

"He was a strong leader," she expressed, wanting to be sure that point was understood, "there was no favouritism with him, he only wanted the best for his country and the people who worked for him…" She tailed off, a tear forming in her eye which she fought to repress. Her reaction tugged at Peter's barely controlled guilt and he quickly changed the subject.

"What about Černý?" he asked. Mirushka took a deep breath and gave a tired laugh.

"Ah, Karol, my dear Karol…" she shook her head smiling. "He is a good man Peter, a national hero. No-one could have asked more of him during the Spring, Herbert often spoke of his bravery. And during the Revolution it was his eloquence that helped Havel rouse our people."

"But?" Peter pressed, sensing she was holding back.

"But...he is a little old fashioned," she answered diplomatically, "he expected the Party to make him the senior partner in the leadership and the press calling him 'the little girl's lap dog' has hurt his pride quite badly. He's probably justified too, I know I would feel angry in his shoes."

With that she picked up her spoon again and continued eating her soup. Peter, without taking his eyes off her, tried to think of a way to assuage the guilt she felt over Černý's treatment.

"You deserve to be leader," was all he could muster to which Mirushka gave a short, sardonic laugh.

"Oh I don't Peter, I really don't," she managed through a half full mouth. "Of all the things I deserve in life, to be leader of my country, to be *his* successor isn't one of them." Her voice was beginning to crack a little and Peter suddenly found he had lost his appetite. He had never been good at consoling women or understanding why compliments so often led to tears and he supposed it was useless to try and change that now. Instead he put down his spoon as quietly as possible and sat, awkwardly watching her, wondering what he should say or do next. Mirushka spared him that decision.

"And what about you my big, strong hero?" She asked, the tear in her eye now returned with reinforcements, "What do you deserve in life?"

The question threw Peter off balance. He knew precisely what he deserved in this world, and the next, but had no way of explaining that to the woman now weeping at the memory of his last victim. After a second or two's composure he gave a small shrug.

"Not my decision," he answered, "I doubt I deserve very

much of anything to be honest. We've all done bad things in our lives, handled things the wrong way; God knows I have. But maybe it's not about the things we've done; maybe it's about making the most of what we've got now. I hope so anyway. You might not think you deserve to be here Mirushka and maybe you don't, I'm not going to try and change your mind. But you are here and maybe you should just accept that and do the best bloody job you can. You might not deserve it but this is where you are, and in my eyes you're still the best person for the job."

Peter found himself pushing forward to lean close to Mirushka, his hand sub- consciously moving across the table toward her. She reached her own hand out to gently grasp it and lifted her cloudy eyes to his, her mischievousness showing behind them.

"Miláčku." She said.

"What?" whispered Peter, his hand returning Mirushka's intoxicating touch.

"It means 'Darling'," she said, smiling at his puzzled face, "I wanted to call you my darling."

Peter knew exactly what he was doing. When he accepted Mirushka's embrace, holding her head and returning her unrestrained kiss, he couldn't be sure what was going through her mind. Infatuation? Misplaced gratitude? Perhaps an escape from the burden of expectation? But whatever it was, he knew for certain that his own thoughts were clear and that he was doing this because he wanted to. As the pair fumbled in disorganised excitement, torn between passionate exploration and the careful undoing of buttons and zips, Peter knew precisely what to expect. Carrying her through the flat and into her bedroom, the guilt boiling in his gut failing to stop him in his tracks, Peter knew that her seeking an escape through him, would lead her to only one place, the place he willingly carried her to now; the inexorable road to hell.

CHAPTER 10

"I DIDN'T THINK YOU WORE LEATHER." Rasti stood next to the seated and battered leather jacketed Peter who looked up and frowned.

"I don't generally hang around with arseholes either, but here I am."

The response was met with a huge laugh and the chef slammed two shot glasses and a bottle of familiar looking spirit on the table. Rasti stepped away to the bar for a moment and Peter took the opportunity to soak up the crackling twelve bar shuffle coming from the speakers. While each night at Smokin' Hot was blessed with live acts, the restaurant honoured its 'Blues Bar' status by playing classic riffs and well blown harps from the tired old CD player behind the bar. The music relaxed him after the tedious six hour journey back to Prague, begun that morning when a rushed morning after conversation with Mirushka resulted in him being driven back for two days off while she remained for the day in Slovakia on government business, before heading back to join the campaign trail in Prague later.

Even two days of semi-freedom were insufficient however

to lift his spirits from the dung heap he found himself in. If befriending Herbert was a mistake then sleeping with Mirushka was a catastrophe, which would only ensure that Peter's mission would become messier and his guilt more profound. He shuddered at the prospect and tried to force his mind elsewhere.

Rasti returned, brow furrowed, scrutinising the front page of a much flicked through newspaper. Unfolding it in front of him, Peter found himself staring at his own face, cringing at the sentimental expression it wore while Mirushka's visage beamed into it.

"Hero of the hour....diligent aide...." Rasti muttered, clearly enjoying his friend's squirming reaction. "You must be very proud."

"Piss off."

"I thought you worked for some EU thing, that 'Institute' you told me about? You never said you were a courtier to my uncrowned Queen."

"You never asked."

"True." Rasti sat down opposite his friend, dropping the paper to the table and pulling a well-worn deck of cards from his pocket.

"How can we play with just the two of us?"

"We'll manage; I want to get my money back for the champagne."

"She's really something Rasti," Peter half whispered knocking back a shot of Slivovice and clamping his gullet hard as it tried to reject the violently flavoured spirit.

"I know she's really something, "Rasti answered, completing his deal. "The woman of your dreams." The Czech's sarcasm radiated from him, extending even to the exaggerated manner in which he dealt the cards.

Peter paused, his fingers touching the freshly dealt hand which lay face down on the varnished wooden table. "Why would you say that?"

Rasti smiled and picked up his own cards. "Well she'd better be. Usually you only pull tourists you've picked up in here, or women you've met on the way home from here; you're sex's answer to a drive through takeaway. You light their cigarette with one hand and dial their taxi with the other. You can't do that with this one…"

Peter grinned like a schoolboy with a crush. Feeling a little sheepish he picked up and carefully examined his cards. "Aye, your right, she's a wonder though that's for sure."

Rasti lifted his eyes from the cards and smiled gently at his friend. Peter knew that despite Rasti's wicked sense of humour and comic insults, his concern for Peter's well being was genuine and palpable. He knew also that Rasti would be thinking that the drink and soft blues playing in the background had the power to sweep Peter into a depression he would be determined to prevent. Peter was grateful for the honest concern of a friend, even if the friend was ignorant as to the reasons behind Peter's depression.

Sure enough, Rasti attempted to probe the obvious distress that had showed on Peter's face when he walked through the door.

"So why did you walk in here looking like an undertaker with piles?"

Peter shook his head in mock despair. "Do all Priests talk like you?"

"Churches might be a bit fuller if they did, but that doesn't answer my question."

"Why do you think? She's a world leader and I'm a..." He tailed off, not wanting or knowing how to end the sentence. "Anyway, work won't be impressed with me."

"Ah, I see." The big man threw a hundred koruna note to the table. "Office politics eh?"

Peter frowned, "What would you know about office politics? You're an ex-Priest and a half-arsed chef."

He threw down a hundred to match Rasti who looked at him with feigned offence.

"I'll have you know I'm an entirely arsed chef," he said indignantly. "I just enjoy the company of my clientele out on the floor, that's all. Spending time with you helps me realise how much I have to be grateful for. And anyway you're not the only one who's had a work place romance; I once had a fling with a nun."

Peter spat his spirit back into his glass. "A nun?! I thought you guys were supposed to be celibate!"

Rasti looked defensive, "You try taking a vow of celibacy then going to work with virgins in sexy costumes and see how long you hold out. And anyway it wasn't a big fling; we stayed friends... any raise?" Peter shook his head and Rasti picked up the deck in front of him. "How many?"

"Three." Rasti dealt them out and took one new card for himself. Peter checked again and grimaced as Rasti threw down a five hundred Koruna note. He covered and in reluctant deference to the game raised his friend another five hundred.

"Anyway, I expect I'll be firmly put in my place for getting too close," Peter mused. "Work prefers me to keep my distance when I'm on assignment."

"You slept with her instead?"

"Pretty much."

"Was it worth it?"

"Absolutely."

"Do you love her?"

"What?"

"Do you love her?" Rasti repeated his question and at once Peter saw his demeanour change to that of a hard line priest pushing to unearth the hidden sins of his flock. He groped for an answer. Did he love her? It had been so long since he had been in love he wasn't even sure that he wanted to be again. Eventually he stumbled on an answer.

"It's impossible."

Rasti pressed on. "Impossible for you to feel love or impossible for you to be with her?"

"Either, both.." Peter felt himself becoming flustered and felt a pang of shame at the responses he was giving. "Anyway, it's not quite that simple mate."

The big Czech responded with a bellow of laughter. "Of course it is! If you love her, tell your 'Institute' that you are damn well going to be with her and they can stick their job up their arse if they don't like it. You can get a job here if you need one; I could do with a new waiter."

Peter smiled and envied the simple outlook on life his friend could afford. It wasn't that simple of course but Peter wished to God that it was.

"Well, she's probably not that into me anyway."

Another belly laugh. "The problem with you Peter is that

you just don't understand women." Rasti matched Peter's raise and sat pondering whether to raise further. "You have worse people skills than the Golem."

Peter was puzzled at the reference. "What's he go to do with it?" he asked.

"He's over there now in the new synagogue. Undisturbed for centuries, a mindless lump of clay, but he knows more about women than you."

Peter thought this probably true and threw down a couple of notes to match his friend's raise. "Maybe we could go over there and ask him?" Peter pondered.

Rasti frowned again, his eyes not leaving his cards. "Nah," he said. "He's Jewish, I'm a Catholic and you're a lapsed Methodist, we probably wouldn't get on."

"What's wrong with that?" he asked, "I wasn't going to ask him to sing Shine Jesus Shine."

"No," said Rasti putting his cards face up on the table, "but the last time he met any gentiles they weren't being particularly nice to his Jewish friends and I suspect he has a long memory. Plus I don't want to have to fight a Golem while you mope around crying about girls. Cards."

Peter looked down to the table at the Full House staring back at him then back at the pair of Kings in his own hand. He dropped them to the table cursing his luck. "Bollocks!"

Rasti scooped his winnings from the table. "Exactly," he said, "the best hand I've had in weeks and it comes on a day when you're being a little girl. I could've taken you to the cleaners if your mind had been on the game! You should never think about women during poker; I learned that at the seminary."

Peter's eyebrows raised at the remark. "Are you sure

you were a priest? What else did you get up to in between hustling cards and shagging nuns? Did you drown puppies in the vestry?"

"I used to punch parishioners who thought they were too cool to fall in love. I've been meaning to get back in the habit."

He grinned his big, cheery grin at Peter, who smiled back and raised his full again glass, chinking it against his friend's. Finally pausing to acknowledge the cavalcade of missed calls and text messages that had buzzed away since he switched his phone back on, Peter briefly rattled off a one word affirmative to the ordered meeting atop the clock tower later that day. Until then, Peter had neither the need nor the inclination to think either about his mission nor his impending chastisement for jeopardising it. Instead, he proposed to confine his thoughts to the fullness of his glass and conversation of his friend. Downing the next shot prepared for him, Peter slammed the glass to the table and grinned across at the Czech chef opposite.

"Fill her up, Rasti," he said.

———

He very quickly lost track of the number of hours he sat there, knocking back glass after glass of spirit, chased with the occasional half litre of cold, strong Czech beer and plates of hot wings for sustenance. He only knew he'd been there long enough not to care about where he had to be next; any lingering throb of worry killed along with a raft of other sensations by an afternoon's hard drinking. Even Rasti, normally stoic as an ox in his capacity for alcohol, was beginning to slur and staggered up, mid sentence, to announce his mission to fetch coffee.

Almost at once, the familiar buzz began to sound against Peter's leg, eventually becoming incessant, latching onto his remaining senses and stubbornly refusing to let go. He knew he couldn't ignore it any more. Rasti had told him to wait for the coffee, but the intoxicated Englishman was in no mood to follow instructions, even those of his closest friend. He was tired of being told what to do. Fuck sobriety and fuck Deprez.

Peter just about retained humility enough to raise his hand in apology, first to Tom, the pianist, for missing his set, and secondly to Rasti, before throwing a crumpled note down on the table and scurrying to the exit to avoid the big Czech's remonstrations.

He knew Rasti would head outside to stop him, so Peter ducked down one of the many side streets that stretched over this labyrinthine part of Old Town, theorising, as best a drunk man could, that the chef would not be able to check them all. Swaying rather than sliding into a convenient stone porch, Peter focussed his blurry eyes back towards Jakubská, waiting to see which direction Rasti would search for him. The buzzing against his leg still penetrating his dulled senses, he slipped the phone from his pocket and switched it off, allowing his head to rest against the graffiti coated wall. Just a few seconds later, Peter saw his friend wearing a scowl fierce enough to subdue the Golem himself and muttering a quite spectacular range of Czech swear words, stomping back to the sanctity of Smokin' Hot, a coffee pot still grasped in his hand.

Levering himself from the doorway, Peter lurched back in the direction of the Square, his brain busy inventing alcohol induced scripts for him to recite to the bastard awaiting him in the tower.

Climbing the stone steps to the top of the tower took a sizeable chunk of Peter's remaining energy and he was breathless and exhausted by the time he reached the top. Finding it deserted, Peter leant against the stone arches overlooking the Old Town Square from high above.

The rain which had started falling as Peter had walked from the restaurant was getting heavier, some driving through the gaps and biting Peter's face. Finally losing what little patience he had, he threw his head back and shouted, "Where are you, you bastard?!"

The echo distorted by the rain, Peter spun around to find Remy Deprez stood before him, a look of undisguised pity on his face.

"Bastard?" The voice was as smooth and calm as ever. "I suppose I should listen to Svobodova's Hero of the hour."

Peter stood still, silent, fully expecting a barrage and reluctant to defend himself from it.

"I need hardly remind you Peter that the Institute does not welcome undue scrutiny, even when encouraged by such noble actions as yours."

Peter said nothing, remaining rooted upright at an unstable attention, his mind not working quite fast enough to produce a response while Deprez spat his condemnations.

"I knew you were getting soft and I certainly knew you spent most of your days drunk, but I thought even you would have held off inebriation long enough to realise that a trip down the Tatra mountainside might just have been advantageous to the cause. If you had kept your hands to yourself you might even have prevented getting them dirtier."

Rolling the keys in his pocket in his hand, Peter finally mouthed a response. "You bloody monster."

Deprez's face contorted; his contempt for Peter mixing with the palpable strain etched permanently onto his features. He stepped closer and spoke with bitter distaste.

"There is only one monster standing here Peter. I have never ordered you to kill; I have never had to because I understand your nature. I am only an administrator, I co-ordinate the requirements of Brussels. The Child gives me the script and I direct my players, players like you." He made no attempt to mask the disgust in his eyes as he looked at Peter. "My days of bloody hands and sleepless nights are many years passed, but yours?" He made a tutting noise and shook his head in a mocking sadness. "You are just a drunken dog, who howls his repentance to the moonlight and goes back to his vomit in the morning."

Peter quietly and forcefully exhaled, his eyes closed and his face twitched in resentment, the fight to keep control of his anger made painful by the slivovice still pulsing through his head. Damn it! How much had he drunk? Peter barely had time to swallow his inebriated rage before Deprez continued.

"As I said," his tone now one of patronising understanding, "some people write the scripts, some direct the play and others play the parts." The Frenchman's faux sympathy drilled into Peter. "You'll let me know if you have trouble reading the lines?"

The rain had surpassed torrential now, hammering against the clock tower and sweeping through the stone window arches beside the two men, soaking them on one side as they stood in antagonistic stillness. They remained motionless as the few tourists who had ascended after Peter, oblivious to the intrigues only feet away from them, hurried down the stone stairwell, joining those scurrying for the intoxicating warmth of the bars below.

The Frenchman gave the slightest of laughs at the impotent frustration on Peter's face. He turned away towards the steps. "I'll wait to hear from you Peter," he said, raising the collar of his overcoat against his neck, "I'm sure I won't be waiting long."

The charming condescension in the Frenchman's voice thumped Peter back to sobriety and he realised, belatedly, that this was a man who had lost his fear. All those years ago Peter knew how scared Deprez had been of him, how he had waited months before assigning Peter a target in the hope that extended, expensed vacation would purge him of the desire for revenge. When that had failed, Deprez had relied on the unseen apparatus of the Institute to deter Peter's wrath, but the fear, the weakness, had still been in his eyes. Not any more. Deprez was more confident around him than before; still wary, still cautious of arousing the beast, but definitely more confident. Peter had pushed the thought back to the shadows alongside his guilt and ordered another drink. This was the result. He himself had allowed his betrayer's fear of retribution to evolve into a contemptuous pity for the drunkard Peter had become. And Deprez was right to feel that way. The hunter had become irrelevant; an aging murderer able to wear a suit and maintain a slender cover, but for the most part lost in a bottle of plum spirit waiting to be given permission to kill.

The sobering punch knocked Peter to the ropes and he stood in solitude, head bowed like a shamed child. His mouth hung open in mute objection, his hollow shell somehow held upright in the stinging rain. It was over Peter thought. Deprez had called his bluff and laid open what he was; a drunken thug, prepared and able to kill whichever target he was pointed at, regardless of whether he received a formal order or not.

The self analysis battered at Peter's senses bringing with them the return of his aggressive frustration. He looked with pure hatred at his superior's back. As if sensing the fury being silently directed at him, Deprez stopped at the top of the steps and glanced back at his chastened subordinate, a look of emancipated amusement on his face. He raised a hand in sarcastic farewell and shouted to Peter. "Say goodbye to your girlfriend from me."

The sentence which began in arrogance ended trailing in uncertainty as Deprez realised the enormity of his mistake. He had Peter beaten, if he had simply carried on down the stairs and resisted the sweet seduction of torment, then he would have won the day. Instead, he had kicked the dog just a little too hard, and Deprez knew it was about to bite.

Peter knew it too. The sudden weakness in Deprez's voice after the verbal barrage Peter had endured was telling and Peter's senses, dulled but not deadened, sparked to life. The Frenchman's tone had changed so quickly from assurance to uncertainty that Peter knew his superior's fear had been buried in the shallowest of graves. With this feeling came a return of the ferocious anger in Peter's soul. A powerful anger at himself, at Deprez and at the entire world for tolerating the filth that had driven him through the slurry of his profession for decades and led him to debating morality with a ghoul in a Prague clock tower.

Homing in on Deprez, Peter grabbed the startled man by his soaking lapels and slamming his body against the hard stone wall.

"You fucking hypocrite!" Peter snarled. "You think that if you don't say the words it keeps you clean. You just shout to the wind 'who will rid me of this turbulent priest?' and scum like me say 'I will.' You think because its not you doing the killing you're some kind of bloody innocent; that you're as pure as the driven snow."

It was Deprez's turn to submit to a verbal barrage and he squirmed under Peter's tight grip.

"Are they all like me? Is everyone you command the same kind of scum who don't need ordering when there's killing to be done? I bet they are you coward. I bet you've got a room full of people somewhere all willing to stab, shoot, throttle and slash until the cows come home if you walk past saying 'if only something could be done.' Anything so you don't have to get your pretty little hands dirty, so that you don't have to give the order to kill. You're just a politician sitting in an office writing out death warrants for soldiers whose arses you're not fit to wipe!"

If ever Peter saw a man's spirit drain from his eyes it was then. Deprez had been so sure of himself, so secure in the safety of his public surroundings, but now the dog had growled and Deprez found himself back in the familiar hold of nervous fear.

"You're every bit the murderer I am. You're murdering a piece of me every single day. Your hands have been round my throat for years and every time you speak to me, every time you look at me, you're squeezing that little bit tighter."

Peter heaved the eurocrat away from the wall, spun him around and, operating on raging instinct, forced his frame through the stone arch so that the Frenchman's head and shoulders hung over the brightness of the Old Town Square below. Peter saw the nervousness in Deprez' s eyes turn into the terror of a man who knew he had avoided revenge for nearly twenty five years and could see no escape now it had finally caught up with him.

"Well those days are over Deprez; if I have to live every day knowing there's shit in the street with more of a right to life than me then so do you! If you want me to kill that woman then order me! Be an honest murderer and order me to kill her! Tell me how you want me to do it, tell me how much you want her to suffer. Do you want her humiliated first? Should she scream for her mother before I slit her throat? Tell me you bastard!"

Deprez' s face was turning paler with each word, Peter's head so close to his he could smell the stale alcohol on his breath. The rain was beating directly onto his head, forcing him to clench his eyes tight from the freezing bullets and the cold made him gasp desperately for air.

"Or how about a quick kill so she never even knows who's hit her or why? So quick she doesn't even have time to think of her family or say a prayer or whatever it is you do when you know you're dead?" Peter allowed the images to play in front of Deprez's uncertain, panicking eyes. "What would you do Deprez? What would you do if I dropped you now onto the square? Would you pray on the way down?"

The Frenchman stuttered before managing a reply, "For God's sake, the people!" Deprez shouted the words, vainly hoping to snap Peter out of his assault or even to be saved by the few scattered tourists who had not yet sheltered from the rain.

"Fuck the people!" Peter spat. "You'll order me to kill that girl here and now Deprez or they'll be scraping you off the cobbles with the horse shit. Or maybe you can go and tell The

Child that you've got a rogue killer on your hands; that your authority's been compromised and the naughty little Brit won't do as he's told?"

Peter saw the fear in his superior's face turn to dread and smiled cruelly. "You don't want that do you Remy?" Peter taunted. "You know what that'll mean don't you?"

Peter grinned in malicious pleasure as he watched Deprez contemplating the prospect of The Child inspecting his affairs as an alternative to ending up as pigeon food smeared across the centre of a tourist spot. The failure of Deprez to keep the firmest control over his players, particularly the British with their inherent ability to sour EU milk, would spell an instant end to his own usefulness. Peter knew about Deprez's fear of The Child, it was a fear that he and many others shared.

"Alright!" The French accent was now robbed entirely of its customary charm and elegance. "Alright, for God's sake!" The words were shouted at Peter who instantly pulled Deprez back through the hole in the wall and let go of his dripping lapels.

"Alright," Deprez said again, this time almost whispered. He breathed heavily and irregularly, like an infant trying to stop itself weeping. Finally, he lifted his head and ashamedly, without looking into Peter's eyes, opened his mouth.

"I order you to kill Miroslava Svobodova. I want it done by the end of the week." The Frenchman's voice was faint and cracking, the rain water that dripped from his hair disguising the salt water in his eyes. "It should look suspicious, so as to harbour mistrust and cause as much resentment and ill-feeling as possible."

Even after all the bitterness Peter had felt towards this man every day since '92, he was embarrassed to be the architect of his humiliation – the man was breaking down in front of him. Deprez spoke again, his brow furrowed and his eyes searching for a place to focus on the wall behind Peter. "I don't care how you do it."

It was clear to Peter that each word Deprez spoke was another slash at his conscience and he stared in disgust at the man in front of him. However hard it had been for Deprez to say the words, for Peter each syllable had brought a curious freedom and he stood apart from his enemy, both men breathing deeply, aching from drained emotions.

Peter straightened up and nodded his acceptance of the order. "Yes Sir," he said calmly before turning on his heel and walking towards the stone stairwell where Deprez had stood only moments before. Just as Deprez had done, Peter turned at the top of the steps and looked back at his adversary, now sitting cross legged and head sunk under the window arch, rain splashing around him. A flutter of pity entered Peter's heart. Despite everything, Peter was amazed to find himself wanting to offer comfort to this man, his former friend whose betrayal ensured he stayed steeped in filth every day of his life. Despite all that, he wanted suddenly to offer some words to ease the turmoil going through this man's head.

Peter opened his mouth to offer something, anything to help.

"Welcome to Hell Remy," were the only words that would come.

CHAPTER 11

AN ACTUAL DATE. After leaving Deprez to his despair and stepping into the rain-soaked square without so much as a backward glance, Peter had rattled off a text to Mirushka asking her out the following evening for dinner, partly with Deprez's order still fresh in his ears, but mostly for an excuse to see her. Not that he actually thought she would or could agree; every second of these last precious days before the election were already double booked – triple booked at some points. All the better, Peter thought as he mopped the sobering rain from his furrowed brow. Her refusal would spare him from making his choice, at least for the moment.

Satisfied with his impending rejection, Peter ducked down the alleyway leading back to Smokin' Hot, his mobile's message alert sounding twice before he noticed it. Slipping it from his pocket he cursed as the rain thwarted his finger's attempt to slide the screen open. Eventually it relented, revealing the message contents to Peter; just two letters, 'Ok'.

An actual date. Peter knew that he owed her that much at least.

———

The nervous excitement that consumed him for much of the next day was a shock to Peter, culminating in him standing in the cold outside Smokin' Hot, dressed in fresh paisley shirt, black trousers and black velvet jacket awaiting the arrival of Mirushka's car.

As it eventually negotiated the tricky, narrow street and pulled up outside, Peter waved a quick acknowledgement to Ivan in the driver's seat and moved to open the door for Mirushka. She stepped out beaming at him, every facet of her beauty and individuality accentuated for the evening. A black, open necked shirt sat beneath a designer waistcoat patterned with many colours in dark shades, while high quality jeans, brown knee length boots and a long, ankle length and feux-fur collared black coat completed the ensemble.

"Is this the place?"

Her voice betrayed her own nerves and Peter leant forward to give the awkward, obligatory kiss that such occasions demanded, thankful that the unannounced change in her schedule had resulted in the absence of paparazzi.

"Certainly is," he said. "I didn't think there was any way I could top the kind of places you're used to so I figured I'd bring you home."

Peter put his arm around her waist and guided her inside, while, from nowhere, black suited security men appeared to stand by the door, Rado disappearing inside to take up his own post.

Small gasps and mutterings abounded as the pair walked in, Mirushka dutifully responding with smiles to those brave enough to make eye contact with her. Rasti came out from behind the bar, an enormous smile on his face, bidding her welcome. Peter was delighted to see he had shaved and was even wearing a shirt for the occasion. Leading them to their table at the far end of the restaurant, Rasti pulled the chair out for Mirushka, who gracefully sat down.

"Be careful of this one," the big Czech said, nodding his head towards Peter as he spoke to her. "The first time I went drinking with him he made me go the bar and ask for a pint of Cocksucker."

Peter's delight disappeared, while Mirushka, thankfully, laughed at the brief display of vulgarity.

"Is that something you stock?" asked, her eyes mischievous.

"Only on special occasions, birthdays usually," grinned Rasti.

"Then I shall know not to be fooled."

Rasti laughed and returning to his bar told them he would be back for their orders presently. Peter could feel Mirushka's eyes turn back to him as he hid his face behind his hands.

"He's lovely," she reassured him, her voice full of fun.

Peter slid his hands down from his face. "Lovely isn't the word. You look beautiful tonight by the way."

"Thank you. You're looking very handsome yourself."

Rasti returned with drinks and took their order, before Peter excused himself to slap an embrace on the musician, busy readying his gear close by the table. "Howdo, Jamie," he grinned, the guitar man returning the embrace and offering Mirushka a smile before returning to the intricacies of his speaker.

As he sat back down, Mirushka captured him in her eyes and began her probing.

"So, tell me about yourself. Who is Peter Lowe?"

Peter winced, not expecting the question.

"The guy sitting with you now?"

She laughed and shook her head. "No, I mean family, what brought you to Prague, girlfriends…?"

Peter took a gulp of his Czech ale.

"Family – none left, Prague started out as good a place to escape to as any and then we fell into a kind of mutually abusive love affair. And girlfriends? Well, nothing serious. Not for a long while anyway."

"Why not?"

Another wince. "That was the reason for escaping in the first place. Anyway, isn't that more of a second bottle question?"

"We're not really doing things the right way round," she smiled, "but if you are uncomfortable…"

"No," Peter shook his head. "It's not a problem."

Peter's eyes drifted as unwelcome memories returned, but feeling Mirushka's hand cover his own on the table, he carried on, voicing words he had suppressed for more years than he cared to remember.

"There used to be one, a long time ago now. She left me. I don't really know why for sure. There wasn't anyone else, not that I know of anyway. She just said she couldn't be the partner I 'deserved', that she wasn't going to be able to be there for me and needed to give me the freedom to find someone else."

"Why couldn't she be there?" Mirushka pressed, gently. Peter dodged the question, dropping his eyes back to the table.

"I hated those words. The freedom to find someone else, like that was ever going to happen. I resented whatever freedom it was she thought she was giving me, I resented the idea that there was someone else for me when all I ever wanted was her and I resented her for arbitrarily deciding what was best for me."

The bitterness poisoning his words shocked him and he stopped himself from saying any more.

"She must have loved you very much," Mirushka said, her voice as soft as her smile.

"That's what she said," Peter replied, his own smile even softer than Mirushka's. "So I decided the best way to spite her great intentions for me and prove her noble sacrifice was a pointless crock of shit was to be as miserable as possible and make damn sure I didn't find this magical 'someone else' she wanted to force on me. I stayed away from women altogether for a couple of years."

Mirushka gave a warm chuckle. "Until when? I get the impression you're quite the ladies man, with this image you have made for yourself, the moody, blues loving loner."

"Those days are gone," Peter grinned.

"Completely?"

"Completely. And I never intentionally cultivated an image, thank you very much, that's just how I am. I keep few friends but love the ones I have, people like Rasti or Jamie. People who've seen a bit of life, who understand the music. And there's no better place than Prague to be lost in a crowd."

Her thumb began to caress the back of his hand as a small silence hung delicately in the air between them, and Peter once more lowered his stare to his glass on the table before him.

"It hurts though" he said softly, "cutting yourself off like I've done. Not just inside, but physically."

He unconsciously withdrew his hand from her delicate stroking and clenched it as he tried fruitlessly to explain.

"It's like you're aching to find a spark of joy in something, anything, instead of just... being hollow. And you start to hate it and hate yourself when you just can't find even a shred of joy in anything, even in the things you used to live for. You could be sat in a pub with your best mates in all the world around you who'd do anything to chisel a smile onto your face, or in bed with some girl who can't say no and is up for anything, but at the end of the day it means nothing. And in the end you do end up like some walking caricature; wrapped up in the image of yourself you've created because that's all you have left and it's all you know how to do." His voice began to trail off, tiring of the effort and self indulgence of vocalising his anguish.

He felt her fingers touching his again on the table and he offered them a perfunctory squeeze, picking up his glass with his other hand to take a deep drink, his frustratingly wet eyes still unwilling to meet hers. Swallowing the lump that had begun to rise in his throat, he sat bolt upright and forced his broadest grin onto his face.

"Never mind," he chirped. "It's all over and done with now, and at least I always have my music!"

"And Rasti," Mirushka replied, her voice calm and patient, while a concerned smile played on her lips.

"And Rasti," Peter conceded, flicking a glance through the archway to the bar area where his big Czech friend had his arm around Michael's shoulders, the two of them laughing heartily at some outrageously inappropriate joke Rasti had doubtless told.

"So what about you?" Peter hurriedly moved the subject on, anxious to clothe the nakedness she had exposed. "What's Miroslava Svobodova's story?"

She leaned back, her familiar twinkle of mischief replacing

the brief look of disappointment, and raised her glass to her lips.

"My full biography is available on the Party website Mr Lowe. I can have my aide forward you the link?"

"My insomnia isn't so bad that I need to read a politician's biography," he said, mirroring her earlier light-hearted brusqueness. "What's the real story?"

"Much the same as yours. One major heartbreak which left me unwilling to get too involved, and a number of disappointments since then. So, I directed my energies elsewhere, firstly as a business manager then into politics with Herbert and now..."

"And now you're the Prime Minister, with the downside that you've cultivated your own image as a mildly eccentric single woman who won't allow anyone to get near."

She grinned at the assessment.

"Image. Yes we all have one I suppose, but it depends on how deep their roots go. I've never doubted the sincerity of yours for a moment, but I could tell, back when Herbert was alive, that there was more to you than meets the eye. Herbert could tell as well, and that, I think, is why he took to you so well. I think your image is more eccentricity than anything, and I love eccentric people."

Peter frowned playfully, wary of having his ego punctured, but knowing full well that his lover was gently teasing him. "What eccentricities?" he replied.

Mirushka's wide grin spread across her beautiful features, "Oh, I don't know," she said, "maybe the clothes... You don't exactly reflect the height of fashion do you?"

"Fashion's for losers," Peter said defensively, still unwilling to give in to her gentle goading, "for people who are so desperate to 'fit in' they'll act however some fashion house tells them to so they don't have to bother developing their own personality. Fashion changes every five seconds, Mod is a way of life."

She returned his grin, pleased at the success of her teasing.

"And anyway," he said, sitting back down and turning his chair sideways as Jamie began the rhythmic strumming of his guitar, his husky voice pulling the attention of the other diners away from staring at the couple and onto himself, "our music's miles better."

———

It was much later that the pair returned to the luxurious sanctuary of Mirushka's hotel, ascending in the lift together to her suite. Peter was taken aback at the comfort the rooms had to offer; deeply carpeted, brightly décored, with the most kingly of king sized beds visible through the open bedroom door. The contrast with Mirushka's family home could not have been more apparent, yet she looked at Peter almost apologetically.

"It doesn't quite have the charm of home," she said, "but I suppose it'll have to do." Her mischievous smile returned to her face as she saw Peter's eyes fixed on the bed. "I suppose even the worst of us should suffer comfort now and then."

Peter turned to her, his boyish grin appearing hesitantly on his face, alongside what he suspected looked like an awkward discomfort.

Mirushka breathed deeply and reached out to gently touch his hand.

"Listen, Peter, if you regret what happened I understand.

We are professional people, we don't have much time for that kind of thing and it's easy to get carried away." She talked quickly, trying to defuse the small spark of tension that had arisen.

Peter stopped her in her tracks, tenderly cupping her face in his hands. "Mirushka," his voice was gentle and calm, "shut up." He leant forward and pressed a loving kiss against her lips. She responded by pulling his body tightly against her own and holding him there, relishing his invigorating warmth through the cotton shirt.

They held on to each other after breaking their kiss, the stresses of their lives pouring out, unspoken, into each other's embrace. Lifting his head from her fragrant neck, Peter held his lover gently by the shoulders.

"I got you something today," he said.

"Mr Lowe," she spoke back in her mischievous voice, "should I accept gifts from an employee of the Institute for European Harmony?"

"It's not from them," Peter snapped, a little too quickly, "it's from me."

He pulled a small, flat box from his jacket pocket and handed it to Mirushka who took it with a look of nervous excitement.

"What is it?" she asked.

Peter's grin grew wider still. "Something to play up your eccentricities," he said.

Mirushka opened the box and looked down at the shining, gold pocket watch within. She laughed gently, appreciating both the gift's value and the sense of humour of its giver. Taking the watch in her hand she ran the chain through her fingers and pressed the lid open to reveal the beautiful glass face and intricate Roman numerals within. On the inside of the lid had been inscribed one word; 'Miláčku'.

"Do you like it?" Peter asked, his nervousness more apparent than ever.

"Like it?" Mirushka's voice trembled slightly and her eyes looked wet. Gripping her gift in her hand she flung her arms around Peter's neck and pressed another kiss against his lips. Looking him straight in the eye she said in a soft, quiet voice, "Lubim ta."

The words were ones Peter had never heard before and his puzzlement displayed on his face.

"What does that mean?" he asked.

Mirushka just smiled her beaming smile back at him. "Guess," she answered before pulling his head back to her own and clasping him tightly to her.

"We really shouldn't," said Mirushka, wrestling her lips free as Peter's hands began to move softly over her body, "I should re-read my papers before the morning.."

"Mm hmm," Peter murmured his agreement as he kissed the nape of her neck down to her shoulder, feeling the tension in her muscles relax at his touch.

"And my speech is still unfinished…" her eyes were closed and her voice was light and distant as Peter's hands moved to the top button of her blouse.

"It has to be a good speech…" she continued, in almost a whisper.

"The best," agreed Peter.

"And I have to work hard tonight."

"Very hard."

Her thoughts of policies, speeches and soundbites drifted

further away from the front of her mind as she lifted her hands to Peter's chest and pushed him delicately and deliberately towards the beckoning bedroom door.

———

Later, Peter watched his hands move over the shoulders of the naked woman lying on the bed in front of him, his eyes wide and unblinking, as though in a euphoric trance. Kneeling behind his lover, Peter's thumbs worked the stress from her shoulders while murderous tension built in his own. His confrontation with Deprez played out again and again in front of his blank, staring eyes as though the back of Mirushka's head was projecting the images. He had won the one small concession for which his conscience had yearned for years; to be ordered to kill and not just have his complicity presumed, and he had humiliated Deprez into the bargain. But what spoils had his victory brought him? He still had to kill this woman, this beautiful, strong, honest woman. Would the stain on his soul be any lighter because he had finally got his order?

He must do it, Peter knew that. Not because of Deprez, but because of the organisation he represented. For as much as Deprez was weak, The Child was not; to cross him was only the act of the suicidal and the stupid. To refuse the kill now would surely mean Peter's own death and it would not be a dignified one. He must kill Mirushka. There was no alternative. If he didn't complete the job, The Child would simply send someone else, someone who would share none of Peter's misgivings. Better for Mirushka that it was him. And it would be so very,

very simple to kill her now, with his hands moving so freely around her soft, delicate neck...

He ran a feather light touch over the warm skin of her neckline, following down and cupping her shoulders as he wrestled with the conflicting desires in his mind.

Mirushka was making a quiet purring sound at the sensation of Peter's fingers. His eyes widened further still, the circular motions of his hands moving closer to her neck until he felt the tension in his fingers as they readied to squeeze.

A contented Mirushka exhaled a deep, satisfied sigh, turning her head to the mirror adorning the dressing table a short distance from them, the movement breaking Peter's concentration, himself now staring into the mirror at the reflection of his own murderous intent.

"Your touch is so soft," she said, "like velvet."

A moaning, howling sound broke his concentration and his body coiled up as he realised it was coming from himself. His fingers clenched shut, centimetres from Mirushka's neck and opening his throat to allow the scream out, he threw himself, in his own nakedness, from the bed to the floor, rolling across and thrusting his tight fist into the offending glass, shattering it into a thousand pieces as the howl within him reached a crescendo.

Then he knelt, knuckles bleeding, arthritic fingers pounding, heaving air into his depleted lungs, shaking, unwilling to raise his head to Mirushka, who sat shocked and frightened on the bed, and whose eyes burned through Peter's back and into his thumping heart.

CHAPTER 12

SHE MOVED TO DISMISS THE SCOWLING RADO, summoned by the crashing of glass and Peter's cry, and turned back to the man still kneeling tensely in the shards. She pulled the bed sheet tight around her as though it shielded her against his words. And his words began to trickle, the apologies dripping from his mouth like the blood from his hand, the confessions close behind.

Peter was an agent, a killer for his sham Institute, whose sole concern was the overall security of the Union and its strategies, the individual aspirations of its members beneath consideration. The Institute had decreed that reunification would destabilise the existing structure and compromise objectives, so must be prevented – Peter was the instrument of this prevention.

The trickle became a flow and Peter recounted his friendship with Herbert and his reluctance to go through with his mission, before he had replaced his medicinal syringe with a tampered version designed to introduce an air bubble into his weak heart. Peter's final job for his employers...

"Until you." He looked, for the first time up from the glass, his eyes puffy and red, betraying his emotions as much as the quiet in his voice.

"With Herbert gone they thought that would be the end of it, but then you took over. I'm supposed to kill you too, but I'm not going to." He looked back at the shattered mirror and at his clenched, bleeding fist. "I've made my choice."

Silence descended which Peter had no desire to break. He had made his confession and given what apologies he could. What happened next was up to her.

She made him wait for a response and when it came it was quiet but firm, the mischievous warmth that infused her voice absent, replaced by cold authority.

"Tonight, the time in Bojnice, all lies?"

"No."

"And I should believe that, why?"

"Because you should believe that it would be far easier for me to have done the job from afar; no personal involvement, just one more face in the crowd. I wasn't supposed to get so close to you, but I couldn't help it. You drew me in."

The answer seemed almost to relieve some of the tension displayed on her face and she swallowed before continuing.

"Did he know, Herbert? Did he know that you'd killed him?"

"Yes."

"But he didn't cry out."

"No."

"Why?"

Peter, still crouched, lifted his head towards her, eyes filling at the memory.

"He forgave me."

Still clutching the bed sheet, she raised her own eyes to meet his.

"So what happens now?"

Confused, Peter shook his head. "That's up to you. If you go public you'll tear the whole system down and they'll burn your two countries in the fall out. You need to make sure you're protected until you can win the election; by then it'll be too late to stop the popular mood and the Institute's strategies will be forced to adapt."

"I meant what happens with you."

Peter nodded to the door. "I'm sure Rado knows how to get rid of a body."

"Suppose I don't do that," her words were quick, business like, "suppose like Herbert, I forgive you. Suppose I let you walk from this room and back to your life. What happens to you then?"

"I'm sure you can guess."

Her clenched hand loosened just slightly and she took a deep breath, steadying herself. "You're killing yourself for me. Either by my order or the hand of your Institute, you die."

Once more, Peter dropped his head, beginning to shiver a little in the cold he suddenly felt.

"I prefer to think of it as laying down my life. Beats taking another person's for a change."

"Why would you do that?"

Peter shrugged. "The same reason I grabbed you at Tatra."

He felt his legs begin to cramp within his awkward crouch and became aware of the shards around his knees, but his body still refused to move.

Mirushka stepped from the bed, dropping the sheet to the

floor and leading him up by his good hand to stand in front of her.

"What are you doing?" he quizzed, puzzlement overcoming him.

"You said I needed to be protected through the election. If you're going to be my protector," she said, "you'll need to get that hand looked at."

"No, you don't need me, you've got a whole squad of blokes out there to protect you without adding me to the ranks."

She stepped closer into him, her naked body brushing lightly against his.

"And how many of them would make the sacrifice you have just made?"

Peter fell backwards on to the bed at her gentle push, his confusion overwhelming him as she lay atop him, lowering her head to kiss his brow.

"Why are you doing this?" he whispered, his tears flowing freely down his face.

"Lubim ta."

"I love you too," Peter replied through his tears, "I love you too."

Surrendering himself to the words and the emotions, Peter lay back on the bed, savouring the embrace, grateful for and terrified of each caress and every kiss from the woman who had torn him apart. And as he responded to her urging, offering her the protection of his arms, he whispered his thanks to her with a quiet 'Ďakujem', for against his expectations and in spite of all he had done, his target had helped him escape from the horror of himself.

———

High above in the skies the nightmare had returned to the ageing traveller, as it always did when he approached this part of the world. He grimaced in his sleep at its expected return. The same horrifying image of a woman that had haunted him since childhood returned once more, her face twisted in agony as though some terrible force were tearing her gut from her body. She was reaching out of the darkness towards him while demonic figures dragged her back down, illuminated only by the flickering flames. More creatures pulled and clawed at the writhing shadows crawling impotently away from the growing fires, howling like the damned begging for escape from hell. Even their terrible sound was eclipsed by the guttural wail of children as they were dragged further and further away from the writhing shadows by the helmeted and uniformed demons. The worst wail of all came from the old man himself who, as always, found himself robbed of his age and becoming a cowering, terrified Child in the midst of the chaos. Ahead of him lay the woman, restrained, her face twisted in pain, staring straight into his eyes, opening her mouth and screaming in a voice that stretched from the Pit to the Heavens. One word, a name, repeated again and again. The name was Marek.

"Marek!" The inevitable crescendo startled the old man awake. Discreetly composing himself he leaned back into his seat, the aircraft's gentle hum acting as a relaxant.

"Prague." He hissed, distastefully, cursing his destination as the plane dipped in the night sky and began its slow descent into the wretched city below.

CHAPTER 13

AWAKENING TO AN EMPTY BED, Peter shook his head free from the blackness that had engulfed it, slipped from the sheets and examined his surroundings. The broken glass was gone, as was Mirushka, and Peter's clothes from the previous evening lay folded on the chair by the wardrobe. Pulling them on and heading towards the bedroom door, the nervous thought pricked him that Mirushka had fled his presence having changed her mind and that Rado and his men awaited him, weapons drawn. Reasoning that it was at least as unlikely as her ready forgiveness the previous night, he resolved to catch up with her at Party Headquarters and put his doubts to rest once and for all. He pulled open the door and marched out into the living area.

Mirushka, Černý and a handful of others glanced up from the paper strewn conference table, the distaste on the old Czech's face as obvious as it was palpable.

"One moment, láska moja, I'm nearly ready for you."

Černý scowled, others suppressed grins, and Peter blushed at Mirushka's words; 'láska moja' – my love. With an air of unconcern, she pressed on.

"As I said Karol, you have been getting some particularly good press these past days."

"Meaning what precisely?" Černý's expression was indignation made flesh. "The Headlines have hardly been universally in our favour since the game."

"Not the Party's, no," Mirushka agreed. "But your own personal image has received quite a boost over the same period; one might almost say too much of one. Even some of the Slovak media has carried that intriguing soundbite that no-one can remember making. You know the one? About you being the true power behind the un-crowned Queen's throne?"

Peter saw the resentment in the old man's eyes and questioned the wisdom of Mirushka's strategy.

"If you have an accusation to make…" His voice was quiet, measured.

"Oh no, no!" She exclaimed, sounding to any casual observer, the very essence of sincerity. "Karol, we're all on the same side here. And to misquote Gerald Seymour, one woman's Leak is another's Confidential Briefing. All I'm saying – to everyone – is that fun time is over; the election is only days away and we must be seen to work together, as partners, agreed?"

All nodded their heads sagely and a smiling Mirushka gestured towards the door. "Then thank you gentlemen, to business!"

"Karol, before you go," she stopped him before he exited, leaving herself, Peter, Adrianna and Rado the only people in the room. "A couple of things."

Peter moved over to join them, a sinking feeling in his gut.

"Your TV speech to the Slovak news this evening?"

Mirushka addressed Černý once more. "I want you to deliver it in Slovak dialect."

Incredulity spread instantly across his thin, lined face.

"I will do no such thing!" Černý spoke in his own tongue. "I was born and raised in Prague; every speech I have ever given in this country has been in my own language."

Mirushka nodded and dropped an offending newspaper on the table, a look of strength on her beautiful face.

"And I was born in Prievidza," she said, "and I was raised to show courtesy to my hosts by speaking their language. You are addressing the Slovak people on Slovak TV; it is not unreasonable to ask you to use Slovak dialect. It's just a little polite deference."

Peter knew she couldn't resist the last few mischievous words and he struggled to stop a smile breaking onto his face at Černý's expression.

"Deference?" Černý hissed in suppressed mortification.

"Yes," she nodded. "It was Peter's idea actually."

Černý turned to glare at Peter who smiled politely back at him.

"Mr Lowe's yes. He advised me that the media are likely to blow up the significance of any instances of inequality between us so as to sabotage the movement, and Čurda would love nothing more than to capitalise on a split between us. You and I may know that we are wholeheartedly committed to each other," her voice was un-tainted by sarcasm, "but I have opted to give all my speeches in Czech when I am in the Czech Republic out of deference to her people. Likewise I think it sensible that when in Slovakia party figures speak in Slovak for the same reason. We wouldn't want to give a bad impression would we?"

Černý remained still and quiet, though his expression betrayed the tumultuous eruption of anger going on within him. Mirushka though simply gave her customary nod of approval.

"That's settled then. Now, the other thing, and this is for you all and no-one outside this room."

Rado and Adrianna moved closer to the table while Peter stayed a diplomatic couple of paces behind.

"Last night, Mr Lowe resigned from the Institute for European Harmony and has agreed to join my staff on a permanent basis. I'm sure you'll all join me in welcoming him to the team."

A cold stare from Rado, a confused smile from Adrianna and a tut from Černý followed.

"Mr Lowe brings with him an expert insight into the region's wider political scene and key information about a hindrance of which we had no prior knowledge. Mr Lowe?"

All four faces turned to stare at him and Peter's gut sank lower still, dreading the re-confessing of sins he had owned up to only hours before. Stripping his words of emotion, he kept his voice professional, business like and offered only the most basic of explanations.

"The Institute doesn't exist in any concrete, physical form. Its Czech address is a room in a suite of offices that never opens to the public and any external meetings are strictly by appointment only. That's because the public image exists only as a cover for a movement dedicated to the internal security of the EU. It exists to root out and eliminate threats to the stability and direction of the Union. Its operatives are controlled remotely, not based in an office. Your movement is just such a threat, considered extinguishable by the elimination of Miroslava Svobodova."

Incredulous silence met his words, until Adrianna's nervous voice piped up.

"So, they want us out of Europe?"

"No," Peter answered, "they want you in Europe, exactly where you are, divided and dependent on their favour for your security. They believe if you unify you'll lead the whole region into a rival power block within the Union that could eventually split the continent back into the old rivalries of East and West."

"That is their reasoning anyway," Mirushka intervened. "Although personally I think the fallout from the Eurozone crisis has made them paranoid. They see things falling apart and are terrified that one of the minnows will try to take over the pond; if our countries reunite then we become the biggest minnow, and they think that Poland, Bulgaria, Romania and the others will eagerly swim in our wake, giving us a top heavy influence at Brussels. All we are interested in is finally giving our people a choice over the future, but I doubt they will take our word for that."

Peter picked up again. "But whatever your motive, the Institute believes that Mirushka is the glue holding the movement together and that without her it will fall apart." He shot a glance at Černý, knowing the last sentence would have stung.

"So," Mirushka continued, "you each have a choice to make. To stay close to me is to put yourself in the line of fire, so to speak. If we are to win this election I need you close, but I will not force you to put yourselves in danger…"

"What do you know of danger?" The words were spat by a Černý who's anger refused to be contained a moment longer. "A few vague threats and you batten down the hatches. I stared down an invasion and am still here to speak of it! This is my country, this is my election! I can win without any help from the likes of you. You have risked everything we worked for, everything Herbert Biely worked for, by opening your legs to a traitor!"

The old man turned quickly on Peter and cuffed an enormous hand across the Englishman's head. The blow rocked Peter who was barely able to steady himself before a second blow came his way. He caught the arm this time, firmly, and stepped close into the old man's face.

"I may have been a traitor, I may have been scum, but I'm doing my best to help now. But you're just an old relic, so trapped in the past that you can't see why this woman is the best person for the job; and so blinded by your sense of self righteous injustice that you're jealous someone made it onto a death list ahead of you."

"Gentlemen!"

They both looked back towards Svobodova, the interruption just long enough to shake them from their mutual aggression.

"Karol, you may detest me and Mr Lowe as much as you wish and for as long as you wish, but that will not alter the fact that you have two choices in front of you now."

Peter observed her looking deep into Černý's eyes, outwardly calm but searching for some spark of indication that he was still with her, that he accepted her terms.

"You can go to the press, tell them everything we've spoken of today and watch in glee as I'm dragged from office in disgrace for taking in a man who worked against us. You can take your place as undisputed party leader; the position your history of service surely deserves. Enjoy all the plaudits your people can throw at you if that's what you want. But as you sit on your throne, you'll watch the party die around you in scandal, and with it any chance to see us as one country again, to see your dream, Herbert's dream, fulfilled. And all the Mečiar's and the Čurda's of the world will revel in their continued privilege, while the outsiders you resent so much, like this Institute which would destroy us, delight that you have done their job for them. All the plaudits and compliments and recognition they cover you in will do nothing but warm an old man's ego as he fades towards irrelevance."

She stepped closer, her voice softer now, Peter silently marvelling at her abilities.

"Or we can stand together, as partners, and fight those who would deny our people their voice. You know about the Institute now, and when one learns of a conspiracy like this, one can either expose it and watch Europe collapse in chaos, or fight against it from within. Either path will have its consequences, but the second option is the one I choose to take. Will you stand with me, Karol?"

The bitter taste of anger still tweaked at the corners of the old man's eyes, that much was obvious to all, but the rest of his face had recovered the cool dignity for which he was famous. Breathing deeply, quietly, diluting the adrenaline that had pumped through him moments before, he turned and walked slowly to the suite door, only to pause and turn his head first to Peter and then to Mirushka.

Looking her in the eyes he said, in a once more calm voice, "The speech will be delivered as you request, and I apologise to you both for my remark." And with that, he was through the door and away.

As he left, Rado, silent as ever, flashed the most loaded of warning stares to Peter and nodded his loyalty towards Svobodova, before returning to his position outside the door. Adrianna, likewise, quietly scooped up her collection of folders and files from the table and scurried to her desk in the far corner where she began furiously scribbling the revised agenda for the day.

Peter couldn't find the words to thank Mirushka. He noticed the chain of his gift, the watch, hanging from the pocket of her waistcoat, an unspoken sign of her forgiveness. Stepping forward he took gently hold of her hand, his head bowed in apology.

"Thank you," he whispered, "But why are you doing this?"

"Doing what?" she whispered back.

He held tightly onto her soft hands.

"Why take these risks for me? A guy with blood on his hands who spent so long working against you."

The nervous excitement of the previous night returned to Peter as she lifted his fingers to her lips and kissed them.

"Your hands are washed clean now," she said. "And if I am the one to help my country reach the Promised Land, I need you with me every step of the way."

As he stood pressed against her, accepting her kiss and her words, a warmth grew in Peter, and with it the thought that they could achieve anything together. And for a while it seemed they could. Černý delivered his speech as instructed and remained silent when the Czech nationalist press derided him for it, while Mirushka and Peter, with Rado and Adrianna their constant companions, bustled from event to event and from photo shoot to photo shoot, moods high and confidence growing by the day that the Institute's machinations were behind them and all they had to do was keep moving and smiling to skip on the stepping stones to victory.

Until the accident.

CHAPTER 14

THE CHAOS OF THICK BLACK SMOKE and twisted metal dominated the TV screen, while a dramatic voiceover solemnly commentated on events.

"The tragedy could have had untold consequences if the Slovak Prime Minister, Miroslava Svobodova, had been travelling in the vehicle as originally planned. Ms. Svobodova had in fact been delayed at a meeting and returned to Prague slightly later than planned by car to join Karol Černý's election campaign."

The day had begun brightly, Peter cradling his lover as she awoke in his arms; their lovemaking carefree and sincere. They had dressed quickly and breakfasted on the move, their now regular companions joining them as they discussed timetables, polls and electoral logistics. Mirushka's mood had dropped slightly at the news of a bullet having been received at their Bratislava hotel. The package had been intercepted by Rado's team and the bullet found to be inactive, included in an A4 envelope alongside a few rose petals and a small silver necklace. Such things were distasteful but not uncommon and Peter was surprised that Mirushka let it affect her, but the dip in her spirits proved a momentary distraction as she completed her full day of appointments before the group made for the helipad and the journey back into Prague. Before they arrived, Mirushka had a change of mind about a cancelled appointment and elected to stay for an interview at a new TV station in the capitol with Peter and Rado, while Adrianna continued on to Prague in the helicopter as planned.

It was as Peter and Mirushka relaxed in the car as it cut through the night that the news came through. The helicopter had crashed midway between Bratislava and Prague. Everyone on board, including Adrianna, was killed. Peter had silently held the weeping Mirushka for the rest of the journey, until she stepped into the Prague night at the door of the hotel and offered Prime Ministerial words of tribute to her fallen aide and condolences to the families of those involved, before retiring to her suite.

Peter did not sleep that night, watching the reports as they came in, hoping against hope that this was just a tragic accident while knowing with absolute certainty that it was not. He knew Mirushka would share his certainty and he cursed his own selfishness at the thought that she may blame this on him. When early the next morning her bedroom door opened, he quickly flicked the images off the TV screen and offered her a weak smile before turning back to the window, waiting an age before risking any words.

"There might be someone who can help us, although I don't know if he would." Peter's words were barely audible as he gazed out at the city. "He's someone who knows about the Institute."

"Who could help us?" Mirushka said in a soft voice, staring

at the untouched breakfast lying on the tray before her, her eyes swollen and unblinking.

"The only people in Prague who know about the Institute apart from us are either dead or next on the list."

She stifled the urge to wretch and pushed the tray away.

"What's the point? Maybe I should just let them do what they want and get it over with."

Peter spun away from his introspection at the window and looked at his lover, properly, for the first time that morning. The sight horrified him. She sat dishevelled in her grief, staring dead ahead at the tray she had rejected. The dressing gown that only nights ago draped over her like the flowing cloak of royalty now appeared as a shroud, clinging eerily to her thin frame, itself frail and robbed of strength. The natural beauty of her delicately lined features had been replaced with a hollow mask of sallow skin, patterned with worry lines and shadows.

"I killed her."

Mirushka had repeated the words since she had closed the door to the press the previous night and Peter had long since abandoned objecting to them. Better, he thought, to let her cry it out of her system.

"I should have sent her away, she was a child."

"You tried, she wouldn't go. End of." Peter had no words of comfort to offer, his merciless sense of analysis not allowing him to formulate any. "I know how you feel, but this isn't helping."

Unmoving, a sarcastic snap came from the wraith like woman on the chair. "And what can? What magic words do you have?"

Peter sighed, hardly wanting himself to mention the name.

"McShade."

Svobodova laughed; a harsh laugh, appropriate to the joyless body from which it emerged. "That's your hero in waiting?" she snorted. "Sir Roger McShade? What possible good could he do? He's already refused to meet either Černý or myself before the results of the election are known; the preservation of Britain's neutrality towards anything European is paramount to him. He's just an aging diplomat who has chosen to flex his ego in Prague in the twilight years of his career."

Peter, though devoid of nationalistic sentiment, smarted at Svobodova's dismissal of both the British Ambassador to Prague, and Peter's recommendation of him.

"Egotistical he might be," Peter responded curtly, "but what did you expect him to do? All he can publicly say is reunification is a matter for the Czech and Slovak people to decide, and he's done that. But it's no secret that he isn't Čurda's biggest fan, and he's one of the most respected men in European politics; at least he used to be. He's got the ear of more than a few of Europe's finest, including the British Prime Minister, and they're exactly the kind of people you need. You've already got their Foreign Secretary onside haven't you? Get McShade too and the battle's half won."

"You're right Miláčku, it's a brilliant idea!"

Peter saw a glass had appeared in her hand and she threw back the vicious shot, slamming the glass down, re-filling it smoothly and immediately from the bottle clamped in her other hand.

"Get as many people as possible involved and 'onside' so I can go on hiding behind my human wall, toasting my own health while you drop like flies around me; all the Queen's Men, lying down before me while I step on your broken backs on my way to destiny. Perfect."

She punctuated her sentence with another shot, swaying a little this time as the glass once more slammed down for re-filling.

Drunkenness in women was a phenomenon which had always unsettled Peter. There was something dangerous about women when in a stupor, which made him nervous and cautious around them. Men were different. In Peter's experience, drunken men were either fun, like Rasti, or a threat, in which he case he would be prepared for them; but women? They were unpredictable, as though the female propensity to confuse menfolk was emphasised with the introduction of alcohol. But with no magic words at his disposal, Peter could only fall back on the brutal honesty with which he typically condemned himself.

"If that's what it takes, then yes!" His voice was louder than he would have liked but it at least served to stem the flow of hard spirits into her body. "The harsh truth is, Mirushka, that every one of us is expendable if it means getting you to stop pissing about at the gate of history and actually walk through the fucking thing. Rado, me and even Adrianna, God bless her. If it's one of us that drops it means you don't, and that's all that matters. So instead of moping about here, acknowledge what she did for you and win the election for her!"

Peter gestured out of the window.

"Those people out there are your people Miroslava. They're waiting for the leader they were promised, for their uncrowned Queen. Černý's name might be the one on the ballot paper but it's you they're voting for; you're the face of the future to everyone in the bloody region!"

Svobodova, draining her glass once more as Peter spoke, slammed it down and finally turned her head toward him, her face skeletal in rage.

"I never asked for anyone to make me their goddamn poster girl! Those 'people out there' waiting for me to lead them to history should take more care about who they make idols out of."

"Oh, they have. This time they have," Peter countered, his temper rising. "Walk into any student bar in the world and you'll see Che Guevara's face staring back at you from a thousand t-shirts like he was some sort of idol. Where are the pictures of Ghandi? Of Martin Luther King? Where are the posters for the workers who built the nation? Of the doctors and nurses who healed it? Of the teachers who educated it? The saints and philosophers who guided it? They're the ones who should be lauded; they're the heroes, not some murdering sadist who looked good in a beret. There's no political heroes out there, not any more, not for most people. But this time, your people had three. And out of them, Herbert's dead, Černý's too old so you're the only one left. Be the hero they need you to be!"

"I've already told you!" Svobodova's voice was frustration itself. "Even if what you say is true, that I am some icon to be protected at all costs, your precious Sir Roger won't meet with me, or with Černý! And what's so fucking special about the British, that the word of one tired, irrelevant ambassador, womanising his way to retirement in eastern Europe, could sway the kind of men who do the things they do?!"

Her words were distorted by the grief which once more claimed her, and she turned away from her silent lover.

Peter watched her shoulders hunch and shake as she tried desperately to control, or at least internalise, her sobbing; and he clawed through his mind again, yearning for something, *anything*, to say. He reached clumsily out, hoping to offer a gentle touch as a substitute for words, only to hesitantly withdraw it. A dozen times he opened his mouth, with his breath the only sound to emerge, and he began to curse his frustrated impotence.

Svobodova stopped shaking and spoke again, the grief in her beautifully accented English replaced with a rising anger that bubbled and threatened to boil over.

"How can they do it?" She asked; her fury quiet and contained. "Kill?"

Peter struggled for an answer but was interrupted as Mirushka screamed her question again. "How could you do it?!"

She spun around to face her murderous lover, throwing the clear, glass bottle at him with furious speed. Peter ducked as it flew past him, smashing on the wall behind his head and covering him with a generous blend of its high proof contents and angry shards. Stunned, he uncovered his head to see Svobodova running at him like an angel perverted by pure anguish; a mask of hysteria clinging tightly to her features and dressing gown spread behind her as wings. She reached him before his mind was able to process what was happening and, surprised, Peter fell backwards onto the broken glass which crunched and stabbed under his weight. Svobodova landed on top of him, hitting his chest and screaming her accusatory question over and over again.

Writhing from the jagged fragments beneath him, Peter grabbed hold of her arms and rolled them both away from the glass, shouting her name into her face, desperate to snap her out of her insanity. Her arms were struggling against his clamp like grip on them, her fingers outstretched, trying to claw into his eyes. She was a strong woman, and in her anger stronger still, voicing her question with as much ferocity as she had shown in attacking him.

"How could you do it?! How could you do it?!"

The words thumped incessantly into Peter's ears, loud and constant until he could bear to hear them no more. With all his might, he forced her arms to her side and himself up, so that she sat on the floor in front of him.

"Because I didn't care, alright!" His bellowed words silenced her in an instant. "I didn't fucking care! I figured all you politicians were the same, that you were all probably up to your necks in some filth or other, so I killed whoever I was pointed at and the bills got paid, that's all I gave a shit about!"

Her resistance waned under Peter's grip and the silence gave way to deep, calming breaths.

Peter, himself breathing deeply, looked into his lover's face and sighed. Her eyes were tight shut, her anguished howls reduced to a faint, barely audible moan, and her hitherto pale cheeks flushed with expended passion. Peter slowly released his grip on her wrists and, when no renewed attack came, cradled her head against his chest, brushing his thumb against her hot, damp cheek.

"Miroslava?" he said softly.

She opened her puffy eyes in response, and looked through the blur of her last tears at him.

"Peter." She replied, her voice as soft as his.

Peter saw the beginnings of her familiar smile forming at the corners of her mouth and as the adrenaline left his system he smiled back at her, both in pleasure at seeing life return to her face, and relief at the end of the outburst.

"It'll be alright," he said softly, hoping to God he was telling the truth. The tightness of her embrace betrayed her own similar hopes.

"But what do I do now?"

"You go out there and you tell them that you're in this for them, that you're one of them. And you do something else too. Something no other politician does in this day and age."

He leaned in closer, his lips next to her ear, faint traces of day old perfume tickling his nose.

"Mean it." He said.

The pair helped each other to their feet and continued their embrace. "And while you're at it," Peter said, "Get in touch with McShade."

Mirushka tiptoed to the bedroom door, carefully avoiding the glass, shaking her tired head.

"Láska moja, what do you think an old has-been like McShade can possibly do to help us? How would he know how to fight the Institute?

"Because he was the one who created it."

CHAPTER 15

"WHAT'S GOING ON?" Jonathan Greyson's question was an understandable one as he stood at the entrance to the conference room of Prague's British Embassy, surveying the collection of people before him. To his side stood an immaculately power-suited young woman, eyes wide in surprise.

Sir Roger McShade rose from his position at the head of the grand, oak table and beckoned the pair inside.

"For those of you who haven't met him, may I introduce the United Kingdom's new Foreign Secretary, the Right Honourable Jonathan Greyson MP, accompanied, it seems, by Her Majesty's Minister for Europe, Ms Caroline Bland. We're all very proud of Ms Bland; straight from Cambridge to Parliament and the youngest Minister ever to hold office. You read 'Political Studies' I believe?"

Peter suspected that he wasn't the only one in the room to pick up on the tainted sarcasm in the ambassador's voice, despite the welcoming smile on his face.

"Never mind that," snapped Greyson, "what the hell is going on here? I dislike being ambushed and this looks like an ambush."

"Believe me, I know how you feel," said the older man. And Peter knew he had reason to.

A few days earlier, he had persuaded Mirushka to contact McShade under the guise of an innocuous call for electoral support. The ambassador, offering his usual bland best wishes, had sought to end the call before Mirushka's insistent voice requested a meeting regarding 'The Institute'. The silence at the other end of the line was palpable, while the eventual response that there were many Institutes and his knowledge of them sparse, was equally emphatic. It was then that Peter had interrupted his bluffing, begging to differ with the ambassador's recollections. Peter knew that his voice would be recognised and stir memories in the older man, and the result was the meeting they all sat in now, McShade going so far as to request the Foreign Secretary cancel the Berlin Banquet and join him. Now that the politician had walked into a conference room to find not only McShade but Karol Černý, Miroslava Svobodova and the unknown quantity of Peter himself at the table, he had, Peter conceded, every right to be suspicious.

"I assure you this is of the utmost importance," McShade began. "I've called you away to discuss vital developments in relations with our European partners, particularly in relation to the Institute for European Harmony."

"The what?" Greyson turned his head in irritation towards Bland.

"It's a think tank," she responded. "They offer advice and promote theories on greater harmonization and relationship management within the EU."

"Is that all?" Greyson turned around and headed towards

the door. "You called me all this way to talk about a think tank?"

"Sit down, please." McShade gestured to a chair.

"Absolutely not! I've got better things to do than be shoe-horned into meetings about pressure groups and lobbyists."

"Sit down man!" McShade's tone was severe, stunning all in the room, including Greyson, who turned slowly back and slipped silently into a chair, Bland alongside him.

"You're posturing is all very well, but there is more than that to foreign relations as you are about to discover."

Peter couldn't help but be impressed by the way McShade took command of the room, as the ambassador resumed his place and began his oratory.

"The Institute, until recently the employers of Mr Lowe here," he nodded towards Peter, "are far more than merely a think tank, and at this present time pose a very real threat to our political ally Miroslava Svobodova."

"Why?" Greyson squinted, assimilating the new information.

"Because Czechoslovak Reunification goes against everything the EU holds dear. It wants to see devolution, declarations of independence, the rise of smaller, more manageable groups, all of whom will defer to the supranational body for their guidance and their enlightenment. Any token importance afforded to the likes of Berlin, Madrid or London is precisely that: symbolism, diluted by a reality that sees power invested elsewhere. Reunification counters that, it creates a popular mood, and galvanises a sense of pride in nationhood. While that's bad enough in any country, here it has the potential to act as a catalyst, bringing the whole of central and eastern Europe with it."

"Are you seriously suggesting we leave?"

"Emphatically not, for the simple reason we cannot

survive on our own, even with the 'support' of our alleged friends in Washington. And even more emphatically the new Czechoslovakia must remain within EU borders to be sure of safety from any further Russian advancement."

Greyson held up his hand.

"Look, we all know that different EU countries want advancement at different rates, that doesn't make them a body of dictators. How is this 'Institute' posing a threat to anyone?"

McShade exhaled his impatience and drew in a lungful of air. "Because rather than being a pressure group for pseudo-intellectuals, the Institute is the body created to aggressively defend the internal and external security of the European Union and its Members, even from themselves and each other, for the long term good of the project."

"What?" Greyson's face was twisted in confusion, "No such body exists! There's no supranational secret defence force for the EU; we can't even agree on a shared army!"

"Not formally no, but it exists nonetheless."

"Impossible." Bland interjected, shaking her head. "Something like that would be traceable, it couldn't exist without a formal infrastructure, and no formal infrastructure could exist on the scale you're talking about without being discovered."

Although others cast disdainful glances at the young Minister, Peter was the only one to vocalise his contempt.

"It exists. I worked for it for decades, and between us and these four walls I killed more politicians, bureaucrats and various other arseholes in that time than I care to recall, including people like you. And right now that same Institute wants to kill Miroslava Svobodova."

Greyson stared, wide eyed and uncomfortable, while Bland coughed nervously.

McShade stared a rebuke at Peter who sat back, satisfied his point was made.

"To put it bluntly," McShade continued, "we were all fooled. The government in the 1980's, of which I was a member, thought that with the Community signing up to the Single European Act the gospel of the free market would sweep across all the continent's economies, eradicating socialism and creating a vast, conservative block to deter the Soviets. We were wrong." He gave a slight grimace as he replayed the memory in his mind. "All it did was give rise to a new political generation of federalists – people who saw themselves as principally European with any lingering loyalty to nation states superseded by loyalty to the nation of Europe."

"And what's wrong with that?" Greyson snapped, still smarting at his embarrassment. "There are many people back home and in every country in Europe who share that view; including on our own benches in Parliament."

"There is nothing wrong in holding that view Foreign Secretary, but there is everything wrong with the manner that some have implemented their vision."

He paused to take a sip of water from the glass in front of him, his eyes raised but never quite meeting anyone else's in the room.

"When the 'Institute,' as it was described, was first mooted we were cautiously optimistic. There was never a chance of us surrendering autonomy to it but it was a useful tool for us at the time, particularly when it came to organising the fallout when the Soviet Union broke up. It gave us an avenue to affect change without incurring culpability through MI6. In the event we played quite a part in encouraging that break up, particularly in this corner of the world."

He shot a glance to Peter, who felt several pairs of eyes burrowing into him before McShade continued.

"But despite the early encouragement, we noted that the Institute was starting to become more aggressive in both its aims and their execution, and their agenda began to conflict with our own. The final straw came when we learned of their plans to assassinate Alexander Dubček. To us such an act was pointless and would serve to jeopardise the future of a potential ally nation. Besides which, several members of the government had a high personal regard for the man and had no wish to see him lying dead at the bottom of some Bohemian ravine. After our appeals were ignored we effectively withdrew from the Institute."

"Or were withdrawn."

The others looked at Peter who had made the aside, but when he offered no more their eyes turned back to the statesman across the table.

"Just like that?" Greyson asked.

"Not quite." McShade shifted uncomfortably in his chair. "We withdrew, or were withdrawn if you prefer, in August 1992 and Dubček had his 'accident' on the first of September. Members of the Foreign Office and our security services made a number of complaints to the Institute, including a veiled and particularly foolish threat to blow the whistle on the operation. It soon transpired that the Minister who'd made the threat had also secretly warned Dubček to be on his guard. Apparently Alexander took this advice seriously and as a result was lying flat across the back seat of his car when it crashed, saving his life, at least in the short term, before he died in hospital some weeks later. Needless to say the Institute discovered the Minister's involvement. Their response was Black Wednesday, devastating the UK economy on September the sixteenth. With one action Britain had been punished for its insolence and warned about the consequences of playing whistle blower. Don't believe for one moment that these players lack resolve or will shy away from attacking those that threaten their agenda. If Black Wednesday doesn't convince you then look at the economic catastrophes across the Euro Zone over the past few years. They'll turn on anyone if they have to, even their own."

He stopped and looked across to Mirushka, Peter squeezing her hand below the table in response.

"If the Institute is set on a policy of prevention by assassination then your only hope is to continue to delay their assault until after Election Day. If your party is elected and reunification assured then the Institute's emphasis will change from violent prevention to persistent obfuscation. Ms Svobodova's demise will no longer be of paramount concern to them and they will review their strategy; The Child is nothing if not pragmatic..." McShade's voice dropped lower as he spoke the last words, but not low enough to be misheard by those around the table, giving Greyson the opportunity to get back into the conversation again.

"A child?" he spat. "What child?"

"The Child," McShade replied, "is far from infantile and is the one against whom we find ourselves standing. He is the seldom seen Head of the Institute, responsible for the internal security of the European Union."

Greyson's impatience lent him an ill-rooted confidence and

he snapped back at McShade, "So who does he report to? I'll open diplomatic channels and we can…"

"He answers to no-one."

"But surely someone in Brussels…"

"Who in Brussels? The Child reports to nobody because there is nobody willing to oppose him. Years back we surrendered responsibility for the internal security of the Union to The Child and slapped ourselves on the back for a job well done. Only with no-one in charge there was no-one to keep him under control, and his reputation has grown to the point where none of the European politicians who even know about him are prepared to say a word against him for fear of being classified as a threat to the Union. To The Child, Europe is a nation and the countries within it merely regions, and he has every right to make sure those regions run smoothly and don't do anything to jeopardise the stability of the Union. To all intents and purposes, he is the de facto ruler of Europe."

"But what has this got to do with us?"

All eyes turned to the young Minister for Europe, Ms Bland, who had almost shouted her question in a tone approaching petulance.

"Svobodova has been threatened and that's horrible, but it's her problem. There's been no threat to Britain, so as long as we don't intervene we won't fall under this 'Child's' radar, no?"

Peter felt his natural contempt for politicians rising in his gut at this nauseating display of self preservation and he squeezed tighter still on Mirushka's hand; she stroking him with her thumb in return. Even Černý looked across in silent distaste while Greyson merely raised his hand to his tired looking face.

McShade offered a thin smile. "Unfortunately, it isn't

that simple. Britain came under threat the moment its new Government, of which, Ms Bland, you are a member, opted to form an alliance with Ms Svobodova's Party in the European Parliament. And the very public appearances since then of UK government Ministers supporting the prospect of reunification means you are very much already 'on the radar'."

"And the meeting today, I suppose?" The anger in Greyson's voice was sharp and pointed.

"It would be foolish to expect your presence here to have gone unnoticed, yes."

Peter watched the dawning realisation that McShade, and to a large extent Mirushka and Černý, had set them up. They were already implicated of course, but the meeting ensured their submersion in the mire and he could only wait, with the rest of them, to see how they would react.

It was Mirushka who spoke first, breaking her silence with soothing, gentle tones. "Jonathan, I know you will feel cheated, but try and see we have an opportunity to take the Institute on now, on our terms."

"If you don't take this opportunity now and challenge the Institute, you will always be the victims, cowering at the conference table for fear of upsetting the wrong person." McShade remained still in his chair but his voice was etched in anxiety. "The choice is yours, Foreign Secretary."

"No." Greyson shook his head and rose from the table, Bland close behind him. "I'm not doing this here, not now. I need time to assimilate this." He strode towards the door, his head continuing to shake.

"Time is the one thing you don't have!" McShade growled.

"But it's the one thing I'm taking anyway!" Greyson shouted

back, wrenching the door open, pausing just for a moment to look at Mirushka.

"I'll be in touch." Then he was gone, his shadow scurrying after him while the door swung gently back into place.

"Well," began McShade, turning to face Peter, whose eyes narrowed in response, "favour returned."

———

Many streets away, at a riverside bar by the Vltava, The Child's diseased memories played out before his eyes as he gazed at one of the many puddles reflecting the city's austere beauty, disturbed only by the approaching waiter.

He detested this place. The sweet, freshness in the air complemented the wet shine on the cobbles and The Child squinted to dilute the glare. A waiter had placed two long stem glasses of deep red wine on the table in front of him. He did not have to wait long for his guest to arrive.

The woman's greying hair and lined face betrayed her mature years but she nonetheless carried her age more elegantly than most. Slender, but not especially beautiful in the classical sense, her magnetism came from the unbreakable strength in her countenance and the intelligence in her eyes. Wordlessly sitting, a thin hand reached out to take hold of her glass, raising it slightly in deference to the white haired, wrinkled man.

"Here's to order," she proposed.

"And those who do the ordering," offered her counterpart.

The toast was as old as their association, of which neither could accurately recall the age, but the sentiment remained as sincere as ever.

"It's of order that I wished to speak," the woman said in her well articulated American accent. "There are things we need to discuss."

"Such as?"

"Such as the Institute's current attitude towards the prospect of Czechoslovak reunification."

The Child paused slightly, his glass at his lips. He lowered it to the table.

"I'm surprised that our approach has come under your scrutiny," The Child said honestly. "It's merely the continuation of the same policy we've employed since the end of the Cold War; divide and control. As I recall the policy has always enjoyed enormous U.S. support."

The American smiled. "Indeed," she said. "And we remain committed to it; we haven't changed the policy, only the direction of its focus."

Realisation spread across The Child's wrinkled features, coupled with a flicker of suppressed resentment at the tipped balance that now existed between them.

"I see." He spoke the words slowly, quietly, and lifted his glass once more to his lips, the cold eyes underneath his now more furrowed brow never leaving his associate for a second.

The American's expression, likewise, remained resolute and cool, her own eyes narrowed with the seriousness of their discussion.

"That should really come as no surprise," she said. "Europe is growing ever larger, and the calls for federalism grow louder by the day from many quarters. Even saddled with the Eurozone crisis you continue to push for greater influence, greater respect; a bigger piece of the pie for This Nation Europe to gorge itself upon. It's only natural such an approach would give us cause for concern, even despite our occasional shared interest in other matters."

"That may be so," The Child conceded, "but it most certainly is a surprise to find America blithely accepting the potential emergence of a focussed Eastern European faction; a prospect which remains as undesirable today as twenty-five years ago."

"To you perhaps."

The Child raised an eyebrow at the response while his counterpart took a deep sip from her wine before continuing.

"Times change and we change with them or die." The American's voice remained resolute and perfectly calm. "In any case, it's no longer a policy that the United States can support."

The American's avuncular inflection irritated The Child and he responded with a curt, "May I ask why?"

She took another deep drink from her glass, her eyes never breaking contact with The Child's.

"Would you believe because we are concerned that the democratically expressed views of the Czech and Slovak peoples are likely to be undermined by the unwelcome machinations of external bodies?"

"No," replied The Child simply.

"Well how about this," the American smiled faintly, "because we say so."

The Child raised an eyebrow, "That would certainly be more typical of American Foreign Policy."

Her thin smile grew a fraction wider, echoed by The Child's own.

"It's always a pity when valued associations come to an end."

"Absolutely," she concurred. "Divide and control, is a policy we have both very much benefitted from. We were happy for the Institute to instigate the split in Czechoslovakia for precisely that reason; the necessity to manage the fall out from the breakdown of Communism effectively, and prevent the formation of new power blocks in Eastern Europe. We have done that. But the situation is different now."

"Different in what way?" queried The Child, dispassionately,

"The problem with enacting policies of divide and control is that sooner or later someone else will enact them on you."

The American, for the first time in the Child's experience, looked uncomfortable and shifted a little in her chair. She picked her glass up and drained it of the last drops of wine, her eyes always upon her counterpart. After an age she spoke again.

"Believe me, it gives me no pleasure at all to give you this ultimatum but it's one you need to be fully aware of. The United States is changing its outlook toward this region and we are now silently encouraged by the prospect of reunification. We see a united country as potentially advantageous to US interests and we do not wish to see such a prospect artificially hampered." She paused briefly. "And it falls to me to tell you that should such a project be disrupted and external pressures found to be behind such a disruption, then extreme sanctions would be imposed on the perpetrators."

The Child's face was impassive. Intuition telling him that she was not yet finished he prompted her with a curt, "And..?"

The American was equally curt. "And you sir, would be deader than the village you crawled out from under."

The faintest sign of distaste appeared on the Child's lined face and then quickly vanished. He rose quietly from the table and threw his black overcoat over his shoulders as the first drops of fresh rain began to fall. He offered his hand to the American who stood to accept it and was drawn close to the old man. When the Child spoke his voice was as deep and cold as ever, but devoid of the malice one would expect from the recipient of a death threat.

"I thank you for your advice," he said in sincerity, the hint of a smile at the corner of his lips, "but you and your associates should remember one thing; I have died once before, in circumstances more horrible than you can imagine. The prospect of doing so again does little to sway me."

With that he picked up and opened his umbrella against the impending downpour and set off along the cobbles, satisfied that although the American approach was disappointing, he at least had the satisfaction of not backing down to their threats. As the heavens opened and the downpour began, the Child's thoughts turned away from the American's threat and his memories forced their way in front of his eyes once again; memories of the old days, of the dead village and a time when a woman called him Marek.

CHAPTER 16

MCSHADE'S DISMISSAL OF THE MEETING was brisk and efficient, like a surgeon performing some well-practiced routine surgery. From there Mirushka and Černý headed straight to the next box-ticking exercises on their electoral calendars while Peter, against his lover's suggestion, took the opportunity for a head clearing walk through the rain to Old Town. It ended with him seated in subconscious homage to the dissidents of empires past at the feet of the Jan Hus memorial, as the pitter patter of the last drops of rain sounded around him. The stories of Hus's martyrdom replayed in Peter's mind; another of Prague's murdered heroes, killed for championing the good of his people against the oppression of outsiders. In days of old, to sit at the statue's feet was to silently protest against the empires that jealously claimed the city as their own. It occurred to him that he himself had long belonged to such an empire and he wondered if someone, anyone, had sat in protest against his former masters. Did they even know that empires and power blocks still claimed dominion over them to this day? And he wondered why he felt his own path towards martyrdom was starkly unavoidable. Was that what he really wanted? The injustice of being offered oblivion as a reward for deserting the horrors of his own reality snarled at Peter and he scowled in anger, dropping his gaze to the floor before closing his eyes and drifting into his memories. He had sat in this spot before, he thought to himself, so many years ago, almost as long ago as the Revolution; back in '92...

"So Mečiar is the better option by far; not for the Slovaks, but certainly from our point of view."

Peter remembered the conversation he had had with Remy Deprez on this very spot decades earlier, as clearly as if it were happening right now. The Frenchman, assigned to be mentored by the level headed Brit, had nodded eagerly along to Peter's analyses, keen to demonstrate his own insightful abilities and understanding that should Dubček become President of a new independent Slovakia, then the entire stratagem would be undermined to the extent that there would have been little point in the Institute having arranged the partition in the first place. As it was, come January 1st 1993, Czechoslovakia would cease to exist and with Václav Havel a shoe in for the Czech Presidency, the last thing the Institute desired was the similarly revered Alexander Dubček holding court in Slovakia.

"So why not take them both out?" Remy had queried of Peter, opining that with Havel the more prominent of the two he was arguably the more dangerous. Peter, always keen to encourage his subordinate, had patiently explained, without condescension, that the Americans were keen for Havel to push for NATO membership, and that taking both statesmen out would create too much suspicion and possibly even create the solidarity they wished to avoid. Ultimately, the Institute wanted there to be suggestions of a conspiracy, but one with people presuming its orchestration was from other sources. Dubček's imminent appointments giving evidence against former KGB operatives provided just such an opportunity. Peter explained that their Head of Region, a Spaniard named Sangre, had informed him that the Institute's strategy was in part to ensure that any future application for EU membership was motivated by a desire to ally with the Old Guard, rather than a unified eastern bloc pushing on mass for entry. While the Americans were content that such a move ensured a fractious Europe, ill-equipped to rival them as a superpower. In short, everybody wins, apart from the Czechoslovaks.

"You mean apart from the Czechs and the Slovaks," Remy had countered, grinning.
Peter had returned his grin, before the mood between the two dipped and the Englishman pressed Remy to be sure everything was properly prepared.

Remy had assured him it was, although, Peter remembered, his voice had shaken at the impending actuality of the plan. Peter's sympathy for his friend's discomfort had been palpable. Remy was no murderer, unlike Peter. The Frenchman was a strategist with a naturally analytical mind and it was clear that he was destined to progress to seniority in the Institute, providing he did as Sangre demanded and 'Bought Into' the project – in other words, got his hands dirty. In Sangre's, and by extension The Child's, mind, an intellectual commitment like Remy's was useless without the practical 'Buy In' that a field operation brought. Dubček was to be Remy's buy in and both he and Peter knew it.

Peter had also known, and understood, his friend's reluctance to murder only too well; it was a burden he had been glad to be rid of, temporarily at least, after Sangre had elevated him to the position of Controller.

With a lack of anything positive to say, all Peter had had to offer was honesty and cold level headedness.

"It's got to be done mate," he'd said simply. "You just need to make sure it's done right."

Peter remembered how his words had held little comfort for his friend and he had noted how the young man was beginning to look pale, as though his body were awakening to the realities of the career it had undertaken.

Peter had tried to restore the colour to Remy by reasserting the likelihood of the young man's rise, offering him an arm around the shoulder and the joke that Peter would one day be answering to him, before returning his gaze to the cobbles and muttering almost to himself.

"You can't do this job forever."

———

It had been several days later, September 1st 1992, that Peter had hurried to Provaznická in search of the traditional Czech tavern in which he'd known Remy would be drowning his sorrows. He had skidded through the door, his eyes darting around to find the Frenchman huddled by the wooden bar, a glass of some spirit or other clutched possessively in his hand. Raising his eyes at Peter's arrival, the drunken Remy had lifted his glass in ironic salute.

"It went wrong."

And it had. All Remy's planning, all the brilliance of his strategic mind, had been for nothing. Dubček had not died. The news had been full of little else; the statesman had been gravely injured when his chauffer driven BMW skidded off the Bratislava – Prague highway in heavy rain. He had been catapulted from the rear window as it spun and was found several meters away from the wreck; the driver was miraculously unharmed.

"They didn't think it was worth checking him." Remy's voice was tinged with sarcasm as he lifted his glass to his lips and cursed the folly of the incompetents with whom he had entrusted the execution of his plan. "They decided that he could not have survived the crash."

Remy had ticked off with Peter each aspect of the plan which had proceeded without impediment: The correct amendments to the car, the selection of a driver with links to the previous regime, the removal from the scene of Dubček's briefcase ahead of his planned testimony against the KGB, the ultimate disposal of the crash evidence; all successfully or soon to be accomplished, but all ultimately let down by the singular lack of a body. Instead, the target lay in a hospital bed recovering from massive chest and spinal injuries.

Peter had had no need to vocalise the extent of the catastrophe. If Dubček recovered he would start asking questions, he would investigate, the media would aid his investigations and their coverage of his recovery would elevate him from mere national hero status to that of a super star. And regardless of that potential outcome, Peter knew that right now, in Brussels, The Child would be seething and that the only way for him to save his young friend would be to ensure the job was finished.

It was not until several weeks after that spirit fuelled conversation that the preparations had been completed, during which time, Dubček had drifted mercifully in and out of delirious consciousness, never cogent enough to lend voice to the general suspicions around the accident. But finally, and irrevocably, Peter and Remy, dressed in hospital whites as pale as the young Frenchman's skin, stood unaccompanied in Dubček's hospital room, the frail object of their machinations lying unconscious, barely a few feet before them. Peter had waited by the closed door, offering the veneer of patience but inwardly desperate for Remy to finish the job so they could make their escape. He remembered silently urging Remy to take action, watching his friend as he stood next to the bed looking down at the figure within it.

Taking the syringe out of his pocket, Remy picked up Dubček's arm and paused, like an unwilling David, reluctant to despatch the stricken Goliath before him, the tip of the needle barely touching the frail, almost translucent skin.

"Come on mate, get it finished!" Peter had hissed, his professionalism offended by Remy's procrastination.

But Remy didn't finish it. He had simply stood by the bed, the old hero's arm hanging pathetically in his grasp.

Peter's spirits had sunk as he saw the tears in Remy's eyes and an eternally brief silence had hung between them, punctuated only by the beeping of the machines hooked into the sedated Dubček.

"Peter I…," Remy had stuttered, "I've never… I don't…."

But the words didn't come. Instead he returned his stare to the lethal syringe he held impotently in his hand.

"This isn't fair Remy," Peter had snarled, trying to keep his voice as low as possible. "This isn't my job anymore, I'm finished with all this crap!"

"But you know how to do it!"

Remy's whispered pleas had sounded more desperate with every syllable; like a schoolboy anxious for his friend's complicity before the headmaster could catch them in the act. The frustration, anger, desperation and pity erupted in a silent explosion behind Peter's surgical mask and he strode forward, snatching the syringe from Remy's hand and taking Dubček's thin, bony arm from the other.

Cleanly, professionally, knowing the situation relied on an absolute rejection of hesitation, Peter had pushed the needle under the wrinkled skin and depressed the plunger, carefully lying the offended appendage back on the crisp sheets before pausing to look at his victim's face for the first time. Restful, serene, Peter had to shake his head clear for a moment before grabbing the still teary eyed Remy and pushing him forcefully towards the door. The final, unheard beep of the machine had signalled the end of a legend just as Peter clicked the door closed behind them. It was done.

———

Their subsequent trip across the border into Austria had been as awkward a time as Peter could remember spending in the young Frenchman's company; a silence stretching over several hours, punctuated only by Remy's tearful apologies and expressions of gratitude, and Peter's grunted responses. After reaching Vienna, they had checked into a small hotel where Remy had immediately retired to bed and Peter had hit the bar and stayed there, quietly pondering why the thirst of his guilt was so much harder to quench this time. In the morning, they had travelled in silence to the office where Sangre was waiting. Peter recognised the bitter taste of resentment beginning to taunt him and quickly washed it down with a plastic cup full of tepid water. He had waited outside as Remy gave his solitary report, nervously hoping the Frenchman would not be treated too harshly; the job after all had been completed, albeit delayed, but when the door opened and Remy walked out, Peter had looked into a face that bore none of the apologetic regret of the previous day, being instead twisted into an arrogant sneer. Wordlessly, Deprez had strode down the corridor, while Peter himself was beckoned in by the quiet, almost gentle voice of Sangre.

It was then that Peter had learned of the betrayal. Not only had Deprez claimed credit for Dubček's murder, which Peter had expected and had been happy to go along with, but he had also pinned the blame for the initial failure of the crash on Peter himself. Sangre explained that the industrious young operative had been so dismayed at the bungle that he had investigated thoroughly and had uncovered evidence that the target had in fact been tipped off about an expected attack by elements within the British government. Although Britain had withdrawn from the Institute, its original operatives remained within its umbrella and it had been obvious to Deprez, and subsequently to Sangre, that conversations must have taken place between some such operatives and their former Ministerial patrons.

Peter's angry denials fell on deaf ears, but Sangre had assured him not to worry; Deprez had personally vouched for Peter's reliability, but nonetheless, in the circumstances it was inappropriate that Peter remain as controller. Instead, Sangre felt, Deprez himself had proven his strategic understanding and operational capabilities and would be the ideal person to guide regional operations into the new era. As for Peter, Sangre felt sure that he would appreciate a return to field operations, the role to which his talents were undoubtedly best suited.

Peter had no choice but to appreciate it, knowing what the barely veiled alternative would be, and he walked from the office swallowing hard on the first of what would be many indignities dolled out to him by Deprez. He had done him up, good and proper. All of Peter's efforts to coach and encourage him had been rolled up and shoved up his backside in what Peter could only imagine had been a long planned exercise in self advancement. Deprez was protected now and Peter, while he may have escaped Sangre's immediate wrath, was submerged once more in the swamp, struggling to keep his head afloat in the thick, black mire of his day job. Reaching the lift, Peter's impotent rage exploded outwards and he roared his objections as the doors slid closed, viciously punching his right hand into the cold metal before him, before rubbing his bruised knuckles in instant regret. It was going to hurt tomorrow.

———

The click of a camera snapped Peter back to the present and he glanced up at the smiling photographer in front of him, taking pictures of the young girl standing on the ridge beside him. Peter waited for them to finish and move on, rubbing his knuckles as the familiar arthritic twinge returned in the cold.

He stood up and reached into his pocket for a cigarette; he was an irregular smoker at best, never truly enjoying it and employing the habit only as a psychosomatic aide to concentration and he cursed to himself as his lighter's flint failed to spark. He hadn't even noticed the leather jacketed man sit down next to him and reach into his pocket until he saw a hand extend into his peripheral vision, accompanied by the words, "Need a light?"

"Cheers," Peter grunted, accepting the offer, drawing the thick, cutting smoke into his lungs and hoping his new companion wouldn't be the kind to make casual conversation. His hopes were fruitless.

"You looked a little lost in thought there," the newcomer opined, a lazy British accent playing on his voice.

Peter frowned at the question but tried not to let his irritation show. "Yeah, just have a lot on my mind is all," he replied, hoping the response would dissuade the stranger from further chat. It didn't.

"I know what you mean," he began, "you must have a lot to think about right now."

The response was an odd one but Peter ignored it, willing the newcomer to shut up, to no avail.

"Beautiful city, Prague," he said, rolling his eyes over the archaic modernity of the Old Town Square. "Don't you think?"

Peter didn't need to think. He knew it was beautiful. Cold, austere beauty; harsh, like that of a mother angry at the hedonistic excesses of her children. A little of the tension eased from his shoulders as he took the time to gaze around the square again and he afforded the stranger a quiet response.

"Yeah, it is".

"This is my first time in Prague," the stranger said. "I've always wanted to come but never had the chance. How long have you been stationed here?"

"Since before the revolution," Peter answered before

stopping as the relevance of the stranger's words hit home. *'Stationed here?'* Peter cursed his stupidity and spun around, fist clenched, ready to smash down on the stranger's jaw.

"Don't bother," said the stranger, and Peter froze at the site of the gun concealed in the arm of the stranger's jacket; small, but deadly and pointed directly at him.

Peter looked at his new enemy, sitting nonchalantly before him, an average looking man in his mid-to-late fifties, thin skin wrinkling over cheek bones and fading blonde hair draping over a skeletal forehead. The face was gaunt, saved only by the presence of the penetrating eyes which once may have bristled with charisma, but now remained resolutely cold and clinical, offering nothing of the personality inside. A simple jacket cradled his shoulders, while a black t-shirt and dark blue jeans completed the ensemble. It was, thought Peter, like looking into the future.

Slowly, Peter straightened up and stood facing the man, whose eyes, and gun, never wavered in their focus on him. Peter became aware of the cigarette that still hung, a little pathetically, from his lip, and he took a deep drag from it, letting the ash fall onto the cobbles. "I suppose I should thank you for a last smoke," he said, his voice thick with sarcasm.

"I don't want to kill you," the stranger reassured him, although the resolve in his stare and the authority in his voice left Peter in no doubt that he would if he had to, "I just want to have a little chat with you."

"Are you sure Deprez would approve?" Peter spat, contemptuously.

"Deprez?" A smile spread over the stranger's thin, mouth, "I don't know anyone called Deprez."

Peter sat back down and tried to keep the emotion from his face as he realised the implication of the man's last statement. If Deprez hadn't sent him then that could only mean...

"The Child?"

"The Child himself," answered the stranger, the cruel smile still on his lips.

Peter remembered the days when the mere mention of The Child was enough to instil fear in his very soul; The Child's presence alone confirmation that someone was to die. But instead of the sinking weight of fear in his heart, Peter afforded himself a brief smile and exhaled in satisfaction. "Good of him to show his face."

"Oh I doubt very much you'll see his face," Peter's counterpart replied. "I wanted to talk to you before we all get preoccupied doing what needs to be done." The note of command was still in the stranger's voice but etched with a probing sincerity.

"Why, will it change anything?"

"No."

"Then that's not much incentive for a cosy little chat is it?" Peter turned away and stared back out into the Square, at the early evening tourists milling around the restaurants hoping not to be ripped off, oblivious to the exchange occurring only yards away from them. A flicker of irritation furrowed the stranger's brow and his voice took on a harsher, more direct tone.

"Look don't get me wrong, mate," he began, his eyes never shifting from Peter's direction and his gun arm steady, "the situation is entirely unchanged. Both of you are going to die." He waited for his words to register with Peter, who gently nodded his understanding. "You can't alter the outcome, but the method is open to a little negotiation."

"What kind of negotiation?" Peter asked.

"You know the kind," the stranger had become conversational, almost avuncular in inflection. "You can die easy or hard, I do both well."

"Never mind me, what about her?" Peter's anger was resurfacing and showed itself in his response.

"Well that's up to you," the stranger answered, his hard gaze latched onto Peter's eyes. "If you do the job yourself like you were supposed to then she can die the quickest, most painless death imaginable. But if you leave it to me, well…" He shrugged and stayed silent.

"Bastard!" Peter spat.

"I'm not a sadist mate, I don't get turned on by hurting people. But I am a professional, and I'm conscious of the need to, *incentivise* you. Call it professional courtesy; a guy who's done our job for as long as you have deserves one last chance to get his shit together."

"What's your name?"

"That doesn't matter; we're all the same guy. Don't think you're the only bugger stuck in some European shithole taking shots at politicians. I've been doing this job for years. I've taken Presidents down. And I've heard all about you too. How the Institute had you working in Prague years before they joined the EU, how you stirred things up at the revolution. Some people would call you a legend. Not me, though."

"And what would you call me?" Peter scornfully enquired, intrigued despite himself.

"Nothing," was the response, "I'd just say you were a bloke doing his job. Just another murdering bastard wandering around Europe, killing suits because that's what some bigwig paid us to do. You're a killer." The last words were snapped at Peter, like the crack of a pistol. "Don't ever forget that, and don't try to fight it. You might be trying to do your best Jesus impression these days, but even if you grow a beard and walk across the Vltava, you'll always be a killer, and you'll kill again before you die."

"Not anymore." Peter turned away from the stranger's penetrating stare and lightly jingled the keys in his pocket. "And I'm not going to kill Mirushka so you can go and tell The Child to stick that idea where the sun doesn't shine. She's protected now."

"By you?" The response was sneering, loaded with contempt. "The only way you can truly protect her is to kill me. Me and everyone who comes after me. Have you still got that in you Saint Peter?"

Peter's anger bubbled and he spun around, ready to unleash a barrage of hateful remonstration, but the stranger was gone. A quick glance from left to right produced nothing and Peter knew it was futile to try and track him now; it would be as pointless as anyone trying to follow Peter. Guys like them knew how to disappear.

Peter spat the spent cigarette to the cobbles and cursed silently. For the first time in days he felt like he needed a drink, a real drink. Adrianna's death in the 'accident' and Mirushka's reaction to it had been stressful enough, but now after seeing McShade again and with the concrete affirmation that the threat continued to be very real, his resistance to the hard stuff began to crumble. Such things were not meant to be dealt with sober and he felt himself moving in the familiar direction of Smokin' Hot, stopping only when the buzz of his phone tingled against his cold leg. He reached into his pocket, intending to rattle off a quick response to Mirushka, but froze when he saw the display. The message lay there, unopened but bursting with potential. It had come from Remy Deprez.

CHAPTER 17

PETER LOATHED THE CHARLES BRIDGE. Not the bridge itself which was beautiful, but the endless hordes that swarmed across it each day from first light until dusk. He hated the gangs of drunken, British stags bullying their way past elderly tourists and shouting boorish profanities at the girls leaning over the sides. He hated the pickpockets who walked subtly behind their prey, waiting for the half chance to slip away a purse or phone and disappear into the heaving throng with their takings while the endless line of Baroque Saints gazed ponderously at the blemished souls below.

But that was in the daytime. At night the Bridge was deserted of souls save for a scattered few delighting in the unspoiled views, and on this night even they were absent. The sight before Peter was one of postcard beauty; the illuminated Bridge Tower standing imperious guard before the cobbled stone walkway which stretched over to the twin towers of Mala Strana – the Lesser Town. It was as though the city had been plucked up, dusted free from drunken revellers and planted in the middle of a gothic fairytale; one of castles and clock towers and creatures lurking in the shadows.

Peter had come to see such a creature tonight, but even as he stepped out from the darkness and onto the bridge he did not fully understand why. Here he was, on open ground, far away from Mirushka's own security and utterly exposed purely on the basis of a texted promise from a man he had humiliated. The message had been brief and simple; *'Charles Bridge, 20:30. Please'*.

Peter had not responded and had at first continued his journey to Smokin' Hot before turning and heading for the bridge. As he started through the illuminated stone archway, Peter began to question, for the first time while sober, his own sanity. He had questioned it on and off for as long as he could remember, but so did most men when the bottle was empty and their heads were resting painfully on the pillow of the latest bar room pick up. But now Peter's thoughts were free of slivovice and he struggled with the notion that coming here tonight proved only that he was suicidal, mad, or both.

He rolled the thought around his head; the thought of the beautiful young leader, an arm's reach from history, assailed from all angles by the murderers who claimed to know better, murderers whose number included Peter only days before. He couldn't die tonight, not yet. Mirushka was his mission now, his crusade, his contrition.

Peter looked over his shoulder in the direction he had just come from. There was no sign of Deprez but Peter knew he would be there; skulking in some shadow or other, waiting for his 'dramatic entrance.' He coughed in contempt of these theatrics and searched his brain once more for an answer as to why he had come. Since the incident at the Clock Tower, a part of Peter had been in shock, not at the assault inflicted on his one time comrade, but one born of the pity he had felt for him as he sat broken on the wet floor. And the realisation hit Peter that he had come precisely because of that pity; that at some level, buried under decades of resentment, hatred and anger, he still cared for his friend of old. The thought stopped Peter in his tracks and he went back and forth as though he were a worried auditor hastily double checking his figures and reaching the same inescapable conclusion; he had come to save Deprez. Resentment rose within his gut as Peter's mind screamed a defiance that his gut would not accept.

The Baroque statues looked down in silent agreement with Peter and he turned his head to look at the one closest to him; a thin figure carrying a crucifix and a golden feather and wearing a halo of five golden stars around his head. The figure held his head to one side and wore on his face a look of concerned forgiveness.

"John of Nepomuk," said Remy Deprez who suddenly stood a few yards behind Peter, "Czech national saint and martyr to imperial interferance. Thrown from the Charles Bridge and drowned at the orders of Wenceslaus King of the Romans in 1393."

Peter had swivelled in surprise when hearing Deprez's voice but stopped still and mirrored the Frenchman's clamness.

"Mate of yours was he?" Peter spoke in a low begrudging voice and turned his head back toward the statue.

"I love this country Peter," Deprez responded. "It's good to know about the place one lives. And dies."

Peter turned back to Deprez thinking to offer a comeback but stopped himself. He looked closely at his adversary. To look at him would not suggest that he was suffering any after effects from the confrontation in the Clock Tower; his black suit and overcoat were as immaculate as usual while noticeably the strain that had been a permenant feature of his face for years had vanished, replaced by a look of surprising contentment. Peter even thought he saw some colour in the normally deathly pale cheeks.

"What do you want?" Peter was disinclined to engage in small talk.

Deprez lifted his hand, to halt any verbal or physical barrage. "The Child has arrived in Prague to personally oversee the completion of the project and ensure a smooth transition."

"Transition to what?"

"Transition from my leadership to someone else's."

The Frenchman's voice was softer, weaker than Peter remembered and he understood why. "So what's going to happen to you?" Peter asked, half predicting the answer.

"I have been offered re-assignment or…"

Peter knew what the other option would be.

"I'm sorry."

Deprez smiled. "It is I who should apologise. I wanted to tell you in person, I'm not sure why."

"And I'm not sure why I came. But here we are."

"My reassignment, of course, depends on one thing."

"You killing me?"

"Oui."

"Good luck with that."

Deprez smiled, a sincere smile devoid of arrogance or sneer.

"I'm not going to kill you Peter, I won't even try. You were right." Deprez looked away, across the Vltava, leaning his gloved hands against the stone wall. "I thought I was keeping myself clean by never going through with a kill myself, never directly ordering a murder. I thought that kept me somehow above it all, above people like you. But in truth, you towered above me."

Peter joined him in looking out across the river.

"None of us can hold our heads particularly high."

"Well I intend to hold mine a little higher in death." He turned back to face Peter.
"I apologise to you for my actions. The only compensation I can offer is to refuse to take your life as ordered."

Peter shook his head, the passionate spontaneity which fuelled his last encounter with Deprez absent, replaced by a speechlessness he could only break by stating the obvious.

"They'll kill you."

"Oui," said Deprez, "but they have been killing me for years my friend, every time they looked at me and every time they spoke to me, their hands gripped my throat a little tighter." He spoke Peter's own words back to him without anger or malice, merely with peaceful acceptance. "At least now they can finish the job."

Deprez reached into his pocket and pulled out a small gun which he held loosely pointed at Peter.

"What's that for?"

"Effect. You should go," he told Peter. "My intentions will soon be clear and I'm sure you can guess what the reaction will be."

Realisation struck Peter and he looked sharply around.

"You're being shadowed?"

"It would be naïve to suspect otherwise. Either way, there is no need for you to stay."

His voice was backed by the inebriated song of a staggering group of Brits, shuffling up from Lesser Town, still some distance from the pair but their voices growing louder by the second.

"Run," said Deprez. "Through your countrymen over there; at least you'll be a moving target."

"I'm not leaving you."

"Then you will leave Ms. Svobodova defenceless. You have your own path Peter, this is mine. Goodbye my friend."

The stumbling collection of drunks was getting close enough to fill their ears with profanity but neither man responded or even registered the innuendo. Peter, a curious desperation sweeping over him, tried one last time to halt his former controller's intentions.

"Remy…"

Before any further word could leave Peter's mouth, the Frenchman had raised the small gun in the air and hurled it into the river below, a tell-tale red light appearing on his chest almost before the weapon had hit the water.

"Go." Remy whispered the word with a smile, just as the group of drunkards reached them, announcing their arrival with exaggerated effeminate whistles, which turned to cries of shock as a bullet whooshed through their number, skimming the bridge as it went. With an agility he could scarcely believe he still possessed, Peter spun around and ran through the close knit, intoxicated huddle, knocking several roughly aside as he sped into Lesser Town and disappeared into the darkness. The sound of his footsteps faded into the distance accompanied by the cries of the startled stag party now panicking and scrabbling to safety.

Remy stood silently alone awaiting his fate.

"Notre Père, qui es aux cieux," he whispered as he turned to face the tower from where the shot had been fired. "Que ton nom soit sanctifié." Walking forward slowly he outspread his arms, inviting his martyrdom. "Que ton règne vienne…"

The shot flung him backwards against the statue and he twisted his eyes to meet John of Nepomuk's and smiled. With a tremendous effort he turned back toward the tower, dark red staining his crisp, white shirt.

"Que ta volonté soit faite sur la terre comme au ciel," he said through his grin. With the second shot he spun again and toppled over the side of the bridge, slipping quietly into the depths of the Vltava, where he sank, silent and un-complaining, through the velveteen waters.

——

It was several hours later that Peter marched down the hotel corridor to Mirushka's suite, to be met by Rado's furrowed brow, his expression hardening further when he saw Peter's own face.

"What's up?"

Peter never broke stride, flinging the door open. "I'm getting her out of here."

In front of him at the writing desk sat Mirushka, a velvet dressing grown flowing around her. She jumped in shock at Peter's entry.

"Láska moja," she said, getting up from her chair and moving to embrace him, "where have you been?"

Peter resisted the temptation to relax into her arms and held her gently at the hips.

"Get dressed, you're not staying here tonight."

"Don't be ridiculous, I'm not going anywhere!"

"They killed him Mirushka!" Peter knew his voice was louder than he would have liked and tried to control the crack he could feel lying in his throat. "They killed him in front of me."

"Who?" Mirushka asked, confused.

"Deprez," Peter shook his head, the adrenaline hampering the collection of his thoughts. "Remy. He was supposed to kill me but he wouldn't do it, so they..." Peter's voice was becoming higher and his breathing shorter and he silently swore at his display of weakness.

Mirushka lifted her hands to his face, cupping it delicately and speaking in her soft, patient tones.

"Calm down Miláčku. Tell me, what happened?"

Peter explained his movements since the meeting with McShade that day; the encounter with the man in the square, his replacement and the subsequent message from Remy to meet at the bridge. She chastised him for his foolishness in attending, to which he nodded in agreement, but when he got to the point of Remy's death he fell into momentary silence.

"He refused to do it," he said after a quiet scramble for words, "so they killed him."

"He sacrificed himself?"

"Some kind of ultimate act of contrition I suppose..."

"Contrition?"

Peter opened his eyes to his lover, "It's an old word, and it basically means deep regret at past wrongs, religious penitence, that kind of thing." He shook his head clear once more and broke free from her arms.

"Anyway, it means they're coming for you now, we've got to get you away. Rado!"

Radoslav appeared at the door, only for Mirushka to hold up her hand.

"Miláčku," she began, "I understand your pain, but I will not give in to paranoia. I have absolute faith in Rado, his team and in you."

She gestured Rado to leave and walked through to the bedroom, while Peter looked on in stubborn frustration.

"You're being reckless!" He hissed.

"I hadn't realised that going to sleep in one's own bed was considered an especially reckless activity," she gently answered over her shoulder.

Peter glowered back. "That's just what Herbert thought about taking his insulin, that's what Dubček thought about chauffer driven cars!"

Mirushka breathed deeply and smiled, acknowledging Peter's heartfelt concern without condescension.

"Láska moja," she began, "I thank you for your concern but this is where I'm sleeping tonight. I would like it if you lay next to me but if you think that is so very dangerous then feel free to go elsewhere."

"I'm staying here with you." He followed her into the bedroom where she dropped her robe to the floor and climbed between the sheets, clamping her tired eyes shut. Switching off the light, he let his eyes get used to the dark while he undressed himself, before perching, cross legged on the bed beside her, his muscles drained and aching but his mind unable to rest. Eyes red and wide he stared into the darkness, waiting for what he was sure would soon come.

———

Though his eyes still stared, stinging and unblinking, several hours later, it was his ears that first alerted him to the danger. The tiniest of clinks on the window glass was enough to break Peter's stare, cocking his head to one side and straining for an encore. As it came, he slid, silently from the bed and stood, naked and barefoot next to the long, velvet curtain, the fibres of the drape brushing against his unshaven cheek as he tracked the sounds behind it. The unrested stresses within him had built hour upon hour, flooding his mind with adrenaline and flushing from it all traces of patience and strategic analysis; instead he stalked his prey on instinct and the primal desire to fight and protect, always keeping the sleeping body of his lover within his field of vision, until finally, as he'd expected, the edge of the drape was pushed gently aside by a silent, steel barrel which raised slowly and deliberately towards the bed.

Letting forth a guttural cry, Peter reached through the gap and grabbed the arm of the would be shooter, pulling it and the man it was attached to through the curtains and hurling him onto the bed. His tired muscles burned in protest but Peter ignored the pain and before the figure could recover, Peter was on him, throwing him from the bed to the floor, away from his now woken lover, who scrambled to the edge wrapping the sheets around her. His feral rage consuming his reason, Peter willingly surrendered to thoughtless instinct and swung blow after blow against the attacker, releasing all of his tension and all of his guilt upon the man who wriggled and grappled in vain to throw off the animal who clung to his flesh.

The door to the room smashed open and Peter became aware

of Mirushka's screams and of Rado shouting in Slovak. Looking up, the haze cleared from Peter's eyes enough for him to make out the sight of Rado pointing his weapon at the man struggling beneath him.

"He's mine!" Peter shouted in a bestial roar.

The man was strong and Peter pushed his smarting, exhausted muscles to tearing point to hold him down and claw himself into position behind him.

"It's you isn't it?" Peter shouted at the figure writhing in his arms, "I know it's you!" He ripped at the black mask covering his opponent's face and yanked at it, his fingers gouging into the eye holes for a better grip and to further weaken the man behind them. Finally succeeding in tearing the black cloth from his face, Peter wrenched the man's head upwards so he could stare down from above into his enemy's eyes. The man in the square. Peter had expected no other but the moment of recognition stilled him for just the quickest of seconds.

"If you let me go I'll kill her!" The figure spat his words at Peter. "Do what you have to do!"

Peter screamed back at his foe, incoherent rage blinding him, preventing him from seeing clearly the two paths in front of him.

The man spoke again against the pressure of Peter's arm. "Don't show me any mercy," he hissed, "because if you let go I will show none to her".

With the last vestiges of effort, and fighting the chaos in his mind as much as the man on the floor, Peter succeeded in forcing his forearm completely under his opponent's chin and, with his back against the wall, he began pressing his throat tightly, violently twisting the squirming gunman's arm up his back with his other hand while he did so. The desperate kicking of the man began to rejuvenate Peter and he felt himself growing stronger again, life seeping back into his body as it leaked from his prey. He knew what would happen, he expected it to happen, *he wanted it to happen*..... He pressed down, tighter and tighter and...

Phut.

The man beneath his grip went limp in an instant and Peter felt a warm trickle caress his forearm, still lodged beneath the attackers chin. The unmistakeable scent of gun smoke began to tease at Peter's nostrils, and all at once, he began to weep; a howl of despair crying forth from deep, deep within him. His forearm, the trickle dripping from it and onto the carpet, still pressed tightly against the un-resistant neck, and as he howled, Peter continued to press it tighter and tighter, for that was all he knew to do. Over the sound of his wailing, Peter was dimly aware of Mirushka's voice calling his name, imploring him to come to her, but he could only shake his head, squeezing his fallen foe even more tightly to him as the death grip became a fearful embrace. Releasing his enemy's arm from behind his back, Peter reached up and cupped the dead man's face, turning his face toward his own. An incoherent apology pushing its way through his despair, Peter leaned his head in close and kissed the rapidly cooling brow, before resting his own against it as the tears continued to fall.

The warmth of his attacker diminished, Peter once more began to hear Mirushka's velvet voice calling to him through the confusion in his mind.

Dropping the corpse to the floor Peter remained crouched, his adrenaline addled mind trying to make sense of the situation.

Looking up, he saw the thin trail of smoky vapour issuing from Rado's muffled gun; the young Slovak still standing frozen in the moment of shooting.

His animal rage boiling over once more, Peter sprang up from the floor and grabbed his colleague by the suit jacket, slamming him against the wall.

"Bastard!" Peter shouted in his face. "He was mine! He should have been mine!!"

Rado was a far stronger opponent than the dead man and easily broke Peter's grip on him, pinning him back against the wall.

"Stand down!" Rado's voice was stern, in command, yet oddly calm. "It's over!"

Peter responded by vainly pushing his spent muscles once more and, unable to break the young Slovak's grip, letting out a scream of rage. Rado stood firm and looked directly into Peter's eyes.

"Stand! Down!"

Peter's scream became a sob and as the resistance in his aging muscles finally gave out, he collapsed in a heap at Rado's feet and felt consciousness slipping away from him while Mirushka's soft voice echoed fearfully in his ears.

CHAPTER 18

MIRUSHKA HAD INSISTED ON STAYING with him that night; through his confusion he knew that much. He remembered hovering on the edge of consciousness, sightless, the hairs of the carpet irritating the still fresh scars on his back, threatening but not quite managing to bring him to, and hearing her soft, wise tones countering Rado's impassioned pleas. He was unpredictable, Rado was saying, unstable, a danger to her and the election. For Mirushka to allow herself to be alone with him in this condition, was, in Rado's view, an unacceptable risk.

Peter had tried to answer, to reassure them both he was fine, but his words wouldn't come, and he found himself unable to translate theirs anymore, as they faded again into the blackness that enveloped him, replaced in his mind by the thousand voices that had permeated his sleep for the bulk of these past weeks. Only this time, instead of the echoing recital of vitriol, the voices simply said his name, over and over again, some shouting, some whispering. And this time there was a new voice, a gentler voice, spoken with a soft, delicate French accent which spoke yearningly, as though desperately awaiting response.

"Remy?" Peter replied as the French voice grew louder,

punctuated by the clashing volumes of the other voices. He strained in the blackness to see his friend, the other voices serving to confuse him when he thought he was close. "Remy?" he shouted again, the Frenchman's voice repeating Peter's own name back at him, louder and louder until it seemed as though he were right behind Peter. Peter spun around in the black, the echoing voices a thunderstorm around him now, hoping against hope to see Remy, to thank him. A shape brushed him and Peter grabbed it, pulling it close to him, an excited joy filling his chest at having found the object of his search, only to turn instantly cold when the face of the shape he held came out of the darkness before him; for Remy Deprez it was not, and Peter found himself once more staring into the deathly pale face of Herbert Biely. Peter stepped back in dread, hoping for the face to rescind into to the darkness, but it remained resolutely with him, stare unbroken, features gentle and reassuring, yet filling Peter only with terror. Slowly the dead mouth creaked open, as if to join the eternal crescendo of voices calling his name, and Peter clamped his eyes closed in pure, unadulterated panic.

"Peter." The voice came, but it was not Herbert's. "Peter," it said again, as fear kept his eyelids from relaxing. It was a trick, Peter thought, and as soon as he opened his eyes, Herbert would be there, accusing him, willing him to join him in death. Shaking, Peter retracted as a soft hand stroked again his stubble lined face, accompanied by the softly spoken word, "Miláčku."

Waking with a jolt, Peter sat up and looked around quickly, taking in his surroundings and relaxing only when he could focus properly on Mirushka's eyes and be sure of the softness of her skin and the sincerity of the grip of her hand.

"You slept all day," she smiled, the worry not far from her voice. "Welcome to the land of the living."

———

"Kajúcnosť." Mirushka said, a short time later as they looked out over Prague, the city relaxing comfortably into the descending gloom of dusk as though it were a favoured blanket.

"What?" Peter asked, his mind's search of his languages drawing a blank.

"Kajúcnosť," she said again. "Contrition; you spoke of your friend's contrition last night. I didn't understand your word at first, but we call it kajúcnos; the moment when regret for our past evils is truly sincere and repentance is possible."

Peter smiled. "Work that out for yourself did you?" he joked, receiving a small laugh for his trouble.

"Never underestimate the power of the internet." She grinned in return, gripping his fingers more tightly in her own. "How do you feel, láska moja?"

"Peter breathed the cold air deeply into his lungs and slowly exhaled. "Better," he said, "not brilliant, but definitely better." He returned the squeeze of her hand and broke his gaze away from the view before him, to look down at his lover, who kept her own stare hovering over the city.

"What happened to the body?" he asked, wanting to ensure business was attended to first.

"It turns out Rado possessed the necessary skill set after all," she replied, "just as you suspected."

"Ah, Rado," Peter's mind drifted to the half heard, barely translated words of the previous night. "I expect he's not too happy about all this."

"Rado is loyal. He'll respect my wishes."

Slipping his hand from hers to lean on the stone balcony rail, Peter took a slow, long breath.

"Why do you stay with me?" he asked, gently.

Mirushka's eyes dropped, for the briefest of flickers, from their maternal guard before she steadied herself and continued to look straight ahead.

"You mean aside from the sacrifice you offered me? You took care of me in my moment of pain, what kind of person would I be not to offer you the same? You are my láska and you were hurting."

"I was dangerous," Peter responded, his voice serious. "I didn't think I'd break down like that, and if it happened once it can happen again. You should have let Rado sort me out, you're too important, I could hurt you."

"I won't leave you to torment yourself Miláčku," was her defiant response.

He delicately touched her face, turning it towards him so he could meet the beautiful, sparkling eyes. She relaxed into his touch and turned her body into his, accepting his embrace and linking her arms around his neck.

"Listen," he said, "I'm expendable, you aren't. Everything depends on you. If I get like that again, for whatever reason, there's no telling what I might do, I could…"

She pressed her lips against his, cutting off his warning, and kept them there until she felt him return the kiss and the tension leave his body. Their lips parted and he rested his head against hers, his eyes closed in introspection.

"I'm sorry," he said quietly.

"I'm not." Mirushka responded. "Remember when you asked me how I could be with you, knowing the things you'd done? And how I acted towards you when Adrianna was killed?"

Peter nodded.

"I am old enough to know that everyone has a past, those in this business even more so. And even though I cannot even bear to think on some of the things you have done, I know that you are as sick of them as I, and that you are sorry."

A tear danced in the corner of Peter's eye before slipping from the lashes and falling down his cheek as Mirushka continued.

"I knew that night when you opened your heart to me that your sorrow was genuine, but ever since then, despite your best efforts, you had been falling deeper and deeper into the pit of guilt and last night you hit the bottom. But, maybe thanks to Rado, maybe not, you avoided returning to what you used to be; you broke through the bottom of the pit and entered into kajúcnost'."

Peter felt the loving brush of her thumbs against his cheeks, drying them of intrusive tears as her soft voice continued.

"I think that Remy was not the only one to have had a contrite heart last night, and I love you all the more for it. For where there is contrition, redemption can grow."

"The trouble is," Peter answered, "I don't know how else to save you. Avoiding them isn't enough anymore; they're coming for you."

"More assassins?"

He laughed sardonically. "Calling us 'assassins' affords us a glamour we don't deserve. We don't drive around in gadget laden cars, sipping expensive champagne; I don't even own a tux."

"Pity," she smiled. He responded in kind though his words retained their severity.

"I wasn't an assassin...I'm...I was...a murderer. At the end of the day that's what all of us in the 'profession' are; murderers and people who arrange murder. There are no 'goodies and baddies', there never were. I read Ivan Klíma once; he was one of yours wasn't he? He reckoned there was no grand battle between good and evil anymore, just two different evils fighting to control the world, and maybe he was right. I can't claim to have fought for Queen and Country, or some grandiose philosophy, I was never interested in saving the world, I just did my job and that was that. I killed people because I was good at it; man, woman, black, white, gay, straight, whatever, I was an equal opportunities murderer. I never asked if they deserved it, I just got on with the job and if my conscience piped up I'd drink it quiet again. All of us are evil in some way, except for you and Herb; the only difference is some pretend to be good guys. But even then they make friends with the bad guys when there's money to be made then go back to bombing them when the headlines get dodgy."

Mirushka pulled Peter around to face her and put her finger softly over his lips. "You're not a bad guy any more." She whispered into his ear before moving her lips down to his neck.

He eagerly returned the embrace, overjoyed but terrified that the best words he had could not dissuade her from her loyalty to him.

"I have to leave early," she whispered as she led him, shuffling, away from the balcony and back into the bedroom, still wrapped in their clumsy, mutual embrace. "I think you should stay here, get more rest."

"No problem," Peter agreed, pushing her backwards onto the magnificent bed. "There's someone I need to talk to anyway."

———

It wasn't too early the next morning that Peter took a sip from his hot coffee, without once taking his eyes from the spectral figures that stared at him from across the road; silent, unmoving, at once accusatory and earnest as they stood forever frozen at the base of Petrin Hill. The small, dark café where Peter and his companion sat was always open, yet never quite bustling; its unique and peculiar ambience, born from its unsettling observers, never quite leaving its patrons completely at ease. Peter scolded himself for his discomfort. It was just one more memorial, in a city of memorials, but each time he sat here, his eyes were drawn to them, as though they were silently demanding he join them in their eternal vigil.

"How far?"

The question snapped Peter back to reality like overstretched elastic, a muffled, "What?" his only response.

"How far will you go for her?"

Across the table, McShade, his jacket, tie and trousers as black as the shadows under his eyes, gave a short exhale of frustration and he repeated his question with elaboration.

"I presume the reason for our meeting like this is to talk about Ms Svobodova? Either that or you're labouring under the vain misapprehension that I owe you some form of apology; in which case you will be gravely disappointed as none shall be forthcoming."

Peter did not doubt that the man's stubborn reticence was genuine and he cracked a large smile. "Yes, I want to talk about Mirushka," he said, "and I'm not looking for apologies.
Although if you feel any pangs of remorse we can always go to a pub instead while you clear your conscience?"

To his astonishment, Peter's attempt at humour succeeded in warming, slightly, the ice in the other man's expression, and he saw the faintest trace of a smile appear at the corners of his mouth.

"So again," McShade said, more softly this time, "how far are you prepared to go for the redoubtable Ms Svobodova?"

"As far as it takes," Peter responded.

"How far is that?" McShade lifted his own coffee to his lips, his eyes ever burrowing into Peter's own.

Though he knew what McShade was driving at, Peter tried to shake off the dogged question with bluster.

"How far do you think?" he said, "I've been practically holding her hand every second of the day, for the past few weeks. I've been protecting her from every threat that comes her way and I've made myself a target by doing it. I've put my life at risk to protect her; maybe you wouldn't know what it means to be prepared to lay down your life for someone."

The words were sincere but laboured, as though Peter knew deep down, that this was one of several losing battles he was fighting.

The diplomat returned his cup to its saucer with a clink, his stare still unbroken; his visage unmoved by Peter's exhortations.

"All risk is quantifiable," he said calmly, "your efforts are all very well but ultimately count for nothing unless you are genuinely prepared to make that ultimate sacrifice."

Peter felt resentment twist his face. "What do you mean?" he hissed.

His stare still un-cowed, McShade dabbed the corners of his mouth with the paper napkin by his hand. "I'm beginning to wonder which of us has had the career in politics," he said. "If someone asked me how far I would go for someone I loved, my response would be instant and emphatic. I have now asked you four times and you continue to dodge the question."

He placed his forearms on the table and lowered his voice; the remnants of his faint smile now wiped away with the vestiges of his coffee. "Are you truly prepared to die for her?"

The question hung there, unanswered for several moments. Though he loathed himself to admit it, and though he had assumed that he was, when the question was pressed, Peter hesitated to answer.

"Yes," Peter said.

"Well that was far from convincing. Come on man, are you or aren't you?" McShade's voice was loud again, invested with all the authority of years at dispatch boxes and podiums; the tone pressing, demanding, the question never relenting as McShade re-asked it again and again until Peter thought his head would explode.

"Yes but I don't want to! It feels like I've crawled through hell, only there's no 'happily ever after' on the other side."

The few others in the dank café turned in surprise at the volume of Peter's exclamation, several openly tutting at the uncouth foreigner before returning to the solitude of their beverages. Peter, embarrassed, looked apologetically back to the few that would make eye contact with him and turned hesitantly back to his companion, whose own body language in contrast to Peter's, had noticeably softened. "So," Peter half whispered, looking down in shame at his coffee, "now you've another reason to despise me."

"Not at all."

Peter looked up to find that the ferocity of McShade's stare had finally subsided and he had relaxed against the back of his chair, his chin resting on his hand. It had been the tone of McShade's voice rather than his words which had raised Peter's eyes; a softness in the inflection which Peter couldn't recall having heard from the man before. He raised an eyebrow at McShade's response.

"Now at least I know you're not just suicidal."

Peter gave a laugh at McShade's crude psychology.

"Anyone can jump in front of a bullet Mr Lowe, but if that person doesn't care one way or another whether or not he lives or dies then all his action equates to is glorified suicide. The rational mind desires its own preservation; I'm glad not to be dealing with a psychotic nurturing a death wish. Besides, The Child is unconcerned by the grand futility of such gestures and there's no reason to believe he would cease his pursuit of Svobodova merely because of your death."

McShade's entire demeanour had changed to one of relaxed conversationalism. Still authoritative, still wary of the earshot of those around him, but nonetheless more genial than at any time Peter could remember, as though he were enjoying mulling over a problem of hypothetical philosophy with his erstwhile protégé.

"Don't get me wrong," he continued, "it's likely you'll still be called to make the supreme sacrifice, but by far the best option would be for you to be true to yourself and kill for her instead."

Again, Peter's face began to contort into a grimace.

"Kill?" he asked, his voice tinged with resentment.

The focus returned once more to McShade's manner and he leaned closer, across the table to his colleague.

"Don't pretend your some kind of reformed apostle," he said, "You've always been a killer and it's still inside you; I know what happened in the hotel."

"Who told y ----"

"That doesn't matter." The older man had command of the conversation and was quick to dispel any insubordinate questioning. "What does matter is that the best way for you to help Miroslava is to use your skills against those who would do her harm. Whether you die or not doesn't matter to The Child, you're only a secondary target for him. And with you dead, they'll still keep coming for her, only this time you won't be there to help; and let's face it, your recent history of reunions with former colleagues suggests you're unlikely to survive another encounter." McShade paused for a moment, to make sure, Peter supposed, that the message was taking root. "Cat and Mouse games are all very well but become significantly more difficult the more visible the Mouse. Ms Svobodova has no choice but to be visible and even if you think you can carry on playing the game with such odds against you, every cat The Child sends will be fiercer than the last, and they'll keep coming until she is dead and the election postponed. We have a unique opportunity to prevent all that by taking the fight to them, an opportunity made possible by your girlfriend's unfathomable decision to forgive you and keep you around."

McShade had drained the positivity from Peter with every word he spoke, snuffing out the tiny flame of hope that had lit inside him after their last meeting, leaving only a sweetly scented, smoky residue. Damn it, he thought, what was he even doing here? What magic words did he think McShade would have to offer anyway, even if he wanted to? No, he didn't want to die, but he wanted to be prepared to if he had to, and killing again was poor preparation for his immortal soul. Peter's eyes flickered as he ran the variables through his mind which was once more becoming flustered; albeit with emotion rather than alcohol.

"Suppose..," he stuttered, desperately reaching for an answer, any answer that could offer an alternative to McShade's 'kill or be killed' mentality, "… you said The Child would alter his plans if Mirushka won the election."

"I said he might alter his plans," McShade corrected him, caution in his voice, "there's no guarantee I'm right."

"So what made you say he would?" Peter continued to press his point, desperate to pluck at any straw which could offer a way out of his dilemma.

"Like I said, he's a pragmatist." McShade downed the rest of his coffee, "The Child doesn't shy away from murder but he's no sadist. I suppose if you were to give him a label then 'disciplinarian' would be the most appropriate. He analyses the political landscape and sets actions in motion which support his objective; often his objective necessitates the death of certain persons, but he prefers to move more subtly than that. At the moment he believes that Svobodova's death will lead to a postponed election and the subsidence of the reunification movement, however if she wins and the countries propose to reunite then it makes more sense for him to ensure the process is procrastinated; your lady friend's death would be little more than petty revenge; that's not his business."

"He wants revenge on me," Peter snorted, only to be met by a laugh.

"Don't flatter yourself Mr Lowe," McShade chuckled, "he doesn't care enough about you to want revenge. You are being disciplined."

"Pretty extreme form of discipline."

"Oh absolutely, but his punishments can vary a great deal. Your desire to 'embrace the light' and lead a pure and holy life has been massively detrimental to his plans, so it makes sense to him that an appropriate punishment would be taking that life away from you. For others it could be loss of career or…"

"Or saddling you with responsibility for an economic disaster." Peter allowed the jibe out against his better judgement and immediately regretted it, even despite McShade's amused re-telling of The Child's punishment philosophies. It had the desired effect of cutting the joviality from McShade's voice and reminding him that Peter was not to be mocked. The older man's expression returned to its default position.

"Quite so," he said, quietly.

Peter sought to limit the damage and get back to the matter in hand. "The election is only a few days away now. If I can get her through them alive then you're saying there's a good chance The Child will let her live?"

"Perhaps," McShade agreed, resentment at his chastening touching his voice, "although punishment will undoubtedly come in some form. But why take the chance?" He leaned forward, the intensity returned to his gaze. "You're a killer Mr Lowe. I wasn't Dr Frankenstein, you aren't my creation; I chose you because of what you are. Accept your nature and do what needs to be done to save her."

Peter once more lowered his eyes, trying vainly to avoid the ferocity of his companion's stare. "Not any more," he protested, "I've stopped all that now."

McShade stared for a moment before he spoke again, patiently but with headmasterly sternness.

"When I was a boy," he began, "my grandparents would insist I accompany them to church each Sunday. They were old fashioned, religious people and the Minister was, shall we say, something of a traditionalist, eager to fill young minds with warnings of fire and brimstone. He would tell tales of evil men, guilty of the most horrendous of sins who became sickened with themselves. Unwilling to turn to the church, they grew so desperate for relief from the horrors of their existence that they sought escape through any means necessary, even into hell itself, believing they could find some eventual release."

"And did they?"

"No, because no such route exists. But like every fool in hell they spent an eternity searching in vain for something that didn't exist, just as you do now. For a wise man, sometimes the only choice is an escape to perdition."

"Not a very appealing choice."

"But an honest one. At least in perdition one has the luxury of being true to oneself and accepting the consequences of one's choices. There is no redemption for people like us and instead of scrambling to find some path to paradise as you burn still further on the coals, you should accept who you are and embrace the damnation it brings you, because at least you've saved someone else from enduring that fate in your place."

Peter broke eye contact as McShade recounted his story, the soundness of his proposition hammering unfairly home, so much so that he had nothing with which to counter it, save for clenched arthritic knuckles and a furrowed brow.

"The Child may instil fear in all he encounters, but he isn't God," McShade pressed on, "and even though his past has been shrouded you can be sure at least that he has one."

Peter's grimace showed little sign of receding. "Don't we all," he muttered, pointedly.

"Indeed, but few as interesting or as unique as his. And particularly his life before The Institute."

Peter raised an eyebrow at the slow tease of information and the old statesman leaned closer in response, his voice low and encaptivating.

"You have motive Mr Lowe, and with the appropriate level of thought and effort, opportunities can be manufactured, even against those such as him. The only question is whether you will allow your conscience to hold you back from whom you truly are or whether you will protect your great love in the only way you surely can. If not she will die, and despite Černý's no doubt sterling efforts, her dreams will die with her. Can you think of any good reason why you would let that happen when it is within your power to prevent it?"

McShade's words continued to pour in their unjustly logical way and Peter clinked his spoon in his empty cup as they washed over him, eyes still averted, face still granite.

"No," he finally said, scooping the remnants of wet sugar from his cup before tapping them back where they lay. "No."

CHAPTER 19

THE PICTURE REBUKED HIM from the table of his Parliamentary office, silently mocking with brutal simplicity. Černý's own self, coldly twisted into undignified caricature, staring back at him; an expression of misery inked onto the exaggerated features. The figure, un-lovingly clothed in scruffy, ill-fitting butler's garb, clutched sadly to the skirt train of the regally sketched Svobodova who stood, radiant, on a podium atop a map of Central Europe; a raggedly dressed peasant poised to lower a bejewelled crown onto her head. The picture hardly needed a caption to deliver its message, but at the top of the panel flew a cherub carrying a flowing banner, bearing the inscription: 'veľký partnerstva' – The Great Partnership.

Černý was used to satire, but this cut him to the core, not least because he recognised the truth of it. However much he may protest its exaggeration, however insistent he may be that this was his election in his country, Svobodova was the one calling the shots. She knew it, the people knew it and deep down so did he. Ignorance may be no defence but neither did awareness offer him comfort as he tried in vain to ignore the picture and concentrate on his speech.

The knock at his door was an irritant, while his ignored instruction to go away and subsequent opening was anger inducing. He raised his eyes, his voice ready to deliver a stinging rebuke to whichever fool had entered, only for him to stare in cold surprise at the figure in the doorway.

"Ms. Hedvikova," he greeted her. Daleka Hedvikova, the Czech Deputy Prime Minister walked slowly but confidently towards his desk, immaculately attired, exuding the air of contemptuous sexuality that saw her hold so many men from all sides of Parliament in her grip, a number which did not include Černý.

"Are you sure the Prime Minister would think this meeting wise?"

"Vladimir is a fool," she laughed, "a puppet. And so is that idiot Čurda, who thinks he pulls the strings."

"A discourteous way of speaking of one's masters."

"But an accurate one," the young Czech countered, a hint of irritation in her voice at Černý's lack of attention to her. "In any case, this is the 21st Century. Why should I submit to anyone's mastery other than my own?"

Looking up at her, the old man took her in properly. She was certainly beautiful. Her hair, typically tied back into a severe pony tail, lay long and dark down her back, brushing her shoulders and cradling her chin. The smile on her face possessed all the mis-chievousness of Svobodova's, but little of its sincerity, and was etched with a trace of cruelty. Not a hint of warmth was detecta-ble behind the striking, calculating blue eyes. She stood, her arms resting on the rim of the chair, leaning slightly forward toward him; the neck of her blouse hanging invitingly close to his line of vision, and asked, her voice softer, for permission to sit.

Černý, unlike Čurda or Rukavice, was no fool and kept his eyes on hers; granting her request to be seated, while declining the invitation of her posture.

"We need to talk about the future," she said, her voice somewhat artificially warm.

"The election is close at hand."

"If it goes ahead."

Her words provoked a genuine reaction in Černý for the first time; of intrigue, yes, but predominantly of disappointment.

"You as well? I'd hoped you were simply ruthlessly determined, rather than a traitor."

"A traitor to what?" Her smile seemed just a touch crueller, her voice a notch harsher as she responded to Černý's jibe. "I simply believe our future lies down a different path than the one you are on, but I would be grateful of company on the journey."

He felt goose bumps threatening to rise on his flesh as she slid her hand gently across the desk to cover his. He looked down at her young, fresh skin, and suppressed the tingle of nerves in his hand.

"I would have thought your 'Institute' friends would be company enough."

"There is always room for one more," she said, her smile widening. "Why not come along for the ride?"

"Madam," Černý began, "while I refrain from passing judgement on those who use their wiles to prey on the weaknesses of others, I would ask you to remember that I am a stronger man than most."

He firmly, respectfully, withdrew his hand from beneath hers and returned it to its position before him on the desk, while a look of puzzled offence flittered across Hedvikova's features.

"I am old enough to be your grandfather and wise enough to know all the rules of the game. I may even have written a few in my time. I find your Institute distasteful in the extreme and its intentions with regard to this election and this country offensive, and your singular appeal, bountiful though it is, is insufficient to sway my convictions. So, if that is all, I shall bid you Dobré Odpoledne."

The puzzlement on Hedvikova's face gave way to a scowl and she quickly pulled her own outstretched hand, now embarrassingly empty, back toward herself. The scowl didn't last long, as Černý expected, and he maintained eye contact with her as her face relaxed into the cold smile that was its natural state.

"Well thank God for that," she said, "I'm not sure I could have gone through with it. You're so… old." She hissed the last word with unhidden disgust, the cold smile unchanged on her face.

The insult, like the short lived scowl, was to be expected and Černý refused to allow her the satisfaction of having caused him offence, instead simply smiling at the spiteful creature before him.

"An advantage of age madam is the ability to gauge whether or not certain sacrifices are worth the price." He paused for a moment. "One imagines your own have proven frighteningly expensive."

This time the smile gave way to a look of vicious anger. She hissed profanities and sprang from her chair, the once seductive arm ready to strike the old man across his face.

Černý's own arm reached up in a flash of age defying alacrity, and his hand clamped down on Hedvikova's wrist like a vice, holding it in the air as she slammed her other hand to the desk to retain her balance, spitting her fury at him, before breaking out into sudden laughter as she collapsed into her chair. Černý relaxed his grip on her and raised his eyebrow at the extraordinary display he was witnessing. After a moment, her laughter subsided and she wagged her finger in a show of mock chastisement.

"Ah, Karol, Karol," she said, "no-one has ever provoked such reactions in me as you do. You are unique sir. If only you were younger."

"You're too kind." The old man responded in mock courtesy.

"And that is why I need you," Hedvikova spoke, suddenly in earnest. "The election is days away and Svobodova will not live to see the votes cast. She will be dead long before and Čurda will have all the grounds he needs to justify delaying proceedings."

Černý stayed quiet, his face reverted to an emotionless slab, shadowed by the ridge of his high forehead, as though the darkness behind Hedvikova's words was reflected on his features. The silence was broken by the crinkle of the newspaper, which the young woman picked up from the desk, unfolding it to reveal the hated cartoon. She shook her head in exaggerated disappointment, tutting just loudly enough for Černý to hear.

"Make no mistake Karol, your party made the right decision in passing you over for the leadership. You are old, tired. A national hero yes, but never quite centre stage; always in Herbert Biely's shadow, even after his death."

Černý's brow furrowed deeper as Hedvikova's words cut into him. She was right; he had always lived in the shadow of his friend. Herbert was the country's darling and Černý had been proud to stand behind him. But in never standing at the front,

Černý had been relegated to the status of support act; a poster boy wheeled out to get the votes in. The party in Prague was his, but he was still overcast by the shadow of another. This time he owed no allegiance to the one casting it, save for her inheritance of Herbert's mantle; an inheritance unearned, in Černý's view, and which kept him from the recognition he deserved. Černý knew that his silence was sugar to the wasp before him, but the resentment bubbling in his throat choked his impotent protest and he remained quiet as she moved in for the kill.

"Svobodova is different," she said, "the face of the future, even though it is a future she will never see. She is a strong woman, who makes even the legends of old speak in her tongue; breaking the men who refused to kneel before Russian tanks."

Černý's eyes dropped still further, while Hedvikova fixed hers upon him. "It must have been humiliating for you Karol," faux concern adding a sickening quality to her voice, "a proud Czech like you, a national hero, publicly submitting to the will of a woman. A *Slovak* woman…"

She tossed the paper down on the desk, to land with the offending image facing the old man. The earnest appeal in Hedvikova's eyes had been diluted, leaving only coldness and she pressed home her advantage while she could.

"You were weak to let her do that to you Karol, the Černý of old would never have made such a concession; the Černý who should have been this country's Prime Minister. But you are not him anymore. You blew your shot Karol; instead of being revered as a great leader of our country, you're just a man who stood in the shadows so long you became one yourself."

Where her feminine charms had failed, her pity was victorious; a potent venom stinging its target. In the chamber of

Parliament, his hunting ground, Černý would have batted aside the barbs of his opponent in a show of imperious authority, his voice booming in total and absolute control. But here he was a gladiator robbed of his arena. He looked again at his caricature, knowing that Hedvikova's words were true; if he were younger he would not have made such a concession. He would not have even been asked to. He would have demanded control of the party on Herbert's death and his colleague's would have insisted he take it. But those days were gone.

"It was right she became leader, but she was wrong to rob you of your respect. And now she has put her own survival above the good of both countries." She moved to stand behind Černý, bending low to whisper in his ear, her breath raising the follicles on his skin. "But she will not get away with such selfishness, and you Karol, can stand with us as President."

Černý's eyes lifted at the words, the spark of curiosity returned.

"President?" he quizzed. "What would your Mr Čurda say about that?"

"Jaroslav is a nobody, a lazy opportunist who enjoys the trappings of ceremonial power while shirking the work such a position involves. He has no love for his people, merely his own position." Hedvikova's disgust was obvious and her display gave Černý the opportunity he needed to restore a more even keel to the conversation.

"A trait the two of you seem to share," he mocked. "Or have you not just extolled the virtues of Svobodova's death, so that you may replace her as the 'Queen of Eastern Europe'?"

"If Svobodova can do it, so can I!" Hedvikova shouted the words, no longer bothering to mask her feelings. "She has rejected chance after chance to come to heel and so she must accept the consequences. We must retain our independence!"

"And what good is a country which vehemently claims its independence, to the point of dismissing its own brothers, but which exercises its sovereign power within limits defined by others?"

Hedvikova's cold smile returned to her face, the passion gone from her voice and replaced with a patient calm.

"Karol, you have a choice. You can stand with Svobodova, the usurper whose skirt train you seem so desperate to carry, and march with her into oblivion dreaming of a Czechoslovakia that will never be. Or you can stand with me, and when she is dead and your party and Čurda finished, take your reward as President of the Czech Republic; the culmination of a career dedicated to our people, a just recognition of your service to the country. The choice is yours."

"Recognition," asked Černý, "or authority without power?"

"The latter of course, Karol," she answered icily. "A fitting position for a political eunuch wouldn't you say?"

She moved quietly to the door, turning her head to the old statesman as she reached it. "I look forward to hearing your answer Karol," she said, "only don't wait too long to give it. The wheels are turning, and I would so hate to see you fall beneath them."

With that, she was gone and Černý sat in the room, his fierce mind analysing every word spoken and processing every emotion felt. And he felt something of which he had only dim recognition. Anger he was used to, resentment a regular bedfellow; but for the first time, perhaps since his youth, Karol Černý was lost in confusion.

———

Confusion was likewise behind the fog in Jonathan Greyson's mind as he bustled into his hotel suite after another stormy conference call with the PM. Greyson shouldn't need reminding, the PM had lectured, that the administration was very new, the government's position already precarious where Europe was concerned. And any provocation of The Institute, which, Greyson thought, the PM was not wholeheartedly surprised to learn of, was precisely the last thing Britain need involve itself in. Furthermore, Greyson, said the PM, should be busying himself with his first big PR victory in his new role, instead of pandering to the egos of relics.

"Get McShade on the phone," he snapped irritably at Bland as he passed by her desk. "Tell him from me that he can stick this Institute business, we're out."

He banged open the bedroom door, and stopped by the bed, hands on hips, willing his stresses away with each breath. "Caroline?" he shouted, conscious that she had not responded to his order. "Are you making that call?"

He stepped out into the main room of the suite, ready to voice his frustrations on his junior colleague, but made it only a few steps before he stopped and recoiled. Bland sat slumped in the hard backed chair, her head awkwardly on the desk alongside a small pile of fine, white powder. It had blown across her papers and smudged the dark material of her suit jacket, while still more clung possessively and startlingly white on her left nostril. Her eyes, wide open in a permanent show of resentment, stared straight at Greyson, who managed to swallow back the vomit once before it returned with a vengeance, spilling through his fingers onto the carpeted floor beneath him. Caroline, he realised, would not be making that call, or any other. Ever again.

CHAPTER 20

MCSHADE RETREATED DEEPER into his black overcoat as the cold wind bit into his cheeks and the grey sky threatened the imminent return of rain. He sat slouched on one of the many metal framed benches alongside the Vltava, nonchalantly allowing the motion of the passing boats to complement his gentle intoxication brought on by at least several large scotches. If nothing else it granted him a modicum more protection against the weather. Even despite the sensation, he was aware of footsteps hurriedly tapping in his direction and had a reasonable idea of their source. They stopped just behind him, replaced for some moments by gently laboured breathing.

"Here at last?" McShade opened. "Ready to damn me for deals done and souls sold?"

"She's dead."

"Where is your security detail?"

"Far away from me and being asked some searching questions as to how she came to die."

The voice betrayed its owner's emotions and his recent tears. "She didn't deserve that."

"Very few of us deserve the fate we receive," McShade

answered. "What precisely was hers?"

"A cocaine overdose." The words were bitter, hateful. "The thing is, she didn't use the stuff, never had; but now that's all she'll be remembered for."

"You can't hush it up? Claim some tragic accident?"

"It was at the hotel, not the embassy. It appears one or two of the staff suffers from loose lips."

McShade gave a harsh laugh.

"The Child's discipline at work; she sought political immortality and now, in a way, she has it, while you can be assured you'll be on the front page of every newspaper in Europe tomorrow morning, just as the PM desired."

"The PM!" Jonathan Greyson snorted and walked from behind the bench and sat down alongside McShade, joining him in staring out over the water. "Why do I get the feeling he knew about this 'Institute' of yours all along?"

"The government has always known, the important branches at least. But their knowledge is less than subtlety tempered by the desire not to rock the boat. So you're the damn Foreign Secretary, so what? You're just there to smile for the cameras and shake hands with whichever dictator turned 'valuable friend' the government wants to see in the spotlight for a while."

Greyson's silence displayed further evidence of his emotions and McShade made no effort to soothe them, relaxing further into his intoxicated observation of the river. His stare was only disturbed by the figure of a toddler, waddling past the benches in front of them, a look of joyous pride in the achievement spread across rosy cheeks. Catching his boot on the stones, the little boy fell forward, palms outstretched, onto the ground. The inevitable cry that followed was cut short when the child's father ran the few yards to his boy and scooped him up in his arms, telling him what a strong, brave lad he was. The child, smiling again, threw his arms around his daddy's neck and clung to him, not wanting to be let go, while the father, just as keen to prolong the affection, held his son close to him with unashamed paternal pride.

Watching the mini drama unfold, McShade grimaced and his eyes followed the pair as they made their way down the street.

"When I was young," he began suddenly, quietly, "I had trouble sleeping. My parents would put me to bed and I'd sleep for a couple of hours but every night I'd wake up, terrified. Alone in a dark room I'd cry in fear, every shadow threatening in its own unique way. My father would come into my room and calm me down by just holding me close to him. He'd kneel on the floor by my bedside, lie me back down and pull the blanket around me. Then he'd just stay there, wordlessly holding my hand, stroking my head until I finally drifted off."

He paused to blink away an intrusive tear.

"Later, when I was a young man, my father became ill, terminally so. He had the best attention money could buy but nothing could be done and he was left to cope with an intolerable level of pain. I moved him into my home to care for him. The first night he called for me I didn't realise the irony, but one night, when his pain was particularly severe and he struggled to sleep, I found myself reaching out and stroking his hair, as he'd done for me all those years ago. I held his hand and shushed him, offering what comfort I could until he fell back to sleep. He never woke again."

The young boy and his loving father were far away now and McShade turned his head back to the emotionless, cold river.

"I was never much of a father to my son." He said. "I never properly explained to him why I left and in truth there were many reasons, the main one being that I wanted to spare him. I hoped to spare him the life I had; one of politics, of filth smeared hands, of dodgy deals with dodgier people. But most of all I hoped that the pain of having an absent father would be immeasurably easier on him than the pain of watching a beloved father die. I hope he understood that."

"Maybe he does." Greyson's voice was still shaky but not unsympathetic and, for a moment, McShade thought the young man was about to put an arm around his shoulders, but no contact came. Instead, he heard the sound of a man composing himself; a man with business on his mind.

"But this has little to do with what's happening here, now. The pursuit of an ethical foreign policy was one of the hallmarks of our campaign and now mere months into our administration, you're asking me to get involved in subversive battles against a dictatorial group of murderers we helped create!"

"Oh, don't be so damn childish!" McShade snapped, his voice restored to its tigerish best. "You're in government now! You can pontificate about ethics or you can pursue foreign relations; if all you care about is ethics then grow a beard, buy a pair of sandals and get back to university."

He sprang to his feet, wobbling slightly with the alcohol in his system.

"You talk to me about ethics and morals and 'doing the right thing'. Well what the hell constitutes the right thing in a world like this? Hands get dirtier with every decision made, whichever side of the fence you're on. Does it matter whether you kill in the name of tyranny or democracy? You're still a killer. Iraq,

Afghanistan and a thousand other lands are filled with the brutalised innocent while soldiers die in their hundreds from incendiary bombs and snipers. What is it that determines if it's right or wrong, if it's all worth it in the end? The opinion of a lawyer? The number of votes in a Parliament?"

He prowled the stone walkway in front of the bench, lost in his own tirade, barely conscious of the nervous discomfort of Greyson who sat, wide eyed and dishevelled looking, staring at the breakdown taking place before him.

"Activists galore condemn governments when they dare to execute murderers but march for the right to murder the unborn, while others cling to millennia old scriptures to justify their own hatred and merrily risk executing the innocent to preserve the principle of an ultimate sanction. Who is right and who is wrong? Whichever path you choose there will be those that praise you and twice as many who vilify, and both sides will insist to the ends of the earth that they are right; that God, or morality or humanistic principle is on their side."

McShade spun around, his temper self-inflamed and leaned into Greyson, his face inches from the younger man's.

"Let me tell you something. It doesn't matter if you entered politics with the purest motives in the world; you're every bit as corrupt as the bastards who put this Institute together, every bit as corrupt as me! And do you know why? Because power doesn't corrupt, it never has. It's the *desire* for power that perverts us. The moment we decide to pursue power, for good or for ill, is the moment we twist ourselves into those creatures we need to be to properly wield it, and we accept that as the price of our authority. And the people, for all their protestations, for all their hatred of the political classes, secretly accept it too because deep down they are glad it isn't they who have to make the choices, it isn't they who have to damn themselves so everyone else can be blessed."

His resources sapped by the scotch as quickly as it had fuelled him, he collapsed back into his seat beside Greyson, the voluminous overcoat shroud-like around him, his voice quieter once more, more measured.

"People arrogate greatness to themselves for being prepared to lay down their lives for the love of others. I laid down my soul."

The silence that followed McShade's breakdown was even more palpable than the passion which punctuated it, and both men felt its intimidation; refusing to break the rigidity of their posture or move their eyes from the stretch of river they had returned to. After an age, the older man spoke once more.

"So Foreign Secretary," he began, "you have witnessed what the Institute would term a mild form of discipline. What do you intend to do now?"

Greyson exhaled, the pressures of the last few days apparent in his sigh.

"I don't really have any choice," he said. "The PM's ordered me back to London where I'll no doubt have the press crawling all over me. He won't let me do anything to take on the Institute then, even if I wanted to."

"And do you want to? To avenge the departed Ms. Bland?"

Greyson hung his head, as if ashamed of his answer.

"Yes, but…Yes."

"Well then, it seems a new conversation with Ms Svobodova should be arranged, as quickly as possible."

"The PM won't be happy."

"Prime Ministers rarely are."

"But I'm supposed to be heading back and in any event what can we do, just us, the Czechs and the Slovaks? This Institute will eat us alive."

"Then widen the playing field," McShade said. "Choose allies, wisely, acknowledging that even the best of political friends will eventually turn on each other, but for now you can serve a mutual purpose."

Greyson nodded through the tension.

"Opportunities can present themselves," grinned McShade as he returned his gaze to the boats slicing through the water, "everyone has a past…"

As he spoke, a thin but visible smile began to form on Greyson's face, the first one in all the time he had been in this city. It heralded the return of the rain as the aching clouds heaved and retched onto the ground below, causing people to scurry and flee until no-one was left except the two men, smiling on the bench, watching the rain drops strike the rippling Vltava.

CHAPTER 21

"MIROSLAVA."

Mirushka stopped dead at the word, as sure of the seriousness to come, Peter imagined, as a child when angry parents used their full name. She kept her back to him but turned her head just slightly to the side, indicating her willingness, however reluctant, to listen.

Inside Peter throbbed with the echoing, hollow sensation of dread, a thousand times worse than when he had knelt in glass and spewed forth words of confession.

He had left his meeting with McShade confused and angry at himself for his inability to respond to the ambassador's bleakness with some small ray of light. But he could find none to offer and McShade's certainty continued to batter Peter's own insecurities as he mulled over their conversation in the subsequent hours, his long walk through New Town unable to inspire the magic words he searched for.

Returning to the hotel hours later, he and Mirushka had fallen wordlessly into each other's exhausted arms, their tiredness underpinning the curious tension in the room, emphasised by the eternity of silence. Neither choosing to break the silence, they had moved to the bedroom where they made love, quietly, sincerely, their sensations heightened and their passions somehow warmer in the coldly austere saturninity of the room. Afterwards she slept, curled up to him, her head on his chest, her hand clutching in sleep as though fearful that the morning would see her empty handed. Peter's tired, sore arm lay around her, in symbolic reassurance and practical protection while he stared into the dark, unmistakeable buzz of silent night; a general contemplating the clam ahead of impending and inevitable bloodshed. When the morning of the battle came, they had both maintained the peace of silence, offering each other genuine smiles and caressed hands, but neither wanting to voice acknowledgement of the nervous tension that had grown in the night, or that each caress might be the last.

Peter had dutifully followed her, along with Rado to the morning's event at Petrin Hill, where they met a similarly subdued Černý for photos against the backdrop of the Tower and the trees wrapped in their autumnal dress. She had shot him glances as she posed and he had smiled back, their eyes telling more than their lips ever could. When a break had been called by one of the legion of advisers, ahead of the Q&A session, she had turned quickly away, pausing only for a messenger to whisper into her ear, while others flocked to the refreshment table to warm themselves from the gnawing cold. That was when he had followed her, calling her by name and waiting in dread for her response.

"Láska," she finally acknowledged, her head still facing away, gazing up at the Eiffel-like tower before them. "I've had a message from Mr Greyson, just now."

"Oh yes?"

"He's arranging something last minute, at the concert tonight. Apparently Sir Roger has convinced the Americans to talk and perhaps the Russians too…"

"Going to share a bucket of popcorn are you?" Peter regretted his words; it was not time for humour.

"Maybe we can share words instead," she quietly responded.

"Maybe. What made Greyson change his mind? He didn't seem very keen at the meeting."

Mirushka hesitated and Peter saw her head drop slightly.

"The girl," she stuttered, "the one with him at the meeting."

"Bland?"

"Yes. She's dead."

Peter's fallen heart sunk lower still. He stood, unmoving, allowing the cold to bite and scratch at his skin, permitting his arthritic knuckles to throb unclenched.

"Another one," he finally whispered.

"Another one."

"I have to go Mirushka." His words were soft, honest; a dignified plea for understanding, for permission.

"You don't love me?"

"Oh God, Mirushka, I love you more than I know how to say; so much that I have to go."

Still she refused to face him, as though only hearing the words, not seeing the man saying them, would bring less pain.

"You can't go," her voice began to shake, "you are my protector now, remember?"

"I do. And I need to protect you the only way I can. Adrianna, Remy, Bland, how many more have to die before I admit what I am and use it to save you? I can't let it go on Mirushka, and I can't let you suffer the consequences of my actions."

"Isn't that my choice?"

"It's a choice I can't let you make. I was kidding myself; there's no redemption for me, there's a reason I was chosen for this work. It's time I accepted that, it's time I accepted who I am. At least by doing that I can save you from the same fate."

"It isn't fair, this isn't right."

"No. You know, you were right, back in the restaurant. I could never understand why she left me, why she said she had to give me the freedom to find someone else, but maybe I do now, because I love you enough to give you the same."

"That's not a freedom I asked for or want."

"But it's the best thing I can do for you now."

"That just makes it worse!" She turned, finally, and ran to him, throwing her arms around him and sinking into his embrace.

They stood there for a precious few moments, unconcerned by the scrambling of photographers or Černý's distasteful glance. An aide's voice called the two minute warning for the Q&A to begin and people began shuffling to their positions.

"I don't know how to say goodbye," Mirushka whispered tearfully into Peter's ear.

"Just win," he answered, surrendering to the crack in his own voice. "Win and remember me."

He cradled her head in his hands and kissed her.

"I love you," Mirushka whispered as the aide shouted for her attendance.

"Lubim ta," he replied.

She slipped from his arms, their fingers lingering together, prolonging their contact for a few precious seconds before turning and striding purposefully, confidently, back to her stage;

the uncrowned Queen, moving ever closer to her coronation.

Peter watched her take her place alongside Černý, holding her court in the palm of her hand, and he turned away from his love, away from his redemption, descending down the autumnal Petrin Hill into perdition's flames.

———

Before entering the inferno, there had to be time for one last apology, one last stop, a final respite before the burning commenced. Striding across the square Peter queried his own sanity as he reached his destination. He couldn't put his finger on why he went back here of all places. In the weeks since Herbert's death, he had barely been able to glance in its direction, not only because of his shame but a nagging illogical fear of being struck down by some divine rage. Nonetheless, there Peter sat in ponderous silence on the back pew of the Church of Our Lady before Tyn. The seat on which Herbert had died had become a shrine, separated from the rest of the row by red velvet cord and adorned with flowers, hand written cards and other tributes. Peter sat in contemplation, allowing the thoughts that had diminished in his time with Mirushka to begin slowly claiming him again.

"I got your message."

Peter glanced up into Rasti's oddly nervous face, giving it a slight smile.

"Alright mate?"

"What's wrong with meeting at the bar?"

"Not a fan of the venue?"

"It's just been a long time."

Rasti squeezed onto the pew next to Peter and joined him in staring at Herbert's makeshift memorial. A few moments passed before the big Czech spoke again, his voice soft, concerned.

"What's wrong?"

Peter laughed. "What's right mate?"

"Woman trouble? You certainly know how to pick them, Peter."

Peter slapped his hand down on Rasti's leg, grateful for his friend being there. "That's just it Rasti. I didn't pick her, she was picked out for me."

Rasti raised his eyebrows but Peter offered nothing more, changing the subject as he continued to stare at the flowers a few rows in front.

"What would you do if you knew you going to die Rasti?"

"I don't know," the big Czech answered, the question taking him by surprise, "probably pull the pants out of my arse and order another drink. Why, what would you do?"

"Don't know," Peter mused. "I think I'm finding out now, but pretty close to the top of my list would be saying sorry to a friend for never being honest with them."

Rasti stayed quiet, letting his friend speak.

"I told you I was a manager at an EU think tank. The truth is I killed for them, for a lot of years; when I used to come and get pissed with you because I'd had to sack someone, it was really because I'd killed them. And the longer it went on, the more I'd drink and the harder I'd lean on you to pick me back up again."

Still no words came from the former priest, his silence, Peter hoped, more intended to keep him talking than it was symptomatic of resentment and horror at the revelation. Fearful of what his friend's reaction might be, Peter pressed on.

"When I did my first job for them, I thought we were the good guys, I really did; the guys who did the jobs the police weren't allowed to do. That's how they trapped you. They sent me to a brothel in Brno, telling me it was full of trafficked girls. I was supposed to get the girls out and take care of the gang masters because the courts couldn't be trusted to deal with them. So I did. My controller drowned me in compliments, telling me what a hero I was and what a difference I'd made, and man did I lap it up. I had nothing in Britain, but here? I was the cat with the cream. But then I found out about another den in Prague using trafficked girls so I ran off to my controller, ready to ride in all guns blazing, and do you know what he said? 'Irrelevant'. He didn't even look up from his desk. Well I got on my high horse asking how could it be irrelevant when he'd had me go in and sort out the last place? It turned out the first brothel was secretly owned by a German politician who'd upset the Institute and they had me turn it over to teach him a lesson. This new place had no bearing on Institute operations so was of no consequence to them; instead I was to take out the German while he was on a trip to Prague because he hadn't taken the hint and was still acting up. Then the bastard offered me a glass of champagne to toast my new mission. I blew my top, said I wasn't just some gun for hire, that I'd thought we were supposed to be looking out for the underdog and I threw the glass against the wall. That's when the shit got real."

Peter paused, Rasti remained silent, having fallen back, Peter realised, into his old role of confessional priest, with Peter in the role of the penitent sinner.

"So I gave in. Totally. But they gave me a concession; kill

the German as ordered and I could take out the brothel. I found him, no problem; a proper sleazy character. I put him in the boot of his car and drove up to the whore house. Once I'd got the girls out I burned the place down with the gang inside it, the German too. It wasn't pretty. Outside, one of the girls crawled up to me and took off this gold cross she'd had around her neck and just knelt there, holding it up to me."

"Did you take it?" Rasti broke his silence, still staring ahead.

"How could I?" came the response. "Not after what I'd just done, after how I'd agreed to live. I could barely even look at it. I just told her that if I'd ever been anyone's knight then my armour was pretty soiled these days and she should save her gratitude for someone who deserved it. Then I left."

Peter drew the church's scented, incense heavy air deeply into his lungs, at once curious and fearful of what his friend's response would be. None came, just more silence, save for the wooden click of rosary beads that had suddenly appeared in Rasti's hand.

"That was years back, before the revolution. There are times I think I've lost count of how many people I've killed since then, and others when every single one of their faces parades in front of me and I can't breathe. But still I carried on, until it was her turn. Then I stopped."

Their eyes remained fixed on Herbert's tribute, Rasti's toying with the Rosary the only movement between them. The big Czech spoke at last.

"What changed?"

"Herbert, I think. He was one of mine. But right at the end, he gave up his chance to turn me in. He could have called to his guards, people would have known it was murder and his legacy would have been secured, but he didn't. He just whispered a passage of the bible to me."

"Which passage?"

"Greater Love hath no man than this…"

"That he lay down his life for his friend."

"Yep, and that's what he did. Sacrificed his chance to ensure his life's work was achieved so that I had a chance to sort myself out."

"And did you?"

"I tried mate, I really did. I told Mirushka everything and she forgave me, can you believe that? She forgave me! And I've been trying my best to save her ever since, get her through the elections. But all around me people keep dying. That helicopter crash, remember? That was meant for Mirushka but young Adrianna got killed."

"I thought that was an accident, the TV reports said it was a mechanical malfunction."

"The report wouldn't say anything else, but it was my lot, you can be sure of that. And then after her, my old controller decided to let himself be murdered rather than do me in, and now that bloody politician, Bland, all dead."

"But not at your hand."

"They might as well have been. Even when I turn my back on that world, people close to me keep dying. But what's worse is that even though I've been trying to be a good man I'm still a monster. There was a guy, my replacement, he came for Mirushka one night but I stopped him; I had my arm around his throat ready to kill him before one of the guards shot him. And for a moment, all I could concentrate on was how angry I was that someone had taken away my prey."

Finally Rasti moved, turning his head towards Peter who looked back, his eyes full of apology. The Czech's typical smile was absent but instead, he raised one powerful arm and wrapped it around Peter's shoulders, drawing him into his chest, cradling him tenderly.

"You tried to change, Peter, that's what's important."

Peter made no effort to resist the embrace, grateful for the warmth of his friend and the gentle rhythm of his heart beat.

"I let you down mate," he said. "I've spent years relying on you to cheer me up enough to go out and do my job again."

"You didn't tell me your job. I didn't ask questions, I was your friend. I still am."

"A friend to a murderer?"

"It's probably better than anything I did as a priest."

"Thank you."

For a moment, Peter stayed relaxed into the embrace before straightening up and looking ahead once more.

"The thing is Rasti, I've still got to save her and there's only one way I know how to do it, and there's only one way that can end."

Rasti looked down. "I see. So why come to Church? To confess past sins before going out to repeat them?"

"I know the score Rasti," Peter sighed. "I'm not some terrorist who thinks he can bomb a pub then nip to confession and think everything will be ok, or blow up a restaurant full of tourists, say ten Hail Mary's and walk merrily home. I know damn well what I do is wrong and I know damn well there's no redemption for me if I go through with it."

"Peter," Rasti began, his voice betraying paternal concern, "I heard a lot of confessions in my time and I know when people are genuine and when they're paying lip service. In fact, that's why I was asked to leave the priesthood."

"Really?"

"It turned out that dragging people from the confessional box and kicking them down the street to the police station after they'd made unrepentant admissions of paedophilia was frowned upon by my superiors as a 'violation of Confessional Sanctity'. We agreed to differ on that point. Luckily I knew how to cook."

Peter laughed out loud, causing the few scattered worshipers to turn and scowl in his direction.

"Good for you mate," he said. "Sounds like you made the right choice." He looked up, away from the flowers and the imposing crucifix which had hung before him the night of Herbert's death. "But I haven't got any choices; I guess I came here to just say sorry and thanks for trying." He stood up and hurried to the door, turning back to Rasti. "And I'm sorry Rasti, sorry for getting you involved and sorry for not being a better friend, but there's no way out of this for me."

He hurried through the doors and out into the street where the rain had begun once more to pour, hammering down onto his head, the sudden cold robbing him of breath. He heard the sound of Rasti scrambling to catch him and soon felt the big man's hand on his shoulder.

"Peter!"

"It's no good Rasti, I've no choice!" He shouted the words over the sound of the falling rain and scurrying tourists, and the chef shouted back, matching Peter's passion.

"Everyone has a choice! Do you want to change or don't you?"

"Of course I want to, but if I don't go through with it she dies and the election is off, I can't let that happen when I've a chance of stopping it!"

"Not if you only rely on yourself!"

Rasti grabbed Peter by the lapels, the Czech's strength taking him by surprise, and pushed him into a small stone alcove.

"Peter," Rasti kept hold of the Englishman, staring directly and intently into his eyes, "I don't have any magic words for you, I don't know what you can do to alter events, but I know that I've fucked up more than a few times in my life and usually because I was too arrogant to ask for help."

"There's no-one who can help me mate," Peter protested.

"Maybe not down here." Rasti pushed Peter down into a crouch, sliding down to join him and fishing in his pocket while rippling pools built up in the cobbles beside them. He pulled a small, half baguette from his deep pocket, crossed his hand over it then tore a piece off and held it out of Peter.

"The Body of Christ."

"You what?"

"Broken for you."

"You're not a priest anymore and does this even work out here?"

"Better here than anywhere, better now than anytime. Take it!"

Peter, flustered, confused, took the proffered, soggy sandwich, chewing it quickly. Stuffing the remainder back into his pocket, Rasti reached into his coat again and produced a hip flask, hurriedly crossing it again.

"The Blood of Christ."

"Mate, I've not done this in years…"

"Shed for you!"

Peter took the flask and knocked a shot back; the familiar warmth of the spirit inside making its way into his body.

"Mate," he said, breathless from the alcohol, "what was the point?"

"It gives you something else to think about, a reminder to yourself that you want to change and that someone else has got your back." Rasti grinned. "Don't just rely on yourself Peter, be the guy you choose to be, not what you think you have to be."

Peter grinned back at his rain soaked friend.

"Rasti," he laughed, "who keeps a sandwich in their coat?"

"For emergencies; you never know when you'll get hungry."

Peter reached his hands up to his friend's shoulders, Rasti reciprocating; the pair leaning their foreheads against each other's as the rain continued to fall on them.

"I love you man," said Peter.

"Right back at you."

"Goodbye Rastislav."

"Goodbye Peter."

Rasti stood straight, giving his friend one last smile, then turned and walked away, rain pounding off him, back towards his bar and restaurant, back towards the sanctuary Peter could no longer run to. Peter watched him disappear then turned and set off to arrange his destiny, uncertain once more if it would see him damned or redeemed.

CHAPTER 22

THE GLOWING RADIANCE of the Smetana Hall in Prague's Municipal House surpassed even its own high standards as the highest of high society gathered for The Concert of Celebration; an evening of works by Czech composers, suggested some time before by President Čurda and, coincidentally, arranged for the night before the election. Those same composers stared down from their portraits at the tuxedoed and elegantly gowned patrons filing into the magnificence of the hall, with its imposing organ and intricate sculptures.

Into the foyer strode The Rt. Hon Jonathan Greyson, alone save for his new security detail, and carrying with him an air of confidence a few notches above what was typically necessary to be a successful politician, and far above that usually displayed by a chastened one. Instantly recognisable to swathes of the audience, many of whom populated the city's various embassies by day, he deftly and skilfully accepted the brief condolences on the loss of his colleague and made his way into his box.

Taking in the ornate spectacle of the hall, he looked down to a box opposite, in which had appeared a balding, burly, though immaculately dressed man, flanked by two men burlier still, but who wore their dinner jackets rather less well. Watching him take his seat, Greyson lowered his chin and spoke softly, into his lapel.

"Konstantin."

"Jonathan," came the response into Greyson's ear, the newcomer's eyes flashing up towards his box.

"It was kind of you to accept my invitation at such short notice."

"It was kinder still to accept your equipment; I would feel more secure with Russian hardware."

"I doubt the rest of us would." A third voice, infused with the unmistakeable accent of North America, joined the pair; Greyson and Konstantin's eyes turning towards another box in which sat a strikingly handsome man with greying hair, alongside a slim, middle aged woman in a black velvet dress, whose own eyes remained firmly on the stage.

"Now, now, Benjamin," said Greyson, "let's not get off to a bad start, as clandestine meetings go this is an historic moment, it's just a shame we can't have any photographers present."

"That'll come later," replied Benjamin Scarlett.

"Maybe, maybe not," Konstantin cautioned. "Are we all here?"

"No," replied Scarlett, "It seems our host is missing. Where is the redoubtable Ms Svobodova?"

"Ah, yes, Ms Svobodova," Greyson said, "I'm afraid she'll be a little late this evening. She's been compelled to attend a last minute event with Karol Černý; election politics you understand."

"Nothing too time consuming I trust?"

"I shouldn't think so," replied Greyson. "I'm sure it'll go off with a bang."

———

The stocky Greek sat behind the steering wheel with his eyes fixed on the road ahead. He had been in position for hours, a short distance from Svobodova's party headquarters, patiently awaiting notification, and nothing could move him from his position. He was a professional. Glancing at the display on the dashboard, he saw the time click to 19:59. Černý's car would be waiting. He turned the ignition key in his own vehicle and sat straighter in the seat, listening to the soft purr of his engine ticking over. 20:00. He placed one hand on his steering wheel, and with the other pressed onto his earpiece, the faintest twinge of anticipation tweaking his gut. 20:01. He continued to wait, anticipation giving way to an equally minute dose of annoyed impatience. 20:02. A crackle of static in his ear, followed by a distorted voice demanding his attention. "τώρα," it simply said.

"Vai," he responded and turned his head toward the street the car would be coming from. Almost immediately, the long, black car glided into view, the tinted windows not sufficient to disguise the presence of Černý and the target in the back. A quick, but detailed glance confirmed Černý's claim of no security; at least none that was obvious, and he pulled smoothly into place behind the car.

He followed it in silence as it swept through Prague and out, north-west, toward its destination, his progress unhindered by the light traffic on the road. He allowed himself to briefly re-run the arrangements in his mind once more; it would be smooth, uncomplicated. He had conducted similar operations on countless other occasions and he did not anticipate any problems this time. It was logical self-assurance, borne not from arrogance but a supreme confidence in both his own abilities and those of his colleagues, and he allowed the smallest fraction of pride to take hold within him.

Černý's car followed the expected path without deviation, and with each mile travelled the Greek's confidence in the operation's success grew. Before long they reached the turn off for Lidice and he drew closer behind his target, to press it forward and limit the opportunities for escape. The Child's instructions were absolute; the operation must take place outside the border of the village. For that to happen, the Greek was reliant on his colleague, and he felt an unwelcome pang of nervousness return as he awaited the intervention. He need not have worried. As Černý's car reached almost the very edge of the village, it screeched to a halt, the driver blinded by the beaming headlights suddenly activated by the stationary car in front of him. The Greek's brow furrowed; this was the point of no return.

Slamming the brakes of his own vehicle, he spun it around behind Černý's to block any chance of reverse, and kicked open the door, climbing out and drawing the gun from his inside pocket in one smooth movement, his actions mirrored by his colleague from the stationary vehicle. Everything had gone to plan, and the Greek focussed on his march to Černý's car for the final stage. Grabbing the handle he threw the heavy door back and looked into the blackness for the target: Svobodova. The hysterical woman sat, blanketed by the darkness in the car, screaming at the unexpected intrusion. He reached his gun into the car and squeezed the trigger.

The shot thudded into the roof of the car and, for a moment, confusion raced through the Greek's mind. The old man, Černý, had taken hold of the Greek's arm and forced it upwards, deflecting the shot away from the target. In his other large, bony hand, he cradled a weapon of his own, pointed at the Greek. The strength in the aged arm was astounding, capturing him totally off guard, while the fierceness in the indignant, staring eyes burrowed through even the Greek's metallic resolve. He struggled to process the information and his focus barely returned in time for him to push the old man's gun arm sufficiently away for his shot to miss. Regaining his clarity of thought, he wrenched Černý's gun from his hand and slammed its butt into the aged politician's head, smashing him into a daze, and then re-aimed his arm at the still screaming target and began to shoot. Bullet after bullet tore through the defenceless body, silencing its screams and decorating its heavy coat a deep, speckled red.

The orders were clear. Svobodova was the target, the driver irrelevant, and Černý was not to be harmed, yet. The Greek leaned past the dazed Černý and put his fingers under the target's neck, searching for any trace of a pulse. Satisfied, he withdrew from the car and nodded to the spectral figure that stood just inside the village boundaries in front of the motionless car, subtlety crossing itself at the fresh carnage. The Greek had done his job. She was dead.

———

"Where is she Jonathan?" Konstantin pressed, irritation rising in his voice. "Much as I enjoy an evening at a classical concert, the orchestra is not the reason I agreed to attend."

"Likewise," Benjamin echoed. "The appetizers are all here but we all seem to be waiting on the main course. I hope you're not jeopardising the Special, Jonathan."

"If the Special you refer to is The Special Relationship between our two great countries, Benjamin," Greyson replied, a dark smile on his face, "we all know that it is most akin to the relationship a dysentery patient shares with his lavatory, with the UK as the receptacle of choice. Gentlemen I assure you, Ms Svobodova will be here presently. Meanwhile I notice that the concert is about to begin, so I respectfully suggest we enjoy the talents on show until her arrival."

The murmur of agreement momentarily settled Greyson's nerves, but they soon returned as he sat back and turned his head to the stage. The plan was in place, the preparations made; *now where was she?*

———

"Bring them here!" The Child demanded.

The Greek grabbed Černý roughly, dragging him through the car door and holding him upright. To the Greek's enormous surprise, he felt the old man straightening of his own accord and begin walking the few steps into the village, looking straight ahead at The Child the whole time. Deciding he was tired of being surprised by a relic, the Greek gave Černý a resentful push, before walking past him and taking his position to his master's right. His colleague had dragged the chauffer from the car, who now knelt in the mud, obviously terrified.

The Greek was forced to admire the resolve in Černý's face as he stared resolutely into the eyes of The Child, presenting quite the picture of the archetypal offended aristocrat. Neither man spoke, preferring instead, it seemed to the Greek, to size each other up. The spark of annoyed impatience re-entered his gut and quickly grew larger. His practical mind required orders, a process to work through and a goal to push towards, and it quickly stagnated when left without a task. Besides which, it was cold and getting colder, and a peel of not too distant thunder rumbled in the air, accompanied by the cold flicks of intermittent rain.

It was the thunder that stirred Černý into speech, never once moving his eyes from The Child.

"Perhaps we should move inside," he said. "Rainstorms and cold night air are no places for old men."

Ignoring the suggestion, The Child spoke with an unusual frustration in his voice. "Your resistance was unexpected Mr Černý," he said. "It seems that Sir Roger neglected to reveal the full intent of this meeting."

He offered a brief glance to the car's bullet riddled and blood stained back seat; its remaining occupant slumped out of view. The merest hint of distaste haunted the deep lines on the old, weathered face, and he quickly returned his stare to the defiant politician.

"In any case, the deviation was far from consequential. My condolences for your loss," The Child said, coldly sincere. "Be assured that her passing was an unfortunate necessity for the greater good."

"I'm quite sure," spat Černý with measured contempt.

The confidence in Černý's voice unsettled the Greek, who

was surprised to see his reaction mirrored in The Child's own features. He had never known The Child to be anything other than in total control, but this night was different; as though the smallest of chinks had appeared in this iron man's armour, and it made his stomach twist in a wholly unfamiliar nervous uncertainty.

"I had hoped that you would see sense enough to understand the necessity of your countries' continued separation and take your place as Czech President, under our guidance. But you have denied yourself that reward." The Child spoke with what appeared to be a genuine sorrow. "I am disappointed in your decision and in the foolish way you chose to exercise your objections. Did you seriously expect to overpower us with just yourself and an antiquated firearm?"

Černý remained resolute. "I would apologise for your disappointment," he said, "but it would be entirely insincere. And as for my expectations, in truth, no, I didn't expect to overpower you; but I hoped I could delay your actions until you understood the full picture."

An eyebrow raised on The Child's face at Černý's words, which were followed by the frantic movement of his other subordinate, waving feverishly at The Child with one hand, the other pressed to his ear.

"What?" the aged figure snapped.

"Sir," the operative said, his voice trembling, "she is at Smetana Hall!"

Realisation dawning on him, The Child motioned to the Greek to continue holding Černý and the kneeling driver at gunpoint, and signalled the other operative to move with him to the car. The operative swung open the door and reached inside to switch on the internal light. There before them, on the torn leather seat laid the bullet riddled body of Daleka Hedvikova.

"My condolences for your loss," Černý shouted from his position. "Be assured that her passing was never a necessity but the natural consequence of men who think they are gods, shooting into the dark in the hope of favourable outcomes."

At Smetana Hall, all eyes turned from the beauty of the music being played on the stage, to the beauty of the late arrival as she entered her box. Her hair long, her face radiant, dressed in a burgundy velvet evening gown and fine silk scarf, she smiled regally to the crowd and sat down, turning her head back to the stage when the musician's tempo had risen with her arrival.

"Gentlemen," said Miroslava Svobodova into her scarf, "it seems that rumours of my lateness have been greatly exaggerated. Shall we begin?"

"This is not the first time someone has pointed a gun at me," Černý said calmly, "and it has yet to impress me. Either pull the trigger or put it away."

"I had no wish for the trigger to be pulled on you." The Child appeared rattled, having taken an age to respond while the rain began to fall around them. "But neither had I wished it pulled on Ms Hedvikova, who would now be unharmed were it not for your intervention. I must ask for full details of your ill-advised plan, before your own termination."

"I would have thought it obvious." Černý, fearless, released his information with every ounce of spite, resentment and superiority he could muster, enjoying the glow of his knowledge. "You had sent Ms Hedvikova to me previously in an unwise attempt to turn my head. I merely allowed her to believe she had been successful and asked her to join me in secret to take the discussions further. She of course agreed. At the same time, Sir Roger contacted you to arrange this meeting, informing you that he had tried to explain from his own experience the uselessness of fighting your Institute, but that no-one would listen to him; except me, consumed as I was by my own resentment at Svobodova's rise. He informed you I would request Svobodova's company at a phantom election photo call here, at which point she would be yours and I would be another of your pawns. I imagine it was hard for you to resist."

"And who is Svobodova meeting with now, in Smetana Hall?"

Černý fell silent, staring ahead.

"You will not answer?"

More silence.

The Child nodded, his aggression replaced with regret. "Then it seems," he said, "that our association is over before it began." He turned slightly to the Greek and curtly nodded his permission.

A sense of satisfaction that there would be no more surprises enveloped the Greek before he turned to Černý and steadied his aim. His practical mind had never felt emotion during a kill, but he quietly admitted that this was one shot he would enjoy. His satisfaction turned back into resentment as Černý refused to close his eyes, instead staring at the man who would be his killer with a look of unashamed superiority on his face. Inwardly furious, the Greek began to press the trigger.

CHAPTER 23

THE NOISE FROM THE GUN cannoned around the field, scattering birds and echoing the thunderous peels that rolled across the valley. But Černý remained standing, unmoved, the faint hint of a smile on his lips.

The Child, his composure intact, looked at Peter Lowe, who stood before him dressed in the muddied uniform of a chauffeur, smoke drifting from his gun into the night air. To The Child's right, his Greek operative was kneeling, clutching his gun arm in pain as blood trickled from the wound through his fingers. Peter saw The Child wince as the blood touched the soil, an unwelcome show of pain on the old, lined face. The Child's remaining associate quickly recovered himself and reached for his own weapon, only to be shouted down by the authority in Peter's voice.

"Drop it!" the Englishman said, his gun arm unwavering and his stare fixed. "Kick it over here."

The man looked to The Child who nodded approval without taking his eyes from Peter.

"And your friend's." The man moved slowly over to his colleague, carefully scooping up the gun which lay discarded at his feet and throwing it and his own weapon, towards Peter's feet.

Peter indicated to Černý to move behind him and the old man complied.

"Go," Peter said. "Go and join Mirushka, go and win that election."

"And what about you?"

"I'll be fine. Just give her my love. All of it."

The Statesman turned, spying the furthermost car, the warm purr of its engine still audible.

"Mr Lowe...,"

Peter glanced at the old man who, for the first time, looked at Peter with something other than contempt. A strong, aged hand clasped Peter on the shoulder.

"You are far from the only person to feel shame at their past actions, and you are right to be ashamed of your own. But far fewer find second chances are afforded them; don't waste yours." Černý turned and walked to the car, sliding in and moving away from the village and back towards his electoral future.

Hearing the car's depature, Peter gestured with his gun arm in the direction of the stone path. It led up to a metal sculpture which stood a short distance away, framed by the trees and cradled in the darkness. "Now move."

The Child's two hard men were the first to react, the wounded one helped by his furious colleague, but The Child himself remained motionless, the hint of pain on his face now joined by undisguised contempt.

"You too," Peter repeated his command, "move".

Again The Child remained still.

"Why?"

Peter revelled in the power he held over the creature who had filled so many people with such dread for so long, and he was damned if he was going to allow him the self satisfaction of facing death with fortitude. He stepped closer, a smile of victory on his lips, the knowledge that his was the job to vanquish the beast, and he growled his answer through gritted teeth.

"So that you go back and face them before you die."

The Child broke his stare to glance up the path to the gloomy monument and, Peter thought, he gave a faint, and involuntary shudder as though someone had walked over his grave. The Child resisted still further, his voice though shaking just slightly, as though scared to permit the emotion behind it from showing itself.

"Is nothing sacred to you?" The contempt on his face had by now turned into a disgust which Peter could almost feel, but he would not allow himself to be dissuaded from his target.

"I murdered a hero in the pews of a church for you," Peter said, "so, no, nothing's sacred in this world anymore. Move."

This time, the thin, darkly clad figure began to move along the path, passing his operatives who had stood waiting for him, and up towards the statue. Just before he reached it, his men caught him up and Peter gave orders again.

"You two!" he said, addressing the shamed bodyguards. "On the floor, faces down and stay there!"

The pair dropped without uttering a word a few feet from the monument. The Child, having reached the statue, turned back to face Peter who pointed once more with his gun.

"Don't face me," he said, his words cold and deliberate, "face them."

The Child's discomfort was obvious and Peter hoped that it increased his advantage. He had ignored Peter's request, refusing to turn to the cold rows of children, their innocence frozen forever on metallic faces. Standing instead in front of them, like a frail and reluctant Grim Reaper come to reminisce.

"It's true what they say about you isn't it?" Peter asked, already knowing the answer.

"What do they say?"

"There are no records about you, you saw to that. Most people who've ever heard of you think you're just another German bureaucrat who didn't mind getting his hands dirty."

"And what do the others say? What do you say?"

Despite the gun in his hand Peter recognised his own interrogation; such was The Child's manner. He nodded towards the metal children behind the aged figure, hoping to redress the balance.

"Which one are you?"

A furrow, small and solitary, strayed onto the old man's brow as the words left Peter's mouth and hovered in the air between them, and his gaze, normally granite like in its rigidity, began to drift, slowly from Peter's own. Though the hypnotic stare was broken, Peter remained transfixed at the sight before him; the old man, this 'Child', turning reluctantly, deliberately to the cherubic smiles gathered behind him, before, for the briefest of seconds, allowing his eyes to clamp shut.

"McShade?" The Child asked, eventually.

"He only told me so much; but the clues are there when you stop to think about it. All anyone knows about you is you're a German bureaucrat who hates the Nazis and has spent the last thirty years defending this nation Europe from all possible threats, inside and out. And you haven't been shy about it. Everywhere you cast your glance you've been ruthless, bloodthirsty almost; you haven't squirmed at sparking riots, provoking coups or whatever, except for here. Oh, you've been a bastard, no doubt. I've killed enough people on your order, implied or otherwise, to know that. I've helped steer this country's destiny more times than I care to remember, whether in revolutions or taking out the men who'd follow a different path to you. But these two tiny little countries have been spared your wildest excesses, even as far back as '92. You've trashed economies, and royally screwed the Ukraine, but the worst you did here was get me to lie down and pretend to be dead to spark a bloodless revolution. Why would you spare Czechoslovakia unless you had some connection to it?"

The old man responded stiffly. "I spared nothing," he spat. "I loathe these countries; that I tore them apart without spilling blood was nothing but pragmatism; why cause a war or a bloody coup when the simple greed of incumbent politicians will work to your advantage? Despite what you may think of me I am no monster and my work brings me no sadistic pleasure, merely the satisfaction of having done what was necessary."

"But why settle for an amicable split when a bit of good, old fashioned violence would have made the separation permanent? You must have some underlying affection for the country to do that, some love or some memory so strong that you couldn't bear to see it destroyed."

No response came, The Child simply looking into the eyes of each tiny metal child one by one, his hands caressing their cold, ossified cheeks.

"Look around," Peter challenged. "Just take a look around.

They're still the same fields you used to walk in, the same woods you used to play in before they came and ripped you from your mother's arms and called you a good little Aryan. Somewhere inside you there's still the boy used to be. What was his name? Marek? He's there no matter how deeply you've buried him. And I can't understand why you'd want to break this country's will and have it come to heel when that's what started it for you all those years ago."

The Child spun back, the authority returned to his voice, the dampness banished from his eyes.

"And I cannot understand, or at least I have a certain curiosity, as to why you have chosen to make your stand for Czechoslovakia." He stood unmoving, a ghoul in the midst of the innocent, his white face and hair granting him an unearthly aura against the black night sky. The Institute for European Harmony is precisely that; our goal is harmonious co-existence. We have done nothing unusual here; indeed we are intervening in a much more humane manner than has been demonstrated at any point in history. Slavic destiny has been manipulated in one form or another for centuries. This country, divided or otherwise, would not even exist were it not for the intervention of outsiders."

"Well I wasn't around then." Peter growled.

"I see," said The Child with cold sarcasm. "Well what should we do to appease you hmm? Revive the Austro-Hungarian Empire? Put the Hapsburgs back on the throne?"

"You wouldn't understand."

"No? Please try me." The Child spoke sharply, resentfully, as though he were an exasperated teacher grappling with an obtuse student's failure to grasp the philosophical questions he was pondering. "If you were to rebel for money it would be understandable, for the murder of a friend or partner almost expected, but you accepted assignment after the Biely operation and have left your lover to her own devices. One can only assume that Biely wasn't much of a friend and your lover not worth your energies."

Peter's anger manifested as a hollow laugh, and he smiled a wicked grin at his opponent.

"Bastard." he said. "Don't forget what working for you all this time has turned me into. I could snap your neck right now and go out for burgers and beer without batting an eyelid."

The Child was the picture of disdain, his tone completely devoid of fear, unmoved by Peter's threat. He remained quiet, just staring at Peter who began to feel nervous, and a nagging sense that he wasn't as in control as he thought began pricking at him.

"You'll forgive me, but your recent actions suggest otherwise. I don't have the time to forge tools Mr Lowe." The Child said. "I'm interested only in purchasing those tools already manufactured. Whatever human tragedy you consider yourself to be, you already were long before your association with the Institute; we wouldn't have been interested in you otherwise."

Peter winced at the truth of the remark and knew at once that his momentary flash of emotion was temptation enough for The Child to continue his assault.

"And now you're older, with a weakness for drink and faced with the reality of your own impending death, and you search vainly around for someone else to blame, when the responsibility is and has always been entirely yours. I may have supplied you with the canvas, but a painter you have always been."

Peter cursed himself, struggling to come up with an answer to The Child's words. "And now you pin your vain hopes of ill-deserved redemption onto the fate of these countries, but what do you truly understand about them? They're just a loose collection of Slavs and gypsies with no great love for each other, suddenly caught up in foolish talk of unification without having thought it through. If they actually find themselves unified do you think they'll be able to handle the position they'll have thrust upon themselves? The other Visegrad nations will hold them up as some sort of guiding light, and they will stumble under the burden of expectation placed upon them by their neighbours. They will refuse to follow our direction, they'll be trampled by America and Russia and there will be dissent in Brussels. They will suddenly find themselves as the new unofficial Leader of the Eastern Block and as a consequence, the Union will splinter. Is that what you really want? Chaos returned to Europe?

Have it your way and the memorial before which we now stand becomes only the first of many."

Despite the nagging doubts, Peter, free from the alcoholic stupor that typically fuelled his anger, was revelling in his ability to control it. The Child's words had been deliberate, calculating, designed to get a rise from him, but Peter was not prepared to give in.

"It doesn't matter what I want," Peter began, "it only matters what these people choose. They've been controlled long enough by people who claim to know better. Austrian monarchs, Nazis, Communists and now the European bloody Union. I robbed them of their choice back when I took out Dubček for you; who knows what might have been if he'd still been around? And I'm damned if I'll let you do it again. If these people want to be one state, two states or servants to some bloody Hapsburg king then it's their business; not yours, not mine. All they really want is what no-one has ever let them have; the freedom to choose."

The Child shook his head gently.

"Not every freedom brings the benefits one expects," he said, his voice sombre, "and that is one freedom these people cannot enjoy."

Peter stepped closer to the old man, his feet squelching beneath him and stirring up the smell of cold, wet mud. His top lip curled back showing his tightly gritted white teeth, framed in a feral display by his dark stubble.

"Because you know better eh? You're no different than the politicians who think they've got the right to go storming into other people's countries toppling regimes and changing governments because they think the way they do things back home is better. They couldn't care less how much innocent blood gets spilled, how many children go parentless or what kind of mob controls the streets afterwards. They just tear everything to pieces then pat themselves on the back for giving people the opportunity of democracy. They butcher thousands in the name of liberal intervention and run off to spend their oil dollars while kids weep for parents who aren't coming home. And no matter how much they protest about their noble intentions and their hard choices, and no matter how much they insist that it's all worth it in the name of democracy, it's never them on the front line is it? It's never their wife or husband or child getting bombed or shot or ripped to pieces. They just send in the troops and tell them to turn three times and start firing, just like you did with me. Fuck the troops eh? That's what they're there for after all, to take the shit. Just like me and all those 'operatives' like me were there to take the shit. You lot think pain is 'agonising' over tough choices while you pocket cash and watch your strategies unfold, but a soldier's pain is a bullet in the gut or a rocket in the face, or living with the knowledge you've killed innocent people. And that's the way you bastards like it isn't it, eh? Well I'm not your soldier anymore. I'm not taking any bullets or any more flak for you. And I'm not crying myself to sleep anymore because you think you know how the world should be run. You want a federal Europe? That's fine with me if that's what the people want. But it's their decision, their choice, not yours. People have grown up, they don't mind getting their own hands dirty, and they don't need you holding on to them anymore. Just let people be."

For a moment The Child remained silent, as though he were, for a fraction of a second actually contemplating Peter's words, before he raised his eyes and spoke again.

"Irrelevant."

"Don't say that word to me."

"Irrelevant!" The Child bellowed. "I care little for your posturing or your soul searching. If I were you, I would be dead now. It seems you sought to bring me to Gethsemane, only for you to be the one to refuse the chalice. There is no soul inside me to search, it was ripped from me here, many years ago, and here it remains, along with the souls of every other child whose metal eyes stare back at you now. This will forever be their playground, and they are always and forever within it; in the trees, in the grass, inside you as you breathe the air they live in. Do not look for Marek inside this shell; Marek is and always has been here, with his friends, with his brothers and sisters, and with them he remains. I am someone else. And I will drink from my cup."

Peter laughed, a sardonic, bitter laugh, and he squeezed the gun tighter in his hand, sending a twinge through his sore knuckles.

"You know what? You're right. All the way here I was trying to think of another way, some way out of this for you, but at the end of the day, if you die, Mirushka lives and that's all there is to consider."

"If you feel she deserves to."

"What's that supposed to mean?"

The Child smiled, an eerie, hollow smile drawn only from cruelty.

"My dear Mr Lowe, you really never worked it out did you? Why you were assigned to this project so late into its development?"

Peter felt his stomach begin to sink and scowled at his enemy, who revelled in his gloating.

"You aren't the only ex-employee I've had who sought repentance for the terrible sin of ensuring stability. If you want advice on how to live with yourself you should look to someone close to you; someone particularly close to you."

The feeling turned to horror in Peter's stomach as a wave of nausea swept over him. No. Not her!

"I don't believe you." Peter's voice was far from convincing.

"Don't you?" Why else do you think she was so eager to forgive your murderous intentions towards her?

"She wouldn't have anything to do with you, she was with Herbert from the start!"

"Actually she was mine from the start, and for quite some

time. In fact before her attack of conscience, she proved quite the mine of useful information. It was only because of her dereliction of duty and refusal to see reason that you found yourself assigned to this mission in the first place."

Peter was struggling for breath, crouching down under the weight of the revelation, struggling to keep his gun on the mocking figure.

"No, that's not true, why wouldn't…why wouldn't she have said something?"

"You'd have to ask her," opined The Child. "Although that won't be possible of course, she'll be quite dead very soon; we always have a reserve plan in place".

Peter stood up, his anger and his sickness overwhelming. He raised his arm, aiming his weapon at the head of The Child, who stood unflinching.

"I'm sorry Rasti," he muttered quietly, "I tried."

Adjusting his frame for to ensure accuracy, Peter's left arm brushed against his jacket pocket, a soft jingling sound distracting him. Pausing, he lifted them out of his pocket and held them outstretched for the old man to see, and the shell of rage he'd built around himself cracked.

"You know," Peter chuckled, "I've had these for years, so long I don't even know what half of them open anymore. Back in the Revolution, they were the most important weapon I had, that any of us had. We used to shake our keys at the soldiers, at the Old Guard politicians, at anything connected to the regime dying all around us. It was just a way of saying 'off you go now, it's time for a change.'"

Peter lowered his gun arm and smiled at The Child.

"What's your Plan B?"

Another smile, a softer one, met him in response.

"You wish to save her? After knowing what she kept from you all this time?"

"Try me."

"You lack the courage of your new convictions Mr Lowe. How easy it has been to provoke you once more into anger, an anger you know to quench only by blood or by spirits. You are no hero, no warrior for God, England and St George and ultimately of no consequence to me, to your young lover or to anyone at all. I could tell you, but only because it is entirely safe for me to do so; whatever posturing you indulge yourself in as we stand here is pointless. With your penchant for introspection you will, I am sure, prove unable to forgive Ms Svobodova for her deception and leave her to her fate, after which I give you my word that we will leave you alone. Leave you to your perpetual cycle of drunken violence and repentant remorse as you drink yourself to death in that bar you so enjoy. Or else of course you will die in some foolhardy attempt to stop the inevitable"

"So what's the plan?"

"The means have always been in place, we just prefer to move with more subtlety than such actions require; heart attacks, car crashes, accidents. Events that make everyone believe a conspiracy is at work but are sufficiently random for such theories to be impossible to prove."

"What's the plan?" Peter said again.

The Child smiled. "As I inferred," he said, "you aren't the only person in my employ."

Peter's eyes narrowed.

"Rado…?"

"Oh no, no, no." The Child chuckled. "I'm afraid he's not

really our type. Far too loyal. Not as amenable to our suggestions as, say, a driver?"

"The car." Peter spat. "Typical. The driver's set a bomb?"

"My lips are sealed," smiled The Child, his words dripping with sarcasm, "but I'd hurry if I were you; you wouldn't want her to go off without you. And I'm genuinely curious to see your decision."

"A gentleman's agreement?" asked Peter.

"More a wager, against you," came the reply. "But of course, you have still to decide what immediate action you will take." He gestured to the gun, still tight in Peter's hand.

Holding it in his outstretched fingers, Peter marvelled at its lightness and lethal simplicity, weighing it up alongside the keys in his other hand. Looking up at the old man who stood as unmoved as ever before him, Peter wrestled away the last vestiges of his murderous resentment and tossed the weapon into the mud at his feet and the keys towards The Child, who caught them in instinctive reaction.

"Decide for yourself," Peter said, then turned and headed back towards the cars.

The bulldog minder sprang forward as Peter walked away and scrambled in the mud for the gun, grasping it tightly and raising it at the still walking Peter's back.

"No!"

The Child's subordinate spun around in shock at the command, the expression on his face pleading for permission to take the shot. Instead, The Child placed his hand on his operative's arm and lowered it to the side, looking at the hurriedly moving figure of Peter Lowe before him.

"This village has seen murder enough," he said.

CHAPTER 24

"I THINK," BENJAMIN PONDERED, "that there is an argument to be made that a natural consequence of the US government's purchase of 28 L-159 planes from the Czech Republic last year would be for a permanent military presence in a new Czechoslovakia in the interests of mutually developing the successor programme. Strictly for research purposes alone you understand."

"Nyet, nyet, nyet!" Konstantin's reaction was emphatic and wholly expected by all. "More transparent attempts to bring American forces to Russia's doorstep, just like your Missile Defence scheme a few years back. You cannot expect us to agree to this?"

"And you cannot expect, my dear Konstantin," replied the soft tones of Mirushka, "for the people of a new Czechoslovakia to sleep soundly in their beds, knowing that an expansionist Russia moves ever closer with every step it takes into the Ukraine? Our memories are long and the people have not forgotten the speed with which our Russian friends arrived to 'help' us in 1968. They might well feel altogether safer if our new agreement with America were extended to include shared military projects. Strictly for research purposes of course."

The conversation had gone well and though orchestrated by Greyson it had been Svobodova who had dominated proceedings. Britain and the new Czechoslovakia would extend their European partnerships, not only sitting together in Parliament but supporting each other in the Council and the Commission, delivering an East-West dynamic unexpected by the Institute. In addition, a joint US/UK investment programme would begin in the new country, with several leading Western companies 'positively encouraged' to take advantage of the generous tax arrangements on offer, while imports from both countries would significantly rise. The only stumbling block was the Russians, with Svobodova insisting on an increased US military presence as a safeguard against any temptation for the ongoing Ukraine situation to move westward, and Konstantin's insistence to the contrary.

"There is no expansionism!" The Russian's frustrations were becoming difficult to mask, despite the orchestral fervour below. "In the Ukraine we have liberated our own people, at their request, from the rise of fascist tyranny; how can there be any objection to that?"

"How indeed?" asked Greyson. "But perhaps there might be a solution, if your President were to acknowledge his somewhat heavy-handed approach to the crisis and make a public declaration to the new Czechoslovakia, and the EU as a whole, that there would be no movement further west, and that efforts towards a peaceful resolution will be redoubled."

"Ah," picked up Benjamin, "now in those circumstances, our President may well see his way clear to downscaling our support in the region to having simply an economic focus rather than military."

"You have authority to speak for the President?"

"It would be more appropriate," all eyes turned towards the American box, where the woman seated at Benjamin's side had broken her silence, "to say that the President has authority to speak for me. And yes, important though the benefits of joint military research are to the US, there is something to be said for the argument that more guns equal more opportunities to use them."

"Tell that to the NRA," sniffed Konstantin.

"However," the woman continued, "were we to make such a concession, we would need to be sure of Russia's intentions towards the region as a whole."

Konstantin folded his arms in resentment.

"Out of the question," he snapped. "Any alleged 'aggression' or 'expansionism' by Russia in Ukraine is merely a matter of perspective. For more than a decade we have seen the effects of Western 'aggression' the world over; in Iraq for example, and Afghanistan. It seems that one country's 'expansionism' is another's 'intervention'. And I see no need for a Russian apology in the noticeable absence of one from the West."

"Well the United States will categorically not apologise for those events."

"Stalemate then," sighed Svobodova, a bitter disappointment in her voice.

"Oh, I don't know."

All eyes turned to Greyson.

"You see, the British government, in which I am proud to serve, was only very recently elected and, like our American cousins, we absolutely will not apologise for events we had no part in orchestrating." He adjusted himself in his seat, taking up a position of obvious comfort.

"But this government didn't orchestrate those events to which Konstantin refers. Suppose, in return of course for a Russian Statement admitting an over-zealous response and guaranteeing no further encroachment, that my government made no effort to halt action against the person who *was* responsible."

"You mean..?" Began Svobodova.

Greyson nodded. "You see, I'm told that the gentleman in question will be in Switzerland next month delivering a lecture on his efforts to achieve peace in the Middle East. Now, if some neutral body were to file war crimes charges with the proper international authorities, and some other neutral official were to see to it they were served during the conference, well, it would be inappropriate for us to stand in the way of the justice system, wouldn't it?"

Konstantin smiled. "Oh it would, quite inappropriate. But such a case could drag on for years; are you certain you are prepared for the inevitable public washing of your dirty laundry?"

"The laundry isn't ours, we are a new administration. And who knows? The case might never even make it to court, but the attention will redress the balance in a way favourable to you and it will have the added bonus of keeping his column inches focused on his own transgressions rather than my government's record."

Konstantin grinned. "Upon reflection you know, I can see how the world might have viewed our actions as a little rash. Perhaps a properly worded address by the President might help alter that view, yes?"

"As long as there is no suggestion of any other 'neutral bodies' hindering US operations, then we agree."

"Here as well," smiled Svobodova. "And Jonathan, can you ensure that your Prime Minister will agree to the investment programme?"

"Don't worry about that," grinned Greyson, "I've already drafted his statement announcing it as the result of his own tireless efforts. As soon as we're done here it'll be released to the press which means he should have the pleasure of reading about it when he has his breakfast in the morning."

"Well then, ladies, gentleman," announced Benjamin as the orchestra played their final note and the audience stood as one to applaud, "I think this could be the start of a beautiful friendship."

McShade had satisfied himself that he'd sown the seeds of fruitful alliance as best he could, but still sat staring from his office window into the courtyard below with a nervous unease in his stomach. Greyson was leading the meeting, McShade insisting that he prove himself worthy of the office he held, but still his guts knotted and twisted in uncertainty as he stared repeatedly at the clock, cursing himself for not attending and then damning his own arrogance. Such was his preoccupation that he failed to notice the entrants to his room until the dreadfully familiar voice rung in his ears.

"I see the years have not diminished your appetite for interference."

McShade spun around, shock on his face as he stared at the creature before him; the hair was a little whiter perhaps, the skin a trifle gaunter, but the eyes were every bit as alive as they'd been all those years ago.

"Nor yours for theatrics. I take it from your presence here that Mr Lowe neglected to avail himself of the opportunity I presented."

"Quite so," confirmed The Child, one of his minders close behind. "My sympathies by the way; it must be frightfully inconvenient to go to the trouble of arranging a funeral, only for the corpse to refuse to show."

McShade gave a wry smile, not doubting for a moment the hostility that lay behind The Child's avuncular words.

"No doubt a replacement cadaver will soon be available."

"No doubt. But first I wanted to know why."

"Does it matter?"

"Outside of my own curiosity, no." A note of whimsy infected The Child's voice and a hint of what looked like regret glinted in his eye. "I had such high expectations for you in the beginning, you had steel, drive. You understood the realities of necessary cruelty for the greater good. But then, like so many others you developed a conscience. Had you the courage of your convictions decades ago you would have accepted the somewhat lenient discipline we meted out and returned to the fold, taking your place as Prime Minister when we engineered the opportunity. But instead you hid in the background, preferring to have your ego massaged rather than take the necessary actions, shying away from the only real contribution you have ever made: the creation of The Institute."

"Your 'necessary cruelties' damn near bankrupted my country!" McShade spat the words in anger, any vestiges of banter eradicated.

"And so you sought to redress the balance now, so many years later, for revenge?"

McShade laughed out loud, his anger composed. "Would you believe for redemption?"

"Were I talking to anyone but yourself, then possibly."

"Well it's something that's been playing on my mind recently; whether it really is possible to atone for past mistakes."

"It seems Mr Lowe's disease is contagious. It seems also that Britain's young Foreign Secretary has discovered his inner fire in recent days. I wonder where he got the inspiration?"

"Who can say?"

"Well, whatever the source it will be a short lived flame; it's always such a shame when so promising a career is cut short ahead of its time."

"Leave him alone!" McShade spat in fury, but it didn't so much as dent The Child's coldness.

"Control is maintained through discipline," The Child said, his voice still un-moved. "The Institute administers discipline for the good of the Union. Greyson is at this moment conspiring with other bodies against us; a meeting arranged through your influence, Sir Roger. By his own actions he has made himself a target. He ignored the warnings, he ignored the order from his Prime Minister to return. To allow him to escape punishment for his interference would be an unprecedented dereliction."

McShade stood feet apart from The Child, fatalistic, his strength exhausted. There was no way out of this for Greyson, The Child would take action.

"Then I suppose," said McShade, calmly, "you should focus your discipline appropriately."

CHAPTER 25

MIRUSHKA'S EYES BETRAYED HER DISTRACTION as she bade what she had so wished to be a fond farewell to Jonathan. Her head was full of Peter; of conspiracies and elections and fury and love and politics and passion. Mirushka gently held Jonathan's arms and kissed him quickly on each cheek, a muttered, "Dobrú noc," her only words. It had taken all her strength to stay focussed for the crucial talks and this wasn't the time for childishness. He looked about to say something but stopped himself, understandable she thought given her demeanour. Instead, a smile appeared at the corners of his mouth.

"Ms. Svobodova," he began, his smile widening as she focussed on him.

"Mr. Greyson," she quietly replied.

"If the new Czechoslovakia possesses the strength you have shown today, she shall be a most valued partner," he said before adding in a softer, more delicate tone as he dipped his head inside the car, "as indeed are you."

Immune to his flirtations, Mirushka fought back the tear welling defiantly in her eye and watched through as Greyson's car swept from before her with the warmest of purrs.

Her fingers reached into her small handbag and fished out the watch, pressing open the lid of Peter's gift before she cursed again, admonishing herself for her inability to even check the time without thinking of him. She hurriedly closed the watch and deposited it back into the darkness before shutting her eyes and filling her lungs with the deepest of breaths. Her mask restored, she nodded to the chauffeur, Ivan, waiting stiffly beside her own limousine. The immaculately dressed driver opened the door and stood, ever patient, waiting for her to take her seat. Mirushka lifted her eyes and muttered thanks as she stooped into the blackness inside, her addled mind only briefly querying why the man was sweating so much. She sat down and the door closed gently shut behind her. With her thoughts now free of the constraints of the talks and unwilling to stay focussed, Mirushka cradled her head in her hands and surrendered to her tears. She sat in morose seclusion, embracing her freedom to weep as the engine started and the car moved forward, flanked by the usual motorcycles. And such was the intensity of her weeping, that it wasn't until she saw the motorcycles peeling away while her limousine took the road heading out of Prague, that she realised the obvious omission; that Rado was not in the car with her.

———

In the seat of his own car, Greyson sat back and poured himself a large, large scotch with which to toast his success and allow the warmth of justified self-satisfaction spread through his body. He felt every inch an architect and emperor combined, and every inch of him revelled in the new role, albeit the orchestrator of an empire whose existence was secret. The story for the public was leaked, the Prime Minister now committed, whether he liked it or not. Damn him, thought Greyson, from what he had learned the PM was either in league with The Institute or else scared into uselessness by them. Well now it would be different. Greyson had tied him into his own dealings and the PM could either enjoy the ride with him or scurry off and bury his head in the sand.

"That was for you Caroline," he said, knocking back the drink, relishing the burn of its passage to his gut.

The journey to the embassy was mercifully short and Greyson lifted the bottle to fill his glass again just as the car pulled into the courtyard, but his movements were stopped by the deafening smash which greeted the car as it pulled to a halt.

A flash of black, white and pink, accompanied by glittering shards of glass like stars in a night sky, fell from a top floor window, *from McShade's window*, smacking down hard on the cobbles below.

Heaving the door open, Greyson leapt from the car and slid on his knees to the broken shape on the deck, a small crowd of shocked onlookers gathering quickly around him. As the young man howled, the figure's arm moved, the cold hand clamping onto Greyson's own with a fierce intensity.

"By my count," McShade began, gasping air into his perforated lungs between words, his voice weak and growing weaker, "this makes for Prague's Third Defenestration."

Greyson could not hold back his cry, squeezing the dying man's hand and shouting useless requests for him to 'hold on'. McShade did hold on, and, though each word brought fresh pain, drove himself to shush the younger man and speak again.

"It appears I am your final warning," he wheezed, "but you should ignore it. It's up to you now," he said, "you young bloods. Make it count, take the fight to them and don't let them stop you. I know you can do it."

Greyson shushed him in return, reaching out with his other hand and stroking McShade's head. The old man managed a last, ironic laugh.

"You know? This is exactly what I sought to save you from, and it isn't any less painful from this side." He reached up, achingly with his free hand, cupping Greyson's face. "I always loved you Jonathan, my precious boy."

The hand slipped from Greyson's face and the vice like grip of his other weakened, the fingers slipping finally to the ground.

"I love you too," Greyson wept. "Goodbye Dad."

———

It was the panic steadily growing in her stomach which most upset Svobodova. There was no escape for her now, she knew that and in truth had been prepared for as much for some time, yet her body's reaction offended her, robbing her of her intent to face her fate with as much dignity as possible.

There was no Peter, no Rado, the police were gone. The tinted windows and the black night sky ensured no-one could see her though the glass, even should she gesture for help; and in any case, what help could anyone give her? Her driver of so many years, Ivan, steered the car onwards, the dividing screen between them stubbornly raised, her phone, left in the car before the meeting, on the wrong side.

The seductive temptations of the city's lights were receding faster into the black until they were only a mischievous glint in the night's eye, before the black woods blocked even that view and the car sped further into the deserted hillside roads, heading, no doubt, for the crash which Svobodova now thought inevitable.

Clenching each facet of her body, she pressed herself back into her seat, whispering a thousand confessions and screwing her eyes closed tighter as the car ran faster, *faster*, until – nothing.

She dared herself to open an uncertain, curious eye as their velocity dropped to a sudden zero, accompanied by the sound of Ivan's door being flung open. Before the treacherous driver could exit however, another shape, a person, flew from nowhere, leaping through the open door and knocking Ivan back inside before he could set one foot out; the pair disappearing out of view. The sounds of the struggle were evident, as was the rocking of the car, but the screen left Svobodova blind to the outcome, until at last she heard a cry and the passenger side door opened, Ivan again seeking to make his escape, this time successfully. She pressed her face to the glass, watching her Judas trip, stumble and blunder into the woods, hampered both by the blackness and the aftermath of his struggle.

She turned back quickly, banging on the dividing screen, screaming in her native tongue for the identity and intent of the newcomer. At first silence, until a crackle on the speaker back in her chair followed by a word, a solitary word, one spoken in a voice she had thought she would never hear again.

"Miláčku."

The screen descended like the reveal on a tired game show, with Peter Lowe the reluctant prize. His exhaustion was obvious, even from behind, his head only half turned towards her. His skin was flushed, sweaty, the day's growth threatening to show on his chin, and he was nursing what looked a very fresh and particularly deep knife wound to his shoulder.

"Little bastard got me," Peter cursed. "I'm getting too old for this shit."

Mirushka sprang forward, reaching through the gap and pressing her hand onto Peter's own, compressing the cut.

"This is too deep," Mirushka frowned, "we need to get you to hospital."

"Not much chance of that," Peter sighed. "The engine's dead, Ivan took off with your phone and mine ran out of power hours ago. Plus there's the other problem we've got."

"What other problem?"

"That we're sat on top of a bomb."

Mirushka's practicality returned with the words, looking impotently around, hoping to see some tell- tale sign of its location, find some way of neutralising the new threat.

"You won't find it, it's underneath the car."

"So you can get out and de-arm it, no?"

"Nope, it's one of The Institute's specials, weight activated. It arms by the weight of two people in the vehicle, and the explosion is triggered for a short time after one person leaves."

"I've never heard of anything like that."

"The Institute's always been good at sabotaging cars; nasty little buggers these, very useful for lulling targets into a false sense of security."

"So what can we do?"

Peter didn't speak, but turned his head away from her. Slipping his hand from his wound he reached across and flicked a switch on the arm of the door next to him. The locks retracting from the rear cracked the silence like bullets in a shooting range.

"Your stop madam."

"What?" She whispered the word, almost silently, her awareness rising as quickly as the locks had sprung from the doors.

"You'd better be quick, the fight might well have unsettled the bomb, it could go off anytime. Just open the door and run like hell."

"Peter, láska moja, no!" Mirushka kneeled by the hatch, her hand clamping pathetically on Peter's bleeding wound, her voice as quiet as the grave. "I can't leave you here."

"Course you can," replied Peter, straining to be as matter of fact as she was quiet and tender. "We can't afford to lose you, no time for rescues, final flings. No time for secrets." Only his last words betrayed his emotion.

"You know." Mirushka dropped her head, as though a weight had been lifted only to be replaced by one still heavier.

"I know."

She slipped her hand from the wound, Peter making no effort to replace it.

"Did you know I was glad when you made your confession that night? I needed to know I could be forgiven. What better way to prove I could than by forgiving you, who came for me?"

"I never deserved your forgiveness, or Herbert's."

"But I gladly gave it, and not just for my own sake. You said yourself, in Bojnice; maybe no-one deserves their fate, but we should make the best of the circumstances we find ourselves in. That's what you did that night, you tried to make the best of the hell you were in and by then I had fallen in love with you so why wouldn't I seek to make the best of that? I could forgive you for the death of the world."

"Did you think I wouldn't do the same?" Peter spoke through his tears, without anger, his callousness smoothed.

"I was ashamed! You had me on a pedestal, you sacrificed everything you had for me, and to be my Protector, how could I admit it was all for one as steeped in dirt as you used to be? I couldn't."

"It wouldn't have mattered, and I refuse to believe you were ever like me."

"I wasn't one of their murderers, but in truth I didn't know what The Institute was. They contacted me one day, when Herbert was putting the party together, and asked me to get involved and report back to them on progress, unofficially. We were small news back then, of no real consequence and they paid me well. But then we started to grow. The people remembered Herbert and he had lost none of his youthful dynamism. Along with Karol, we built an effective movement, a popular one, one that started winning seats. That's when they started demanding more of me; strategies, plans. And then came their suggestions for changes I could make, ideas I could tweak. But by then I'd been captured by Herbert's vision; I believed it, shared it. So I refused and hoped that in time I would forget how I'd betrayed him."

"You must have known you'd be a target."

"I didn't really know who I was dealing with. I had my suspicions after you arrived, but it wasn't until Herbert's death that I knew. I wanted to ask you, to confide in you the night of his death, but how could I admit my knowledge to you? I didn't know what to say. And I couldn't risk raising any kind of official investigation, for fear of upsetting the campaign, so I thought to keep you close to me."

"But afterwards, you could have said something, you could have told me anything."

"I wanted to and I nearly did, but then there was the crash and Adrianna. You see, that morning, the death threat I received, you remember? It contained a silver necklace."

"So?"

"It was the necklace I'd bought myself with the first payment The Institute ever sent me. I thought it was at home in Bojnice, but to see it there…I knew they wouldn't stop coming for me. So I resolved to end it then and there and spare as many people as possible. I contacted The Institute and told them I would not be travelling on the helicopter as planned, that I would stay on and return to Prague later. I'd planned to send you and Rado back separately and travel alone, giving them the opportunity they wanted, but instead…" She wept as the memory returned.

"Instead they went for the copter and killed her anyway."

"Why would they do that?" Mirushka howled.

Peter shrugged. "Psychological?" He shrugged. "A warning of what was coming your way, that you'd involved too many people? Who knows."

"I killed her. Because of my actions that young girl is dead. After that my shame was too great to tell you."

"You didn't kill her." Peter's voice was becoming quieter as the blood continued to flow from his wound. "They did. But if you don't get out of that door and win that election, you'll be letting her die in vain. Don't let that happen."

He turned again, twisting his body painfully towards her, shocking Mirushka with how pale he had so quickly become.

"You go!" She cried. "Leave me here where I deserve to be." She pressed her forehead against his, reaching through and clutching his cold hands.

"I'd never make it down the hill," he smiled. "And your country needs you."

"And I need you."

"I'll still be knocking around in here," he whispered, tapping his brow against hers. He reached into his jacket pocket, pulling a crumpled, tattered page from it.

"I want you to have this," he said.

"What is it?"

"A gift Herbert left me. Keep it close. And take care, be careful who you trust and make it worthwhile. The Child is still out there and he won't be happy."

"You didn't…?"

"No. I could have, I wanted to, but no."

She kissed him softly, cupping his head in her hands.

"See?" she whispered, tears on her cheeks. "You have changed after all; you don't deserve to die here."

He smiled the softest smile she had known, taking her hands and delicately kissing them, holding them tightly in his own through the gap.

"We don't get what we deserve."

"Not in this world, maybe in the next?"

"I'll pop over and find out." He laughed through his tears. "I'll let you know in a few decades, eh? Now go."

Her face contorted, her throat aching, she nodded her silent acquiescence, slipping from his touch and opening the door to the heartless night outside. She crouched at the door, turning back to her love one final time.

"No happy ever after?"

"Not for us," his smile, still gentle, his face devoid of fear, "but maybe for them. God bless, Miroslava."

"And God bless you, Peter. You know? It was the very best love."

"None greater," he whispered back.

She wordlessly pressed her lips to her fingers, holding them up to him, before turning to the freezing blackness and stumbling and sobbing as she flailed down the wooded hillside, her feet ripping through weeds and bracken as she ran.

Inside the car, Peter watched her leave then turned back to recline in his seat, dizzy, faint, but content. The remnant flavours of his rain-soaked Communion played at the back of his throat and he closed his eyes, allowing the delicate caress of sleep play flirtatiously with him as he waited for the inevitable. Drawing into himself a deep, final breath, Peter grinned widely.

"I hear music," he said.

The explosion thundered and echoed, illuminating the hillside in a bright orange hell, sending thick black smoke into the blacker sky and knocking the still stumbling Mirushka to the ground in a storm of broken twigs and leaves, where she lay sprawled, weeping into the dirt at the loss of this man sent to kill her, and of whose heroism she could never speak. Dragging herself to her knees, she strained her eyes in the glow of the flames to read the crumpled, blood stained page he had given her; his final message to his love, her sobbing growing harder as she translated the words of John, 15:13 in her mind. Sirens began to sound in the distance and though she knew she should wait, she clambered up and set off through the woods again, ready and determined to honour his sacrifice.

CHAPTER 26

SHE HAD DISAPPEARED. Not a soul in Prague hadn't heard of the explosion, or that Svobodova's body was not among the wreckage, only that of an as yet unidentified man. And the rumours had started, the theories concocted. This had all happened before, people muttered, just like with Dubček; the vehicle's remains given only the most cursory of examinations before destruction, the driver unscathed. Moreover he had vanished.

Looking down onto the city from his imperious office in the Castle, President Čurda was worried. It was election day, Daleka was nowhere to be found and her advice was incomplete. The election should be called off, she had said, when Svobodova was dead. But who knew if Svobodova was dead at all and while he knew he should still make the call, the throng of people gathering below in Malostranské náměstí had him nervous. Headed by the obstinate Karol Černý, they were quiet, almost silent. They simply stood, en-masse, staring up at the castle, at Čurda, as if daring him to deny them their voice.

He snapped in irritation at the knock on his door and a young aide came scurrying in, breathless. "She's been found!"

"Daleka?"

"Svobodova."

"Where is she?" Čurda's three words carried a world of dread and he silently willed the young man not to answer, but to no avail.

The aide stretched out his arm to the window and pointed to the growing crowd below.

"Out there," he said.

———

The people present parted for her, and in her wake she brought others, the buzz of their confusion punctuating the stunned silence. Around her she could hear people quietly whispering of the Return of the Queen, or bestowing on her a new title, 'ona jefénix'. Miroslava Svobodova stood, silent, looking around at them, taking in as many of the faces in the crowd as she could, wanting to look each of them in the eye, in the soul. Her delicate makeup betrayed the streaks of her tears, her skin was scratched from her descent, her outfit from the previous night's concert tattered and brushed with the greenery of the hillside, yet still she was regal, still commanding, still in control.

Černý looked down from the small platform made up of crates and boxes on which he stood, as silent as she, an unused loudspeaker poised in his hand. Reaching the spot beneath him, Mirushka looked up into the old, proud eyes and offered him the gentlest of smiles; reaching out her own arm toward him.

"Karol?" She asked in uncertainty, wondering and hoping along with the crowd that he would accept her hand and have her stand alongside him.

For a moment he remained still, the great eyes burrowing and unreadable, his gaunt face an emotionless slate. All muttering in the crowd had ceased, and every head had turned to stare anxiously at Mirushka's outstretched fingers, as though she were the leading lady in some romance, desperate for the embrace of her man.

A cheer erupted when he reached back, accepting her hand in his own still powerful grip, the touch tender, fatherly, and for the first time in her memory, she saw warmth when she looked into his piercing eyes. She stepped up onto the ramshackle platform and he pulled her gently level alongside him, the pair relaxing into a mutual smile while the crowd around them roared their bottled up approval.

"Děkuji Karol." Mirushka whispered, leaning forward to kiss his cheek.

The old man's smile widened further. "Prosim Mr Lowe?"

She shook her head and blinked away a tear. Černý bowed his head in genuine regret.

"I'm sorry." He pressed the loudspeaker he still held into Mirushka's hand, and moved to depart the plinth.

She tightened her grip on his other hand and looked quizzically at him, suddenly nervous at the thought of his departure, wanting to hold onto his presence a while longer.
He returned the squeeze of her hand and leant down to whisper back in her ear, "You were the face of the future," he said, "now be the voice of the present."

With that he slipped his hand from hers and stepped off the plinth, turning to face her at the bottom, alongside his fellow Czechs; looking up at her, excited and expectant.

"Many of you are wondering where I have been," she began.

"Well in truth that doesn't matter. There was an accident, a man died, a good man. But what matters now is that we are together, together at the end of our campaign. And it was our campaign; your brothers and sisters in Slovakia fought it with you!"

Cheers bellowed out and Mirushka held up her hand for calm.

"We made mistakes, Karol and I," she said, the crowd silent once more, drinking in her words, "mistakes between ourselves and mistakes with this campaign. When you look around Prague, around the Czech Republic, you'll see our faces smiling back at you, like your Slovak brothers and sisters saw Herbert Biely's last year. TV, the newspapers, all bestowed great titles upon us, titles like Europe's Un-Crowned Queen, or Hero of the Prague Spring, and we clung to them jealously; we used them as weapons to beat down our opponents who couldn't hope to match our personal glories for themselves."

She paused, scanning the crowd, allowing her words to be properly digested in the silence.

"Yes," she continued, "Herbert Biely was a great man, yes he was a hero to our country. So too is Karol Černý who stands before you today, asking to become your Prime Minister. But the faces on our posters should have been yours, not ours."

A few sporadic cries of agreement broke out through the crowd, imbibing her with the confidence to continue.

"They should have been the faces of the doctors and nurses who healed us when we were sick, of the teachers who taught us when we were ignorant, of the parents who set examples for us. We should have seen the faces of our old who pass us their wisdom and of their families who return their care in old age.

We should have seen the faces of our young, who inspire us with their drive and optimism, and their unwillingness to accept the inequalities of this world. We should have been looking into the eyes of the shop worker, who has packed our food each week for a lifetime, of the man who has swept our roads since his youth! We should have felt the warm smile of the friend, whose shoulder was there for us to cry on, or the priest who comforted us in our despair, or the tram driver who got us home safely! We should have seen the Czechoslovak people, whose sweat built a nation, only for it to be torn in two by the greed of selfish men!"

The sporadic cries had become cheers now, finishing each sentence Mirushka spoke with affirmative exclamation. She looked around once more into the eyes of the crowd, waiting for the applause to subside.

"But instead," she began, when the buzz had dipped, "like in every other election, we politicians smiled down at you from our billboard thrones, desperate in our desire to have you believe in *us*; to put your trust in *us*; but just as important is that you put that trust in *yourselves*. Trust in your ability to piece together our two nations into one again. We, Karol and I, can put the pieces in place, but you are the glue that will hold it together, through your trust in yourselves and each other!"

Looking down, she saw Černý's lined face smiling proudly back up at her, freely offering her the respect he had previously begrudged her; the new found warmth in his eyes a now constant shine. Smiling back, she lifted the loudspeaker once more to her lips and revelled in the crowd's excitement.

"A good man once told me that if I was the Un-Crowned Queen of Europe then all of you are Princes and Princesses. We are the same; all of us. Whether Czech or Slovak, whether our roots are Austrian, Moravian, Hungarian or Romani; we are one family, with one future!"

The crowd bellowed their approval now, and Mirushka held up her hand, appealing for quiet.

"Right now, in his office, President Čurda wants to cancel the election; claiming grounds for a state of emergency. I say that it is the desperate act of a man who doesn't want to see his people enact their will!"

The cheers were replaced by boos, the crowd turning their heads towards the castle, venting their anger at the President.

"They call me the Face of the Future. Well that face has a voice too, and that voice says that we will not accept a delay, we will not accept postponement! So raise your voices with me now and say to President Čurda, that we demand our right to choose!"

She roared the words into her megaphone, her stare fixed defiantly on the castle. Stepping down from the crates, she linked arms with Černý and marched through to the front of the crowd, the people making way for them, where they stopped, in the shadow of the castle. As the throng joined their leaders in linking arms, it was Černý who started the singing, before Mirushka and the crowd joined in; heads back, joyous and unashamed, they sang their anthem, the anthem of the old Czechoslovakia.

Up in his office, President Čurda chewed on his thumb as he watched the play unfold below. Behind him, the nervous young aide pressed.

"Is the election to be postponed Sir?"

The President continued to chew.

"Sir?"

———

It was much later that night, long after the polls had closed and the declaration of victory a formality, that The Greek, his arm freshly bandaged, caught up with Ivan and slid a knife into his kidney. He admired his new target. He had been quick to discard his uniform and make an effort to blend in with the tourists. But though he did feel some pity as he clamped his hand over the surprised mouth, alas, he had been spotted too quickly and The Child dictated that all failures must be punished. He bundled the dying man into the boot of the waiting car and set off to the river. Pulling him out, the effort making his sore arm sting in objection, he heaved him unceremoniously into the water, standing back to catch his breath.

The Greek staggered forward, as though he had been punched hard in the back, and he looked in incredulity at his feet, searching for the source of his stumbling. Then another punch, and another, and he fell head first into the freezing river. Shock tore the breath from his lungs and he gasped as the bitter cold was matched by the searing, painful heat which burned a trail inside him from the three punches. He tried desperately to kick but his legs no longer responded, and he strained to lift his head from the depths. Straining his blurring eyes in the darkness, he saw his target bobbing alongside him, weak, his resistance to the river almost exhausted. With a tremendous effort, the Greek reached out and grabbed hold of his victim, who responded in kind, pulling a heavy arm around the shoulders of his killer. Seeing the faintness he was feeling mirrored in the flailing man's eyes, the Greek pulled closer to him and pressed his lips tightly to his cheek. "συγνώμη." He wheezed to his victim, who tightened his own grip around his new comrade, in mute acceptance of his apology. The victim and murderer clung tighter to each other for comfort and in fear, as their thrashing stopped, and the dark, cold waters of the Vltava closed over their heads.

On the shore, watching the scene unfold with a bitterness in his mouth, The Child crossed himself in brief respect of another fallen at his command. His operative quietly slid his silenced weapon inside its holster and turned back to his master, who gestured him to start the car. Reaching into his pocket, he drew out the keys thrown at him by Peter, weighing them in his hand for a moment before hurling them far and deep into the waters.

The bitter cold masking the dampness in his eye, The lost Child of Lidice turned and walked briskly back towards his waiting ride, as the last drops of the season's rain began to fall.

CHAPTER 27

RASTI WAS IN A DAZE from the second he read the paper. Not because of the triumphant headline saluting the victory and extolling the virtues of the now impending reunification. Not even because of the sizeable column inches devoted to Svobodova's car. Only after reading, at the bottom of the third paragraph, the name of the aide killed did Rasti become numb.

"Peter Lowe," it read in Czech, "a Relationship Manager seconded to Svobodova's staff from the Institute for European Harmony, was believed to be travelling alone in the vehicle at the time of the explosion."

Rasti's heart plummeted like a boulder in the ocean and a haze blanketed his senses to all around him. His eyes on auto pilot, Rasti somehow managed to stumble through to the next few words.

"Ms Svobodova has been said to be deeply upset by Mr Lowe's death yesterday and told reporters that Mr Lowe had been an, 'exceptional man who could not have shown any greater love for the Czech and Slovak republics. Neither the new Czechoslovakia nor I will forget him'. Police say there was no trace of the driver's body in the wreckage and they are anxious to locate…"

Rasti's eyes blurred and he found himself swallowing ineffectively against the lump lying defiantly in his throat. He walked out of the restaurant into the bright daylight, his body oddly aching and his mind as distant as if he had enjoyed too many beers on a warm day. As he walked, the soft blues drifting out from his bar was overwhelmed by the sound of cheering. People were running past him from every side towards the noise, all laughing, shouting, some slapping him on the back and urging him to hurry up. Hurry up to what Rasti didn't know but he kept on walking, following the stragglers through the cobbled maze of Old Town until he reached the bottom of Wenceslas Square. There he saw why the people cheered.

A multitude had gathered. As if following some collective homing instinct, the people had gathered here where they had always gathered on momentous days. They had been here in the Spring, they had returned for the Revolution and now they came again at the dawn of their future; a unified future. His mind still dazed, a smile came slowly to Rasti's face and the grief in his heart gave way to the beginnings of joy. The square was alive again in the fresh morning air. Rasti raised the paper he still clutched in his hands and looked at the headline – an echo of the great Herbert Biely, 'A Family Reunited, A Future Shared!' it declared and the lump in Rasti's throat melted into a hearty laugh. Peter had done this. After being so nearly destroyed by the deeds of his past, Peter had done this! A people were one again, rejoicing in the streets, overcome with a joy and an optimism not felt since that golden day in 1989, and Peter had given his life for it to happen.

Rasti knew it to be true. Pushing his bulky frame to the front of the crowd, Rasti looked up at the grand frontage of the Melantrich building where years before Václav Havel had brought Alexander Dubček out onto the balcony to acknowledge the crowd. Today, Miroslava Svobodova would soon stand on that same balcony, waving to her ecstatic supporters below and Rasti's smile became a grin. Looking back down at his newspaper, his bottled up emotion, that intoxicating mixture of grief and jubilation, burst forth. The paper was hurled into the air and he threw his head back and cheered, a long, passionate cry of anguish and joy, subsiding to a calm peace. As the shouting and laughter continued around him, Rasti closed his eyes and smiled, offering a prayer for his friend Peter, his hard drinking, foul mouthed, secretive, blues loving friend. Rasti thanked God for him and for the good that Peter eventually, after so long in the dark, had done.

"Well done mate," Rasti whispered quietly, "I'll open a bottle for you tonight."

———

Mirushka stood just inside from the balcony of the Melantrich building, a simple net curtain separating her from destiny. Karol Černý stood just behind her, to her right hand side, having refused her request to go ahead of her to thank the people. "It's you they want to see," he had said, like a grandfather, proud of his descendant. "The future has arrived, and it needs a face."

Inhaling deeply, she crossed herself and began to move forward, only for Rado's voice to distract her.

"Ma'am!" His cry was barely audible over the roar of the

crowd coming through the open balcony doors, but was enough for her to stop and turn. Rado stood by the room's entrance, his head bandaged from the blow that had incapacitated him the night of the attack, flanked by two newcomers; the first of which Mirushka instantly recognised as Herbert Biely's adult son.

"Jozef!" She exclaimed, smiling at the unassuming, conservatively dressed fifty-something. "How wonderful of you to be here! You must come with us on to the balcony…"

"No, thank you Mirushka," he quickly interrupted, which offered no surprise. Jozef possessed his father's natural modesty, but none of his desire for political attention. "I apologise for interrupting, but my father wanted me to introduce you to someone." He nodded to the second figure, a grey suited middle aged man whose hair and moustache precisely matched the colour of his suit.

"This is Branoslav Kral, lawyer and executor of my father's will."

Mirushka was puzzled but nodded a greeting to the strange little man who stood possessively clutching a leather bound document, and who seemed remarkably un-intimidated by his presence in a room of dignitaries during a momentous occasion. Without hesitation, he stepped forward and held out the document to Mirushka.

"Herbert Biely stipulated that in the event of his death, the content of his will not be made public until after the election, and that then it should be released to the leaders of the party."

Taking it from him, her puzzlement continued. "Well thank you," she said, "but can't this wait until later? We have one or two things to attend to this morning." The still rising volume of the crowd stifling her words.

"I think you should read this before you go out there; both of you." Jozef addressed Mirushka and the curious Černý who stood alongside her. He continued as they opened the binding and began to read the contents within.

"You see, father wasn't just dismayed by the break up of the country, he was devastated by its after effects too; the corruption, the backroom deals, and the asset stripping. When he saw our heritage being robbed in bungled privatisations, and slush funds, he grew angry. That was the whole inspiration behind his movement, his business empire; investing his fortune to bring some of these assets back, and hiring people like you, Mirushka, to manage their growth, while building the party up with you, Karol."

The pair continued, open mouthed, to read the fine print while Jozef continued.

"But just buying it back wasn't enough. He wanted to turn the clock back, erase as many transactions as he could that took our assets from our country's hands. My father was a wealthy man, he ensured that his children and family would be comfortable after he died, then planned for the bulk of his assets to go elsewhere. That plan is in your hands now."

Mirushka was speechless as she and Karol read the words in her the folder, each beautifully scribed character articulating Herbert's plan in his own hand; his last gift to his country.

"Father willed," began Jozef, "that after his death, the complete ownership of his spa's, resorts and land in High Tatra and around the country, revert at once to the Czechoslovak People, to be administered by the elected government of the day."

The two politicians were speechless, looking in turn at

each other, at the document and at Jozef, who stood smiling his father's gentle smile at them. From beyond the grave, Herbert had given them the perfect gift, and the perfect way of solidifying their victory.

Černý's words were almost inaudible in the ever growing noise from outside, "This was his plan all along?"

"People accused father of flirting with the more extreme forms of capitalism after the revolution," Jozef said, "but it wasn't true. He just looked to enact his social responsibilities in a different way. He didn't want anyone to know about it before the election, in case he was seen as bribing the people; he wanted the future to be decided by the strength of the arguments, not material gain."

Unable to speak, Mirushka simply embraced the smiling, quiet man who stood before her; kissing him once on each cheek and holding him close, as though the tighter she held him, the greater were her thanks to his father.

Laughing gently, Jozef released himself from her grip and smiled at her. "And now," he said, "as you say, you have one or two things to attend to today; I hope our chat will help."

"Yes," Karol Černý, shaking himself free from his amazement stepped toward her, "you must tell them now; let the people know that the country is theirs again."

Mirushka slowly nodded her head and walked back towards the balcony doors, before stopping and turning to the old man behind her. "No Karol," she said, the noise from below now almost unbearable, "we must tell them." And she held out her hand to him, as she had done at the plinth only hours before.

Karol Černý reluctantly did as Mirushka requested and joined her at the doors. A quiet gasp was his only utterance as he looked through the thin, transparent curtain in awe at the heaving, cheering multitude covering Wenceslas Square in a blanket of adulation. Tears welled in the eyes of the old aristocrat and he knew he should be reproaching himself for his unguarded display of emotion. He felt the fingers of Mirushka's left hand gently clasping those on his right. Karol's mind drifted back to the day decades earlier when he had stood on this very same spot with his heroes. Giants like Dubček, Havel and Biely, as they celebrated with the people the Velvet Revolution and the end of Soviet rule. And now here he was once more, himself about to be hailed a hero by the people he loved – a people soon to be one again. His voice distant and dreamlike he whispered to Mirushka, "It's just like the Revolution."

Their hands clasping tightly as they prepared to step forward, Karol, not used to such sentimentality, felt compelled to offer comfort to the remarkable woman alongside him. Paying her the greatest courtesy he could think of, he lowered his head to hers and spoke in her Slovak dialect. "He truly loved you."

Mirushka blinked away her own tears and smiled at the gentlemanly kindness Karol offered. "I know," she said, gripping him tighter, her eyes never leaving the ecstatic crowd below, "he laid down his life for me."

She relaxed in Karol's paternal company and prayed a silent prayer for Peter and for what would soon be Czechoslovakia again. Her anguish at his death began to be surpassed by contentment that he now finally had the peace he had ached for. It was thanks to Peter that history had been made today. Thanks to his bravery, to his love and to his contrition; a contrition that had saved her from death and ensured the chance of her own redemption by leading a new Czechoslovakia into the future.

And as she and Karol stepped through the curtain together to be met by their ecstatic people, she knew that by leaving behind his bitterness and violence, and showing instead the depth of his love and the extent of his mercy, Peter had found true contrition.

AUTHOR'S NOTE

January 1st 1993 saw the end of the much abused Nation of Czechoslovakia and the birth of the Czech and Slovak Republics. Despite, or arguably because of, its artificial nature, Czechoslovakia was hardly a blameless nation (and I'd struggle to name any countries who could claim that mantle), tensions between its component racial and cultural groups proving particularly problematic, but in its brief history it found itself sinned against on far more than its fair share of occasions.

While I personally think the break up to be a great shame, others hold a different view and those interested in finding out more would do well to read Mary Heimann's excellent review, "Czechoslovakia – The State that Failed". Whatever one's opinions though, what remains true is that the split was not pre-empted by a vote or referendum, nor was there any mass movement for separation, so where did the impetus for what became known as 'The Velvet Divorce' come from? Certainly not from Václav Havel, the legendary Czech dissident who proved so influential during the Revolution and who resigned the Presidency rather than preside over the break up.

While, in my humble view, the separation was a mistake,

it provides a few clues as to the activities of The Institute for European Harmony prior to our story.

Peter Lowe finds himself injected into historical events, some fictional, others grounded in reality, and is occasionally guilty of stealing the thunder of others. During the demonstrations of November 17th, a Secret Police Officer named Ludvík Zifčák was found lying motionless on the floor, providing the source for the fast spread rumor of a dead student, which proved such a significant trigger in furthering the protests. For the purposes of our story, it is Peter who takes Ludvík's place on the cobbles.

Likewise, the tragic early demise of Alexander Dubček is shrouded in at least as much mystery in reality as in our tale. The real Dubček was indeed the victim of a car crash, caused (officially) by 'aquaplaning' as his vehicle lost traction while travelling at very high speed on a wet surface. The driver, Jan Reznik, who did indeed emerge largely unscathed, received a Twelve Month sentence for speeding as a consequence, while rumors and hearsay continue to abound. A useful summary of the case, including then current calls for its re-opening can be found via the archives of Radio Free Europe:

http://www.rferl.org/content/article/1090401.html

The Child as well borrows from history, a still more tragic one at that. In 1942, the Czech village of Lidice was accused by the ruling Nazi powers of harboring partisans and aiding British sponsored members of Operation Anthropoid, who had assassinated the hated Reinhard Heydrich. The Nazi response was the utter and complete elimination of the village in an act of nauseating inhumanity. All adult men were executed, the women were separated from their children and sent to concentration camps (the pregnant women undergoing forced abortions), while the children faced death in the gas vans at Chelmno, unless they were one of the few selected for 'Ayranisation (taken to Germany to be adopted and raised by 'suitable' families'). Days later, a second village, Ležáky, suffered the same fate. Quite miraculously, these children were found and repatriated after the war, The Child however, is a victim of the atrocities who never returned home.

The Lidice Memorial referenced in the story is really there, work beginning on it in 1969 and continuing into the year 2000. Originally the work of Czech sculptor Marie Uchytilová who completed the work in plaster in 1989, she unexpectedly died of a heart attack just one day before the Velvet Revolution of November 17th. After her passing, her husband, Ji í V. Hampl, continued to work on it alone. Operation Anthropoid also lends a name to our fictional President Čurda, the name originally belonging to Karel Čurda, a Czech resistance fighter who betrayed Heydrich's assassins for One Million Reichsmarks and a new identity. He was tracked down and hanged after the war. Those wanting to know more about this key event of the Second World War may wish to read John Martin's, "The Mirror Caught the Sun: Operation Anthropoid 1942".

Regular visitors to Prague will be familiar with the plethora of jazz and blues bars lining the streets and the many talented musicians plying their trade within them. Smokin' Hot is an homage to one such establishment, sadly no longer with us but still alive in the memories of many. My thanks to my wonderful wife, Miroslava and to Jamie Marshall, Phil Speat, Michael Lechaciu and others, all so very intertwined with that place, for permitting me to reference them, obliquely or otherwise and, hopefully, capture a little of what it used to be like, back in the day. Rasti Vojtovic too deserves my thanks for allowing me to turn him from an Isle of Wight based Slovak Chef to a Prague based Czech one. To the best of my knowledge he has never been a Priest. And thanks, of course, to the real Peter Lowe, a chap who couldn't be more unlike the character if he tried, but who is blessed with quite the most perfect name I could have asked for.

In one of life's coincidences, a new campaign has begun to be noticed in both Republics, with the intention of bringing a referendum on reunification to coincide with the planned 2018 elections. It will be interesting to see how this develops and whether fact mirrors fiction. For Miroslava Svobodova, the future is a blank canvass on which to draw the shape of the newly rejoined country while she works towards her own redemption and the betterment of her people, although I'm sure The Institute has other ideas. Mirushka, Czechoslovakia's new Phoenix, will most certainly rise again. For Peter though, the journey is over, at least in this world, and any tales of his now lie in the past; and I hope that one day we will learn exactly how he found himself in Prague to influence those famous events of 1989; a young British killer, trying to survive in a strange land of falling Iron Curtains and Velvet Revolutions.

James is an HR professional and former DJ for modradiouk. net, with a neglected talent for the harmonica. Hailing from the North, he read Politics & Modern History at the University of Manchester before embarking on a career which has taken in retail management, high level technical recruitment, and a plethora of public sector roles. After making a reluctant peace with the fact that he probably won't be the next Doctor, James indulged his passion for story-telling, encouraged by his regular trips to the Czech and Slovak Republics and his delving into the rich history of the region.

Those trips, and that history, helped inform Escape to Perdition, James's first novel which (he hopes) reflects his love of Prague and all its highs and lows. He is happy to leave further speculation of its motivations to the reader.

A fan of God bothering, rum and Manchester City, James

possesses the skill of always pulling into traffic behind a bus and still loves spending as much time as possible in Prague and Bojnice.

When not writing, James flirts with the idea of a return to internet radio and educates his two spectacular kids in the irrelevance of most forms of 21st Century music. He has a day job, dreams of writing full time and composes a regular column for Doctorwhoworldwide.com.

He very much hopes you enjoy this book and he might, just might, still be the next Doctor.

Urbane Publications is dedicated to developing new author voices, and publishing fiction and non-fiction that challenges, thrills and fascinates.

From page-turning novels to innovative reference books, our goal is to publish what YOU want to read.

Find out more at
urbanepublications.com